The Eight of Pentacles

Eloise Hill

ISBN-13: 978-0-9836065-0-5
The Eight of Pentacles
Copyright © 2011 by Eloise Hill

This is a work of fiction. Names, characters, places, and
incidents are either the product of the author's imagination or
are used fictitiously, and any resemblance to actual persons,
living or dead, business establishments, events, or locales is
entirely coincidental.

The Eight of Pentacles cover illustration
Copyright © 2011 by Myla Lara

www.eloisehill.net

In memory of my parents

In memory of my parents

Prologue

The voice was high-pitched. It came from somewhere down the corridor, past the point where the concrete walls disappeared into shadow.

I hesitated and took a step forward. The sharp keening rose and fell away again and the hair on my arms jumped to attention.

Silence settled over the empty hallway. It was a nervous, edgy quiet, waiting in the dark to be broken, and I waited with it for the muffled sobs to return.

Overhead a bare bulb swung, rocked back and forth by a stale breeze. I reached for the pull chain and the walls buckled.

I staggered, my arms splayed out before me.

Muck bubbled up through the carpet, brown in the jaundiced light. Mottled ooze flowed over my feet, engulfing them in the stench of rotten eggs.

I stepped sideways and slid, my right heel scraping debris that pierced like shattered glass. Matted fibers clawed at my ankles and raked the skin as I wrenched them free. Purple droplets blossomed and trailed, crisscross, down my legs.

The crying was louder now and I propelled myself toward it, lifting my legs high, one at a time, like a demented stork. Icy water stung torn flesh and whorled past, glistening over the surface of the doors I now saw lined the hallway.

I paused at the first one and placed my ear on the moist, grainy wood. A young woman's voice rippled past it: tear-choked and thick with despair. She whispered a word I didn't recognize, over and over. I pressed against the door straining to hear and it splintered and gave way, and I twisted, free falling, my head exploding with light.

My heart hammered against the mattress. I fought off the cocoon of blankets and flopped over, hot and still clumsy with sleep. The night wind tapped the bedroom window and leaked past it, prickling my arms and neck and eyelids. It was always the same sensation after a nightmare: that feeling of being hurtled through space and slammed back into my body, as if there hadn't been enough time to make the shift from one reality to another.

A ricer gunned down Piedmont Avenue and backfired once on its way toward downtown Oakland. I forced my eyes open and eased upright, one vertebra at a time. My mother used to joke that I was such a late riser—a sin in 1960's rural Virginia—because I spent more of the night making up "stories" than sleeping. But when several of those "stories" foretold the death of my Grandfather Smith, at the age of fifty-two, and the birth of a baby to the unmarried daughter of our church's pastor, the joking stopped. And I learned to keep the subjects of my nocturnal visions to myself.

Not that all my dreams amounted to second sight. That was the problem with being intuitive and human. It was still sometimes difficult for me to distinguish between authentic psychic input and, say, the cumulative effects of a late-night dinner and the eleven o'clock news.

On the ground floor, the ancient elevator rumbled to life and began its phlegmatic climb upward. The neighborhood was quiet tonight, unusually so for the week after the Fourth of July. No leftover bottle rockets or spinners popping out in the street, no feet pounding on the rickety, wrought iron staircase, no late-night TV rumbling through the walls. Only the contented snoring of the fat British blue shorthair sprawled across the foot of my bed.

I ruffled the dense fur between her ears and Audie grunted in protest. I tucked my feet against her rump and she emitted a long-suffering sigh at this second assault upon her person. The warmth from her body seeped through the covers and the muscles in my neck and back began to relax. I pulled the blankets around my shoulders and closed my eyes, lulled by the sound of soft, feline breathing.

Outside, a branch from the maple tree brushed against the window as I sank into the pillow and drifted toward that sweet spot between consciousness and slumber. Half-formed images sailed past, intermingled with snatches of nonsensical conversations. Darkness curled over me, pushing me down into a deep, bottomless sleep.

And then I heard it, spoken as clearly as if she were standing next to my bed . . . the word, the girl in the dream had been whispering. It was "Ari".

Chapter One

"Murp!" Audie lifted her nose to the warm breeze blowing in from the Central Valley and sniffed.

We were sitting on the landing of the back steps, two stories above the riot of color in the yard below. In the western corner of the oblong lot, a Meyer lemon tree shaded the hot pink trumpet vines cascading over the wooden fence that ringed the property. Fuchsia, star jasmine, and yellow and lavender iris lined the northeast side of the garden. A cranberry bougainvillea spilled down the back of the building above the creamy heads of a stand of calla lilies and blue asters. Beside them, a bird of paradise glowed orange and purple in the morning sun.

Casa Mariposa was the three-story apartment building Audie Murpy and I called home. Built in the 1930s, it had sustained damage in the Loma Prieta earthquake and remained in constant need of repair. Hot water was a scarcity at certain times of the day and wall insulation was nonexistent. The ancient windows leaked air and the bathrooms collected mold and mildew at a rate that would rival that of any petri dish.

Still, it had a certain eclectic charm. The stucco exterior had been painted some years back by the landlord's nephew—an art student, on summer break—and was covered in Magritte's trademark blue sky and puffy clouds. Across this serene backdrop sailed four-foot bowler hats, green apples, rocks, and tortoiseshell combs displayed at contrasting angles over the front, sides, and back of the building. In an area known for its architectural nonconformity, Casa Mariposa still managed to turn a head or two.

I took a hit of jasmine-scented air. With the exception of some lower lumbar stiffness, my back felt pretty good. It was a fog-free morning and the bills were paid, at least for the month. My client referrals from the salon had picked up, and I had several private readings scheduled in the weeks ahead. And while I wasn't generating anywhere near the kind of income my nursing career had provided, prior to my worker's comp injury—or the one I would have preferred, perched precariously on the edge of forty-three—being able to just about cover the bills was a big improvement over the last three years.

Plus, I'd polished off a load of laundry last night and, with the exception of some Audie hair on the futon, the apartment was clean. I wasn't due back at work until Friday and the thought of two gloriously unplanned days stretched before me like an unexpected holiday.

I was steeping my second cup of black currant tea when the phone rang.

"Eileen McGrath?" The crackle on the other end of the line told me the call was coming from the security entrance downstairs.

"Yes."

"Sergeant Burnette from the Oakland Police Department. My partner and I would like to ask you a few questions."

I paused and then pressed the nine button on the handset. A wisp of steam clouded the blue glass mug. The OPD in Casa Mariposa? I hadn't heard of any police presence in the building for a long time. Or in any of the apartments on Glen for that matter. If anything had happened, Jessamae would—

The brass knocker rapped out a sharp staccato on the front door and I jerked, sending a spray of warm amber droplets down the front of my white tee shirt. I watched, in horror, as the thin fabric sopped up the fluid. *Oh, crap.*

I grabbed for the dishtowel on the oven door and bumped Audie's bowl. It wobbled, tipped, and rolled into the kitchen chair. A trail of kibble flew over the scarred linoleum.

The knocker sounded again: three, short, impatient taps.

"Just a minute!" I shouted and swiped at the spots. A beige smear streaked across my right breast.

I threw the towel on the counter and dashed for the living room, cat food crunching under my bare feet. Through the peephole I could make out the fish bowl images of two men: one Caucasian and one African-American. I yanked back the deadbolt and pulled the door open.

The one I took to be the senior officer—a wiry, middle-aged man with wavy salt-and-pepper hair—didn't wait for me to catch my breath. "Ms. McGrath?" he said, flashing his badge. "I'm Sergeant Burnette and this is Sergeant Johnson." He indicated the younger, taller man beside him with a slight tilt of his head. "May we come in?"

I seldom take an instant dislike to strangers, especially those of the public servant variety, but there was something about this man that irked me. Like he was paying lip service to the question mark at the end of his sentence. Like he was issuing a command instead of making a request. Like he already had a search warrant folded neatly inside the inner pocket of his well-tailored suit and seeking permission to enter my home was a mere formality. I held my ground.

"What's this about?" I asked.

Sgt. Johnson, hands clasped in front of him, shifted his thick frame. "Ms. McGrath, we're conducting an investigation into a possible homicide and we have cause to believe you have information that could help us."

Homicide? I studied his broad cheekbones while my brain absorbed the impact of the word. The neighborhood had its fair share of crime, to be sure: car theft, vandalism, a little drug dealing, even some domestic violence. But murder? This had to be some kind of mistake.

I stood aside to let them pass. The cat door in the kitchen creaked and Audie bounced in, fresh from her morning inspection of the backyard. She took one look at the square set of Sgt. Burnette's shoulders and froze in position, her gold eyes round as dinner plates. She emitted a squeak, moon walked a few paces, did a split second turn, and disappeared, in a blur of grey, into the bedroom.

The policeman arched a thick, dark eyebrow. "Nervous cat," he said and eased onto the futon.

Sgt. Johnson coughed into his fist, looking for all the world like a man who was trying to maintain a serious expression.

His partner leaned forward and extracted a small picture from his suit jacket. "Do you know this woman?" he asked and handed me a worn photograph.

I examined the creased image. It was a high-school headshot: a blond teenager in a turquoise drape, posed self-consciously for the camera. Her brassy, badly-layered shag was unfamiliar, but I recognized the wide, blue eyes and the lopsided smile.

I handed the picture back and seated myself in the butterfly chair opposite him. "Yes, I know her. Her name is Laura. Laura Neff."

"And what is your relationship with her?"

"I've done several readings for her."

"Readings?" Two small scars at the top of his nose drew together in a sharp, inverted "V".

"Yes," I said, with a bit more attitude than I would've liked. "I'm a psychic."

It was now Sgt. Burnette's turn to try and keep a straight face. Only I got the impression that he wasn't making much of an effort. In fact, I got the feeling that he wanted me to know exactly what he thought of my choice of professions. And short, redheaded, tee shirt-stained tarot card readers everywhere. If this was an interrogation technique designed to throw me off-balance, it was working.

He suppressed an arrogant smile. "So, you're a psychic counselor, then?"

"No, I'm not a counselor. I do psychic readings for clients at the Paul Roberts salon, in Montclair. And I do private sessions, here, on request."

"Was Ms. Neff one of your regular clients?"

"I guess that depends on what you would call regular. I saw her several times. Once at the salon and once here, at my apartment."

"Did she appear emotional during these meetings?"

"Emotional?"

"Upset?" he snapped. "Depressed? Worried?"

"Actually, she seemed quite upbeat," I said, ignoring the heat prickling my cheeks. "And before I answer any more questions, I'm going to have to know what this is about."

For the first time since the interview started, Sgt. Johnson spoke. "The woman you identified was found this morning, by a jogger." He paused and cleared his throat. "She drowned in Lake Merritt sometime last night or early this morning."

A rush of frenetic energy hit me between the eyes, as if a window had been thrown open and a gale force wind was forcing its way through; I had to fight to hold my head up. From above the chair, I could see my body sliding down, my spine scraping the corduroy fabric . . . and the policemen on the futon watching me. I blinked and rubbed my forehead.

"Are you all right?" The futon frame creaked as Sgt. Johnson leaned forward, tensing his body to stand.

Sgt. Burnette, however, stayed put; his grey eyes analyzing, dissecting the curious specimen before him.

"I'm fine," I heard myself say above the ringing in my ears. There was no point in explaining. Not to these two.

I sat upright. What did they want from me? There were no words to explain this kind of senselessness; at least, none that I possessed.

"Has her family been notified?"

Sgt. Johnson shook his head. "No, Ma'am, there was no

identification on the body, only your business card and that picture, in her purse, at the scene. We would appreciate any information you might have."

The noon sun slanted through the front window and threw a path of light across the hardwood floorboards. I shivered, wishing I was still on the back steps soaking up its warmth. Funny how the mood of a day could shift so quickly.

And now it was about to change for the loved ones of Laura Neff in ways I didn't want to imagine; on a date that would be etched in their memories, forever. And it seemed wrong that I, a total stranger, be made privy to such an intimate loss before them. I tried to focus on the last time I'd seen her, here, in this apartment.

"She came to see me about three weeks ago, around the middle of June, I think. She wanted a general reading, just some feedback about where her life was going. She was from the Knoxville area, in Tennessee."

"Any family in California?" Sgt. Burnette asked.

"No, I don't think so. I had the impression she was very much on her own."

"And why is that?"

"Because there was nothing in Tennessee she wanted to go back to. She described her parents as heavy drinkers who fought a lot. Her father died when she was young and, after his death, it sounded like her mother spent the majority of her time partying with her boyfriends."

"Any boyfriends of her own?"

I had picked up a strong emotional connection around Laura, but in my current state, I wasn't clear on the details.

And I didn't want to disclose anything from the actual reading until I'd had time to think things through. Plus, I was pretty sure the sergeant had zero interest in information he suspected had been acquired psychically. I choose my words carefully.

"None that I remember."

"Did she talk about her living arrangements?"

"No. But she must have lived with someone because she was late for her appointment and, when she got here, she said she had to borrow her roommate's car."

"Did she give you an address?"

"No, but I might have a phone number. Would you like me to check?"

"Please." Sgt. Burnette pulled back his sleeve and glanced at the face of a silver and black TAG Heuer.

I took that as a sign that the interview was over. I excused myself and went into the bedroom to retrieve my daybook from the nightstand. The tip of a broad, bluish tail poked out from under the bedspread.

"Coward!" I whispered and bent down to copy Laura's phone number on a notepad. An unfamiliar ring tone pealed out in the living room. The tail promptly disappeared from view.

When I returned, both men were standing by the door.

"Thanks for your help," Sgt. Johnson said. He took the sticky note and handed me his business card. "If you think of anything else, please don't hesitate to call."

"I won't," I said and returned his smile.

His partner gave me a curt nod.

I can honestly say that I've never been so glad to see the

back of anyone. And I mean that sincerely. For my last glimpse of Sgt. Burnette was that of a well-dressed man striding out into the world with a muscular grace: the back of his dark, beautifully-cut trousers covered in a fine coating of grey cat fur.

Chapter Two

"Slow down," I shouted, over the deafening strains of urban soul.

My bangs beat frantically against my contact lenses, threatening to dislodge them. The curtain of hair in my face obscured the speedometer, but from the rate at which the San Francisco Bay whipped past the glare screen on the top of the temporary divider, I knew the Mercedes SLK 350 was well past the legal limit. My neighbor, Jessamae, floored the accelerator.

She examined the pearly frost on her perfectly contoured lips in the rear view mirror, then veered right across two traffic lanes without signaling. One long silver fingernail tapped out the baseline on the steering wheel as she sang along to the radio, her head swaying back and forth to the pounding rhythm. The midday sun glinted off her bronze skin, her platinum tennis bracelet, and the titian waves that capped her head.

Gravel sprayed in all directions as the silver convertible exited the Eastshore Freeway and raced up the Albany off-ramp. We paused at the intersection for a nanosecond, then swerved right and bounced off a pothole. Jessamae braked suddenly for a red light.

I released my death grip on the creamy leather upholstery. "Don't you ever worry about the CHP?" I gasped.

She peered at me over the top of her metallic, wrap-around shades. "They'd have to catch me first!" She laughed, her smile framing the slight gap between her front teeth.

The tires squealed as she maneuvered a sharp left onto San Pablo Avenue, less than a foot from the bumper of the UPS truck in front of us. Two blocks down the street, we gunned into a parking lot, narrowly missing a red BMW backing out of a space. Temporarily diverted from her close harmony work with Luther Vandross, Jessamae waved at the driver and threw him her most seductive smile, then slid into the spot next to him.

How she and the other inhabitants of the Bay Area had survived her driving for the past thirty years was an ongoing source of fascination to me. She claimed to have never been in an accident and I hadn't spotted so much as a scratch or a dent on any of her immaculately-maintained automobiles. I'd come to the conclusion that there was a benevolent spirit somewhere whose full-time job it was to keep her from meeting the pavement; a force, I hoped, whose protection extended to her passengers as well.

The smell of saffron and bergamot greeted us as we walked through the door of Persia. We took a table at the front of the restaurant, in the enclosed porch facing the street. The sun bounced off the cut-glass panes and threw a spectrum of light across the celadon walls. Behind us, a small terra-cotta fountain gurgled amid the rising volume of lunchtime chatter. A young man in black dress pants and a loose, white shirt approached with a full tray of platters heaped with steaming khoreshes.

"Uh huh," Jessamae said, watching him bend to place the tray on the serving stand next to our table.

"Are you talking about the food or the waiter?"

She surveyed me through a sweep of lashes. "Girl, you know what I'm talking about. Those are some fine looking glutes!"

"You're shameless." I lowered my voice as he walked past our table. "He couldn't be a day over twenty-one."

Her eyes followed his path across the dining room. "A healthy appreciation of the opposite sex keeps you young," she said, in a voice loud enough to turn the heads of the two businessmen at the next table. "And the day I stop looking, you better call up the preacher 'cause I must already be dead. Besides, it wouldn't hurt you, Miz Eileen, to pay a little more attention to the men in this world."

She glared at me over the top of the menu. "With that cute little figure of yours and those green eyes and red hair, you could have a different man knocking on your door every night of the week."

Before I could protest, our waitperson—a decidedly female waitperson—appeared from the back bar with two glasses of water. Clearly offended by this gross oversight on the part of management, Jessamae proceeded to demand a recitation of the daily specials and a full breakdown of their ingredients, followed by a haughty cross-examination of every entrée and appetizer on the menu. By the time she settled on a chicken kabob and a diet Coke, my blood sugar had hit single digits.

She inspected the flatware for cleanliness while I placed my order, then returned to the subject at hand. "When was the last time you had a date?"

"Last weekend."

"Dinner with your gay boss doesn't count!" She stabbed the linen tablecloth with an elegant index finger. "I'm talking about a real date with a man who can appreciate, girl."

She leaned forward, her brown eyes round with sympathy. "Honey, you are living like a nun and that's just not natural."

"I'm too busy for a man in my life right now."

She snorted. "Doing what? Playing with Audie?"

"Doing readings."

"Oh yeah, I forgot you were seeing people at your place now." She pulled the pink cloth napkin out of its paper ring and smoothed it across her lap. "I had an auntie like you back home, in Louisiana. She had the gift, too. She used to call it her 'mixed-up blessing'."

The picture of a blonde teenager with a heart-shaped face popped into my head; an image that had refused to stay submerged in my subconscious for the past twenty-four hours, no matter how many times I shoved it back down there.

"Well, I'd have to agree with your aunt on that one," I said. "Sometimes it feels like a gift, but only if you can do some good with it."

"Isn't that what you do?"

I hesitated. Jessamae had a big heart and an equally large love of gossip. The details of Laura's reading making the rounds of the neighborhood would do nothing to alleviate the metric mooseload of guilt I'd been carrying around since the police visit. Or make the nightmares stop. Still, it would be a relief to talk to someone.

I took a deep breath. "A client of mine was found drowned at Lake Merritt yesterday morning. I did a reading for her a few weeks ago and I feel like I should've seen it coming." There, I'd said it.

Jessamae reached across the table and her tennis bracelet slid down her forearm. She patted my hand. "Darlin', you shouldn't blame yourself. Aren't you the one who's always telling me that people make split second decisions, everyday, that change how their lives turn out?"

The clatter of metal and stoneware signaled the arrival of our food. The waitress set a platter full with falafel, hummus, dolmas, tabouleh, and naan in front of me: an irresistible combination of hot and cold, texture and spice. I selected a dolma and took my first bite of warm rice, pine nuts, grape leaves, and turmeric.

The mixture went dry on my tongue.

I reached for the ice water. "I guess what's bugging me is that I'm usually pretty aware, psychically speaking, if the person I'm reading is in danger or having a crisis. I can't believe I could have overlooked something like murder."

Jessamae forked a plump piece of grilled chicken breast from the skewer. "You think she was murdered?"

"The police who came to my apartment seemed to think it was a possibility."

"What about suicide?"

I picked at the tabouleh. "Maybe, I mean, she could have. But given what I know of her, I don't see it."

"Why not?"

I put down my fork. "Her father was an alcoholic who died in a head-on collision when she was a kid. Her younger brother incurred brain damage, as a result of the accident, and ended up becoming a ward of the state. Her mom couldn't cope—started self-medicating with booze and pills and men."

"Oh, Lord."

"And, when she was sixteen, one of her Mom's live-in boyfriends got a little too friendly. So she ran away from home."

Jessamae shook her head. "That poor baby."

"Yeah, she got handed a pretty raw deal. But from what I saw, she didn't get hardened by it. All that stuff she had to endure seemed to ratchet up her determination to not end up like her parents."

"So, how'd she get here?"

"She pieced together enough to take a Greyhound cross-country. Started waitressing, got her GED, and went back to school for training as a medical assistant. Oh, damn."

"What?"

"I forgot to tell the police about her job."

And there it was again, that sense of dread. Massive, heavy, sucking me down into the center of the earth.

"Girl, are you okay?" Jessamae pointed at my platter. "I don't see any food leaving from that plate." She narrowed her eyes. "Is your back acting up again?"

I conjured up a smile. "No, my back's fine. It's just that I have this nagging feeling that something is wrong . . . about the drowning, I mean. And it's not just guilt or because she was so young. What I remember of her reading pointed toward positive movement in her life. I don't recall anything that signaled depression or suicide."

"Maybe you should tell the police that."

"And say what? That I have a *feeling* foul play was involved in the death of Laura Neff?"

Jessamae toyed with a slice of charred red onion. "Well, you are a psychic. Don't the police use you guys in their investigations sometimes?"

I flashed on Sgt. Burnette's smirk. "I appreciate the vote of confidence, but I doubt that most of the OPD would share you opinion. I'm pretty sure the lead detective would be more likely to follow up on a tip from that guy." I pointed at a tan pug waddling down the sidewalk on the opposite side of the street.

Jessamae grinned. "That bad, huh?"

"Let's just say the minute he heard the word psychic, all my cred went out the window."

"What about the other detective? Could you give him a call? Maybe he'd talk to you about what they've turned up so far. For all you know, they may already have it handled."

She was right; I was probably obsessing over nothing. I had Sgt. Johnson's card on the coffee table. I'd call him tomorrow on my lunch break.

I took a bite of falafel. It was nicely browned, still warm and crunchy. My stomach gurgled in appreciation. This disclosure thing was working; everything was going to be fine.

Outside of the window, traffic moved slowly, steadily down Solano Avenue. A middle-aged couple strolled past, talking and exchanging spoonfuls of pastel-colored gelato. The pug danced on its leash while his pet mom adjusted the sleeping baby in the denim Snuggie on her chest. God was in his heaven and all was right with the world.

So why did I feel like I was whistling past the graveyard?

Chapter Three

The eight-story police station loomed over the corner of 7th and Broadway, near the heart of Oakland's Chinatown. Diminutive, and less gaudy than its more famous cousin across the bay, the retail district teemed this hot afternoon: its crammed storefronts hawking everything from hand-cut jade to dim sum to Buddhist pamphlets to ancient elixirs guaranteed to restore male vitality. Exhaust fumes from idling downtown traffic clung to the air, embellished with an overlay of dried herbs, fresh seafood, smoked duck, and the saltwater tang drifting in from the Oakland estuary.

The sidewalks were congested with businessmen, office workers, and shoppers winding their way past street construction and the city's homeless. Produce piled high in the streets as deliverymen scrambled to disgorge the contents of their trucks. Hordes of elderly Asians scurried past with pink plastic bags bulging with goods, routinely darting out into the path of oncoming traffic.

I had, in fact, barely missed clipping a tiny, wizened couple in matching madras sun visors on my third circuit around the Webster Street block in search of parking. A serious underestimation of the time it would take to drive from the salon to downtown in Friday commute hour traffic had left me ten minutes late for my appointment with Sgt. Johnson.

Ten minutes and counting.

Suddenly an empty space materialized in front of the Cathay Bank. I shifted into reverse, wrestled my battered Mercury Lynx into place along the curb, leaped out, and pushed a handful of change into the meter. I tossed the receipt onto the dashboard and headed for the station at a run—or as close to one as I could manage in the three-inch sandals I'd picked out in an attempt to make myself more presentable than on my last encounter with the detective.

My watch read 4:13 p.m. as I stepped into the cavernous lobby at 455 7th Street. The California and U.S. flags hung on pedestals inside the doors, the folds of their bright fabric in sharp relief to the charcoal granite walls that lined the impressive space. To my right, several uniformed policeman huddled in conversation beneath the face of a large clock sporting bold black numerals. At the far wall, a group of teenagers in hoodies, despite the heat of the day, milled around a bank of elevators.

I approached the Hispanic policewoman behind the desk. "Hi," I said, breathing hard. "My name is Eileen McGrath. I have an appointment with Sgt. Johnson."

She smiled, revealing a glimpse of dimples. "We have two detectives with that name. Do you know which unit he's with?"

I handed her the detective's card. She lifted the phone and pressed the keypad.

4:15.

So much for winning points for punctuality. The second hand swept above the tight French braid that restrained her gleaming hair as an indistinct voice emerged from the earpiece.

"I have a Ms. McGrath here for Sgt. Johnson," she said.

The elevator doors whirred and dinged closed behind me and I strained to hear. I could make out the register of a male voice, rising and falling, but not much else.

4:17.

What was taking so long?

She returned the phone to its molded black cradle. "Sgt. Johnson is unavailable," she said. "But his partner, Sgt. Burnette, will see you." She pointed toward the opposite wall. "Homicide is on the third floor."

The little top hats on my kidneys shot into overdrive: adrenaline, adrenaline everywhere. I stared at Officer Ruiz's nametag and scanned my brain for escape options. Unfortunately, she had given Burnette my name, so to bolt now would well and truly convince him I was a flake. If I wanted to get Laura Neff off my conscience, I had to go through with this, even if meant enduring further condescension at the hands of the O.P.D.'s most arrogant cop.

Fine. I would simply tell him what I remembered and leave. If five minutes spent in my presence offended his delicate sensibilities, so be it. I was, after all, here to provide him with information that might be relevant to his investigation. He should be grateful for my assistance, especially since it was he who had come to me. I crossed the room and pressed the up button.

On the third floor, the elevator doors slid open to reveal a brightly lit corridor with stark white walls and a yellow 'Wet Paint' sign taped to the back of a chair planted in the middle of the hallway. An arrow on the sign pointed to the right and, several yards in that direction, the hallway opened into a crowded room filled with desks, half of which were occupied with plain-clothed policemen. A desktop computer monitor flickered here and there, and the unsynchronized ringing of phones cut through the rumble of primarily male voices.

I was about to ask for directions when I spotted Burnette leaning against a soda machine that had been pulled out from the freshly-painted wall. Energy drink in one hand and corded biceps crossed in front of him, he looked like he was posing for the cover of one of those 'fitness over 40' magazines—an impression not wasted on the pert little brunette gazing up at him. She was playing with the strap that secured her ID badge to her slender neck, and it didn't require psychic ability to see that her rosy complexion had less to do with the day's warmth than with the proximity of a certain detective.

As for Burnette, he seemed to be enjoying the attention, that is, until he caught sight of me. Upon recognition, his spine stiffened and what I took to be a flirtatious smile morphed into thinly disguised irritation. He glanced down at his watch and muttered to his coworker. She turned and did a quick inventory, her dark eyes flashing annoyance at the interruption.

Burnette motioned for me to follow him and began to shoulder his way past the group of teenagers I'd seen downstairs, who'd now formed a bottleneck at the entrance to the room. They scattered as he approached, leaving a path for me to pick my way through. He disappeared into a cubicle in the far right corner.

I paused at the entranceway for direction and, when none came, seated myself on a metal chair that had been pushed back against the mauve, fabric-covered walls inside the cramped space. The air conditioning blasted artic air directly overhead. Cold seeped through the silk top and skirt that barely separated me from the thin chair pad.

He sat back in the tall, sueded chair behind his desk. "Sgt. Johnson told me you had an appointment," he said. As in past tense . . . just in case I hadn't noticed how inexcusably tardy I was.

I decided to skip the apologies. "Yes. I remembered some things I thought might be of help . . . about the Neff case."

He tapped his pen on the surface of the slick, red file in front of him.

I plunged ahead. "Laura mentioned working for a doctor in Marin. A plastic surgeon, I think."

Rap-tap. Rap-Tap. Rap-tap.

"She also talked about an ex-boyfriend, someone she'd broken up with several months ago. She said he'd been calling her recently, trying to get back with her."

Rap-tap. Rap-tap.

The muscles in my neck and lower lumbar tightened; my body's response to the frigid air and warm welcome and the initial offering of more intense sensation to come, no doubt. I shifted in the chair.

"He was a rap producer, in Emeryville. She said she broke

it off with him when she found out he was dealing drugs on the side."

The pen paused in mid-downstroke. He opened the file. "Name?"

"It was like a rapper's name. Fo, Fo . . . Foze, I think."

Burnette looked up from the file, and then flipped it closed. Without noting my statement. "Anything else?" he said.

A tiny pulse began to pound at my left temple, syncing to the rhythm of his pen. *Rap-tap. Rap-tap. Rap-tap. Rap-tap.* He really was being rude. And for no good reason. Well, this had been productive.

I stood up, nearly toppling in my heels. "No, I guess that's about it. But I do have a question I'd like answered."

He returned the pen to its holder, an organizer that contained two others: each one a different color and each one with its own designated compartment. It was immaculate, like the rest of the desk. No paperweights, family or pet photos, or messy personal memorabilia to mar its pristine surface; just a laptop, a wireless phone, and a stacking tray with two perfectly aligned manila folders.

"Do you think Laura Neff was murdered?" I said, pressing my palms into the shiny wood.

He pushed back his cushy chair. "Considering the evidence we have on hand, I would say it's more likely a suicide. Or an accidental death."

"And why is that?" I asked, leaning forward.

Burnette stood and opened the file drawer behind his desk. I guess I'd violated as much personal space as he could stand. Good. Let him be the one to feel uncomfortable for a while.

He cleared his throat. "Your, um, client was found with a significant amount of amphetamines on board. More than enough to impair her judgment and coordination."

Amphetamines? The word ricocheted around my brain like a bullet. Laura, on drugs? Not possible.

"Then there's something wrong with your findings. Laura didn't do drugs."

He dropped the file into the hanging folder. "Ms. McGrath, I don't know what goes on in your sessions, but—"

"I'm telling you there's been some kind of mistake," I said, my voice carrying well over the cubicle walls. "Laura Neff didn't do drugs or alcohol. She hated them. They destroyed the lives of her entire family."

Burnette turned back to face me. "Familiarity can breed more than contempt," he said.

So that's how it was: *Cracker see; Cracker do.* A fait accompli. Poor White Trash, No Inquiry Necessary.

I took a deep breath. "Are you saying that Laura had some familial predisposition to drug abuse?"

"What I am suggesting, Ms. McGrath, is that Miss Neff's upbringing might not have provided her with the best set of coping skills."

"So if Laura had been raised in Montclair or the Oakland hills instead of a trailer park in east Tennessee, she might warrant a bit more of your attention?"

He closed the drawer. "Miss Neff's case will be accorded the man hours it deserves."

A muscle spasmed above his jaw line—only a flicker and constrained quickly—but its presence told me my comment had struck home. And that the interview was officially terminated. It was done and I was leaving with nothing but the knowledge that no further effort would be expended on Laura's behalf, no matter how much I protested.

I had really screwed this up. Until now I'd had a pretty good track record dealing with difficult people, both as a nurse and an intuitive. So, what was going on here? Why was he putting so much energy into making me feel small? And why was I letting him?

And then I saw it, in the middle of his chest.

An iron ball with spikes. A maul. It was positioned in the upper part of the cavity behind his ribs: heavy, smudged, and covered with a scarred shell that had partially peeled away, exposing a red hot surface. I watched, open-mouthed, as it glowed like fresh lava.

Heat flared in my chest, searing my flesh like lit matches. I stared, half-expected to see him tear at his shirt or fall to his knees, screaming. But Burnette didn't flinch; he just stood there and glared with those cold, colorless eyes.

It took all my willpower not to bolt from the office. At the elevator, I pressed the down button and swept the room for a distraction—anything to clear my head. The herd of teenagers had disappeared but there was an Asian kid, not much older than them, slumped in a chair at the desk nearest me; his wrists bound by white plastic, jet-black hair swept up into a topknot. The set of his face mirrored the tattoo on his right bicep: a snarling leopard with a limp rabbit in its claws, fangs dripping blood. It was probably a gang tat, meant to intimidate, but it felt like a cartoon compared to what I'd just seen.

What was up with the elevator? I pressed the button

again and it dinged, the doors finally parting to reveal an empty compartment.

Thank God. I had to get out of here.

Chapter Four

I pried open my eyelids. "What's up tuna breath?"

Audie stood on all fours on my chest and peered down at me. Her chubby face was a study in feline concern, her pupils huge in the semi-darkness. I could feel her breathing slow as I floated up to full consciousness.

Apparently satisfied that disaster had been averted, at least for the time being, she hopped off onto the bedspread. She glanced out the window, her rounded belly and the pointed tips of her ears silhouetted in the streetlight pouring though the sheers. Sighing, she turned around twice and scrunched her considerable backside against my right hip.

I pulled my arms free of the covers, which I'd somehow managed to wind around me, and reached out to scratch the top of her flat, furry head. She began to purr, drool dampening her chin.

"Go easy on the industrial lubricant, furbag."

From the expression on her face you would think I'd told her that she was the most wonderful cat in the world. Which, of course, she was. She bumped her head against my hand, her eyes half-closed in kitty bliss.

I'd probably been crying out. I'd had the dream, again, and for the second night in a row since my visit to the police station. I knew, by now, that the voice was Laura's and that, for some reason, I was picking up on the distress she'd felt in the last moments of her life. What I couldn't figure out was why. Of all the people she'd known in her short life, why was her death being replayed, over and over, to me? And what did the images mean?

A snore erupted from the folds of the bedspread. Audie was already down for the count, her nose tucked discreetly under the end of her tail. Being the chief cat and human watcher was obviously taking its toll. I eased out from under the covers and tiptoed into the living room, closing the door behind me.

It was pretty clear, given the drowning, that the water currents in the dream represented Lake Merritt and the stones and scratchy carpet were the lakebed and its vegetation. But the yellow light, the long corridor, the sweating doors, the explosion in my head—her head—I wasn't getting.

And the name, Ari. And the way she said it, like it was the last thing of real value to her in a world that had shown her precious little kindness . . . one she'd barely had time to sample.

I had to move this sensation out of my body. I needed comfort and grounding. And an energy shift. I padded across the cold kitchen linoleum to the snack drawer and reached inside for the black wrapper with the gold foil: instant serotonin, packaged neatly in a square of fifty-six percent cocoa bean confection.

The moonlight sprawled across the futon. I could see Laura sitting on the end of it, her bare legs drawn up under her, one flip-flop dangling from her toes, speaking in that soft drawl. She would have lost it in time, more's the pity, but she was fresh enough out of the South that it hadn't yet homogenized into a less traceable accent.

The way she spoke, the openness in those wide eyes, her courteous manners—I'm sure made some people mistake her for a hayseed. But she was no hick. Just a sweet, young woman who'd been taken advantage of her entire life . . . by her father, her mother, her killer, and now, by Burnette. Failed by the people who should have protected her, again and again.

I rubbed the goose bumps on my arms. There was a reason I kept having the dream; one I could no longer push away. Laura was reaching out to me and with good reason. Because she knew that I knew I'd let her down, too.

I had to help her. If I could only figure out where to start.

Chapter Five

"So is communing with the dead not doing it for you anymore? Now you're trying to bogart my territory?"

Atticus Spencer crossed his long legs and planted his size fifteen Birkenstocks on his desk; no mean feat considering the narrow spaces between the piles of paper stacked on top of it. Wisps of strawberry-blonde crept past his hair tie and brushed the collar of his lime green Hawaiian shirt. He took a long pull on a super-sized latte.

"Speaking of spirits, your grandmother's a little concerned about the whole pierced ear thing." I pointed to the ruby post in his right lobe. "She wanted to know if there's something you've been keeping from her."

He fingered the earring. "If I didn't know better, I'd think you were dissing my God-given right to be a GQ'd heterosexual."

"I think that's called metrosexual."

"Metro, hetro, what would your spirit guides know about it?" He mimicked a hip-hop gesture with his large, boney fingers. "You're like old school, *dawg*, strictly twentieth-century."

Atticus loved to harass me about being a psychic, even though he'd benefited from my services. We'd crossed paths last year when a client referral, a child abduction case gone cold, and a healthy dose of frustration had brought him to my door. I'd assisted him pro bono and I was hoping he'd be willing to return the favor now.

He reclined in his creaky wooden chair. "Did you tell the OP about the whole medium thing?"

"Sure, Atticus. Right after I got out my crystal ball and made Audie levitate in the middle of the living room."

He let go a belly laugh. "Okay, okay." He held up his hands in mock defense. "You're preaching to the choir, here. I know you've got game. I'm just trying to figure out why they're giving you such a hard time."

"It's not the whole investigating team," I said, taking in the sheer volume of books and manuals crammed onto the shelves lining the left wall of Atticus' office. "Just some jerk named Burnette."

His enormous sandals plunked on the floor.

"Daniel Burnette?"

"Yeah, you know him?"

Atticus chuckled. "We both went to Chipmann High, in Alameda. And we hung out some when I was with the department."

It took a minute for his disclosure to sink in. Somehow I hadn't pictured Burnette as being from the Bay Area. Or as having a community of friends.

"So, he's a local, then?"

"Well, as local as military brats get. His dad was a big deal at the old Navy base. Daniel blew into town his junior year. Made star running back before the end of the season. Kind of a BMOC."

"Big Man On Campus?"

"Yeah. All the ladies were hot for him." Atticus grinned, relishing the look of disbelief on my face. "He ended up marrying my brother's main squeeze."

I flashed on the cozy scene at the station. "He's married?"

"Well, divorced now."

"Let me guess, one woman was not enough for a man of such intellect and charm."

He took another swig of coffee and considered my comment. "Nah, that's not Daniel's style. He's too Catholic for that."

Atticus stood up and walked to the window behind his desk. He pulled the cord on his blinds, raised them a few inches, and released a spray of dust motes into the bright sunshine that spilled through the glass.

He stifled a sneeze. "He and his wife hit a pretty rough patch some years back when their kid died."

"Oh, jeez." A prickle of heat welled up inside of my chest. "Now, I'm going to have to feel guilty for all those evil thoughts I've been thinking about him the last three days."

He shrugged his broad shoulders, creating a ripple effect that ran the width of the tiki mask and thatched hut motif on the back of his shirt. "No sweat, Big Ron, you had no way to know."

The prickle grew hotter and radiated toward my sternum. "Well, I did have a hint at the police station."

"A hint?"

"Yeah, I sometimes pick up sensations from people. Kind of like catching the flu." I paused long enough to will the heat out of my chest cavity. "Now I understand what I saw."

Directly sharing the pain of another human being is never easy. Having an experience that intimate with someone you dislike is downright unsavory. I felt like I needed to take a wire brush and disinfectant to my psyche every time I thought of my encounter with Burnette.

I decided to spare Atticus the gory details. The images I get seem to be specifically tailored to me, like the kind of symbols that repeat in your dreams. For example, metal represents emotion held in check: the more battered it is, the longer the individual has been lugging it around and the thicker or heavier it is, the more effort it takes to keep it under wraps. Sharp points always mean pain. Fire or smoke translates to feelings that linger, like a smoldering sensation. From what I could tell Daniel Burnette was in a world of hurt; one he kept locked down so tight he couldn't get free of it.

"You okay?"

Atticus lounged on the desk's edge. From this angle, I could make out gold flecks floating in the outer edges of his iris and a few freckles splayed across the bridge of his nose—holdouts from childhood, no doubt. I could imagine him as a kid: the gangly daredevil who was on a first name basis with the nurses at the local ER . . . the boy with the bright blue eyes and his own designated chair in the principal's office . . . the kid you kind of envied, because he was always where the fun was.

"McGrath, are you all right?"

I jumped. Ye gods, how long had I been staring at him?

"Guess I'm a little sleep deprived," I said, faking a yawn. Given the last couple of nights, I wasn't that far off the mark.

I stood up and stretched, taking in the second story view of the street. The black, block-letter signage of A. Spencer Investigations overlooked Lakeshore Avenue, a heavily trafficked strip of retail less than a mile from where Laura had drowned. The tired facade of his building, although not as outstanding as some of the Art Deco theatres, stores, and apartment houses that studded the area between Lake Merritt and downtown, displayed the green tile and geometric symmetry typical of Moderne architecture. Except for being located on the wrong side of the Bay Bridge, the office had Sam Spade written all over it: the wheezy old elevator down the corridor, the frosted glass pane in the door between the inner and outer offices, the solitary sink on the wall opposite Atticus' bookshelves—all looked like throwbacks to the 1920s. That, and some rather impressive layers of dust.

I eyed the corn plant next to the window, all brown-edged leaves and drooping pathetically. "Is that a failed attempt at feng shui?" I asked.

I retrieved an old coffee cup from the scraps of paper overflowing the top of his trashcan and filled it from the sink's tap. Slowly, I poured the contents on the cracked surface. The water disappeared below the soil line as soon as it hit dirt.

Atticus observed my attempts to revive the one piece of greenery in his workplace. "If I didn't know better, I'd think you were trying to impress me with your mad domestic skills."

I threw him a dark look. "What I'm trying to impress you with is the fact that I need your help in figuring out what happened to my client."

"Okay, okay, let's go over what we've got so far." He fished out a legal pad and pen from under a pile of papers.

"Laura Neff is a Caucasian female who drowned in Lake Merritt sometime on the evening of July 5th or in the early hours of July 6th. She was nineteen years of age, a native of Knoxville, Tennessee and had been living in California for approximately three years. She gave you no indication, during your readings, that she was depressed or inclined toward recreational drug usage. Correct so far?"

I nodded.

Atticus scanned the pad. "Did Daniel specify what type of amphetamines they'd found?"

"No." I grimaced. "It's a miracle he gave me that much."

He scribbled a note. "The ex-boyfriend, FoZ. He's an Oaktown wanna-be. Into rap. Shouldn't be too hard to track down. We'll start with him and build out our guides from there."

"Guides?"

"Yeah, pieces of information that tell us about the vic and her lifestyle . . . point the way to what happened. You know, *guides*. You're not the only one who uses 'em, ya know."

"Could you be a little more specific?"

"Stuff. Data." He pointed the pen at what he'd just written. "Look, it's Monday—which means Daniel and his partner have probably gotten in four or five days worth of legwork since your client got herself drowned. With the phone number you gave them, they'll have located Laura's address and her roommate, her family and employer. And it's likely they'll have the preliminary lab work detailing the pharmaceuticals she had onboard when she died. That's a decent start."

I rubbed my fingers over a dust-covered leaf. Was it my imagination or did it already look perkier? I tossed the cup into the trashcan.

"So how do I get access to what they have?"

"Don't worry your pretty little head about it. The A-man will hook you up." He gave me an exaggerated wink.

Against my better judgment, I laughed. "Okay, A-man, any suggestions for what I should be doing in the meantime? Other than finding a new home for this poor, neglected plant?"

He reached under his desk to an opened cardboard box and wrestled out an oversized paperback entitled *Under Cover With the A-Man: The Extreme Guide to Urban Espionage.* He thrust it at me.

"Review Chapter Three on interviewing techniques. When we start following up on suspects, there's stuff in there you're going to want to have memorized."

We? I didn't know which was scarier, the title of the book or the thought that I was actually about to participate in a murder investigation.

"Don't worry." Atticus grinned. "It will be Big Fun."

There was that word again.

Chapter Six

Anne Berel started as I turned over the Death card.

I patted her hand, eying the charred skeleton grinning up at us. "Remember, I warned you about jumping to conclusions."

Anne was a Thursday regular at Paul Roberts, a retired hospital administrator with whom I'd occasionally commiserated over the sad state of our health care system. A willowy, sixty-something, there was a nervous energy about her this morning when she'd shown up for her weekly hair appointment and asked if I could fit her in; an energy I'd seen before. When people are visibly uncomfortable about being "read" it's usually for one of three reasons: they view going to a psychic as a possible sign of weakness; they're concerned they will reveal more of themselves than they would care to; and/or they're afraid of the outcome.

In Anne's case, I suspected all three.

"So, what is it that you'd like to know?" I asked gently.

"Well, I guess I'd like to know what you see going on in my life right now. In general, I mean." Her voice sounded like it was about to take wing and fly out the window.

The concern in her deep-set brown eyes reaffirmed what

a quick survey of the cards had already told me. She was, for the second time in her life, passionately in love. And at loss for what to do about it.

"Would you like me to tell you what I see?"

"Yes, please." The pale apricot fingernails of her right hand tightened over the ring finger of her left.

I pointed to the first card in the spread: a woman in a purple tunic dress and a gold circlet, silver-streaked hair flowing down her back. The figure pressed one hand to her heart and extended a red rose in the other. "This card is the one that represents you, in the layout. It shows a woman who has overcome the insecurities of youth, one who understands what it takes to sustain a long-term partnership. She no longer sweats the small stuff or fights over incidentals; she knows what's important and freely offers up the gifts of mature love."

I tapped the pictograph of a jewel-toned spiral on the card next to it. "The general influences surrounding you in regards to your question are those of positive change that has already begun. The message here is not to resist the energy associated with this change; that which is underway is favorable and will ultimately enrich your life."

I laid the Death card across the first two cards. "This position represents obstacles or opportunities and, in this case, indicates a supportive influence. It shows me you're in the process of releasing old sorrows and, in so doing, opening the door to new possibilities."

Anne burst into tears.

In my business, tissues were a staple. Anne was my seventh client at the salon since Tuesday and my supply had taken a pretty good hit. I handed her what remained in the iris-covered box and my hand brushed hers.

The image of a young man with a blonde crew cut, in olive drab, popped into my head. His shirt was unbuttoned, revealing dog tags and an undershirt: the front covered in a triangle of sweat. A metal helmet dangled from the chinstrap of one hand and, behind him, a pack mule carried canvas bags crammed with mangos and coconuts. He smiled directly at me, his palm forward, shielding his eyes from a fierce sun. I let go of the box and he began to fade.

"I'm sorry," she said against the wet folds of the tissue. "What you said about letting go, it reminded me of my husband, Billy." She blew her nose softly.

"Anne, was your husband ever in the military?"

She nodded. "Yes, he was stationed in Guam in the late 1950s. Why do you ask?"

I described what I'd seen.

"There's a photograph of him like you described . . . in my scrapbook at home." Her tears gave way to incredulity. "But why would you see him like that? The picture was taken more than fifty years ago!"

"I'm not exactly sure," I said. "But if I were to make an educated guess, I'd say that's your husband's way of letting you know how he'd like to be remembered—healthy and vigorous."

Anne smiled through her tears. "He was so handsome in those days, like a young Paul Newman." She pulled another tissue from the box and dabbed at her eyes.

I needed to go easy on this next part.

"It looks to me like you've been worrying about Billy

quite a lot lately. And what he would think about the new man in your life."

Her jaw dropped. "I . . . I don't know what to say."

I smiled across the table at her dumbfounded expression. "Well, I'd say that you're a lucky woman, finding two good men to love in one lifetime."

I touched the card in the relationship area of her spread: a gentleman in a fur-lined houpelande, sitting with his lady in front of a roaring hearth fire. "I think your husband would like your new friend very much. It appears to me that they have a lot in common, especially their discriminating taste in women."

She laughed and shook her head. "How could you know all this, from these cards?"

"That's a good question. Mostly, I use a combination of things to help me answer your questions as accurately as I can. Sometimes I see images, like with your Billy, or hear a voice that relays information. Other times, I get a sensation in my body, like a gut feeling that lets me know I'm on track with what I'm saying. During some readings, I experience all three. Then the cards help me fine tune the details of what I've sensed."

Anne's face conveyed complete overwhelm. Maybe I'd save the spirit guide portion of my explanation for another day. I got up and walked to the counter behind her, to the electric kettle I kept plugged in, rain or shine. "Would you care for a cup of tea?"

"Yes, that would be lovely," she said.

I poured the hot water into the bone china cup that I kept for such occasions and scanned the collection of teas on the shelf above it for the coral-colored tin. Ginger peach: the perfect blend for a lady of refinement. The sachet sank into the water and the smell of ripe citrus bubbled upward. I let it brew for two minutes, added a dollop of raw, clover honey, and sat the cup, saucer, and spoon in front of her.

"Are you doing okay?"

She accepted the tea from me. "You must think I'm a silly old woman, reacting this way." Her voice quavered. "I'm not quite sure what I was expecting, coming here." Her gaze drifted across the narrow room.

My boss had done most of the decorating himself, softening the sharp corners of what had been a supply closet with textiles he'd accrued on his world travels; all hand woven and dyed in brilliant hues of blue, berry and green. The translucent quality of the hangings and the diminished light from the one small window lent the ivory walls a velvety appearance that transformed the space into a cocoon: a sanctuary, set apart from mundane interruptions, where it was safe to reflect and express what needed to be said.

Anne relaxed back into the overstuffed chair opposite me.

"Things were so simple when I met Billy. I knew he was the one on our first date. We got married before he went off to the Navy, and started our family almost as soon as he was discharged." She took a delicate sip of the hot beverage. "Things weren't always perfect, of course, but we were what was called, in those days, *simpatico*."

She eased the cup back into the saucer. "The years flew by, what with working and raising the children. I never thought about anyone else—romantically, I mean. When he got sick, I kept focusing all my attention on him getting well. I realize now I was simply refusing to consider a future without him."

She sighed. "When he died, there was a hole inside of me a trolley car could have driven through. I could hardly get out of bed. After a while, I realized that I was upsetting the kids so I started to try and act more cheerful for their sakes. For months, I kept going through the motions."

"Then one day a friend invited me to a game of bridge at her house and Edward was there. He was tall, like my husband, and outgoing. After the game, we got to talking and, for the first time in over a year, I realized I was enjoying myself."

She looked at me, her eyes warming. "One thing led to another and it wasn't long before we were dating. Now Ed wants a formal commitment." Her forehead wrinkled in concentration. "Neither one of us is comfortable with the idea of living together, so I guess I'd like to know what you see ahead for us as a couple."

"Let's take a look at the rest of the spread, then." I pointed to the fifth card in the layout: a winding country road with multiple intersections and road markers. "I see that confusion is part of what brought you here today. This card indicates that you need to reassess your priorities. Once you do, it advises you to stick by the path you've chosen."

I directed her back to the gentlemen's houpelande and the heart, cross, and anchor emblazoned on the back of it. "I believe your friend is a good man. He is capable of deep commitment and values family as much as you. I think that you're evenly matched in your abilities to give and receive love and because you are equals you will experience your relationship as an extraordinary one."

The frown on her forehead softened. She took another swallow of tea. "Do you see anything about the children? I'm concerned about how they are going to handle this."

I indicated the ninth card: a walled castle on a hill, surrounded by a deep moat. "This is the position that pertains to your fears and it shows me that you're going to encounter some resistance initially, from one of your offspring. Do you have a child that's a Capricorn?"

She nodded. "My oldest son."

"Do you remember when your children were younger and you and your husband would have to set limits with them and present a unified front?"

"Oh, yes." She laughed.

"Well, parameter setting is the message, here. Your kids need to accept the fact that you and Edward are capable of making your own decisions, especially in regards to taking your relationship to the next level. If you guys stick to your guns, I believe things will be resolved by autumn. As a matter of fact, I think this will help your children see you as a more powerful woman, in your own right—not only as the woman they've known as 'mom'."

"It's funny that you should say that. My oldest son has never liked change of any kind. When he was little, he wanted to know everything that was going to happen in advance. If you tried to surprise him with a birthday party or even a gift that he wasn't expecting, he would get upset. I have often wondered if my husband and I didn't pamper him too much, being the first baby and all."

"Well, this will be an opportunity for him to let go of some of that insecurity and need to control. You can help him by being loving and consistent, like you did when he was a little boy."

The vision of a plump-cheeked cherub popped into my head.

"Do you have a grandson with black, curly hair?"

"Yes, a three-year-old named Ben." She smiled, as if picturing him in her mind. "He's my oldest son's boy."

"Well, I think he's going to be in the wedding party. I see you and a tall man at the altar with a robed official and a little boy coming down the aisle carrying a velvet pillow, tugging at his bowtie."

Ben's grandmother reached for another tissue.

On the drive home I thought about Anne and the gift she'd been given. Statistically, people who have had one successful marriage stand a far greater chance of creating another one than those of us who have never made that kind of commitment, like they possess a secret knowledge or inner confidence that pulls the right partners to them. In my mind's eye, I could see her Billy; muscular and tan, sweating under the noonday sun, posing for the camera with the cocky assurance of a man who still had most of his life's adventures ahead of him. His picture had been stuck in my head all day.

Which was my psyche's way of letting me know that it wanted me to notice something. But what?

I tried breaking the photograph down into its basic elements: a soldier, a mule, the sun—

The car in front of me screeched to a halt and I slammed on the brakes, my heart flailing at my chest wall. I craned my neck out the window and peered at the road ahead. There were no flashing red or blue lights on 580 and, thankfully, no signs of carnage. I slouched back into the seat and eyed the four solid lanes of traffic between me and Glen Avenue. Welcome to the parking lot.

My hobo bag had flopped over the edge of the passenger's seat and deposited my tarot card pouch on the floor mat. With one hand on the steering wheel and one eye on the road, I leaned over and picked it up. The yellow silk slid from my hands and onto the passenger's seat. I reached over to tighten the drawstring and a card slipped out. It was upside down, but I recognized the imposing figure, standing next to the horse: the soldier of fortune dismounted, at ease, bareheaded in the sun—The Eight of Pentacles.

My scalp prickled. The universe was speaking in its Big Voice. The card was a clue about Laura's murder. Like Anne, the first time she laid eyes on Billy. I just knew it.

Chapter Seven

In 1867, the mayor of Oakland built a dam across the neck of an estuary known as San Antonio Slough, effectively cutting it off from the San Francisco Bay and creating the only salt-water lake within a metropolis in the US. In an attempt to increase the value of the land along its shores—some of which he owned—Samuel Merritt financed the construction of the floodgates necessary to regulate water levels and decrease the salinity of what had been a tidal lagoon. Substantial real estate development followed and, in 1869, he had the area declared a national wildlife refuge, to the relief of north shore residents who were tired of dodging stray bullets from hunters on the south end of the lake. By the 1880s "Merritt's Lake" was ringed with stately Victorian homes replete with private gardens, stables, and boathouses.

Unfortunately, the dam he had orchestrated so severely restricted the volume of the lake's tidal flows that the hundred and forty acres of standing water often sat stagnant and polluted. This led to low oxygen levels, high salinity and periodic fish kills that lasted for decades. In the 1990s, a decision was made to leave the floodgates open for regular tidal flushing, and a more suitable habitat evolved for the fish, crabs, shrimp, clams, and other delicacies enjoyed by both the local wildlife and those traveling the Pacific Flyway.

Today the lake was playing host to a women's crewing team at practice, their oars slicing the smooth green water in time to the cadence called by the leader at the prow. Several sailboats and a couple in a lone paddleboat drifted by as joggers, bikers, and race-walkers circled the three-mile shoreline. The thermometer had risen to eighty and, thanks to the kielbasa roasting on the grill behind me, the park smelled like a slice of heaven. It was the kind of Friday afternoon intended for lounging on the grass with a cold drink, soaking up the sun, and people watching—which made it all the more difficult to get on with what I'd come here to do.

Atticus had called last night to give me a heads-up. According to the police reports, Laura's tox screen had shown no significant abnormalities, except for the presence of 4-methylenedioxymethamphetamine. In the back of my mind, I'd been holding out hope that Burnette had screwed up or was, for some inexplicable reason of his own, winding me up. Listening to Atticus reel off the word brought the truth, and the lump in my stomach, into sharp focus; I had to accept the fact that Laura had ingested Ecstasy a few hours before her death. And now, I had to figure out why.

Her body had been pulled from the north end of the lake. I could see the area detailed in the report not fifteen yards from where I was sitting: a stand of cypress trees next to a lamppost, at the edge of the retaining wall, across from the utility shed. From my seat at the picnic table, I had a perfect view. But twenty minutes had passed in the shade of the oak above me, and I still couldn't seem to propel myself closer to the spot where Laura had died.

The plan was to hone in on any energetic impressions she might have left behind the night she was murdered. Problem was, I wasn't that keen to relive her drowning one more time. Experiencing the dream in the privacy of my home was one thing, but dealing with a psychic hangover out in public could get tricky. On the other hand, if I didn't go through with it, the nightmares might never stop.

I stood, stretched my quads and stepped down onto the graveled path. The three cypress trees sat a few inches from the retaining wall and I stepped into the alcove formed by their gnarled, twisted trunks and overhanging foliage. A good six inches of head clearance extended above me and the lowest part of the branches, making it possible for an adult as tall as 5'8" to have stood upright inside the curve of trees and be well-camouflaged, even in daylight. After sunset, they'd be all but invisible.

Clear water, no more than four feet deep, lapped against the retaining wall. Green moss, jagged rock, twisted tree branches, and a broken Budweiser bottle dotted the lake bottom directly below me. Between the small, oval leaves of the center tree, I could make out the boom that cordoned off the bird islands from the rest of the lake, stretched across the water; the white tubing stark against the brown stain on the segment closest to me.

I took a step nearer the water's edge, squinting to see the

smeared surface more clearly. Up close, it had a reddish cast, like rust. Or dried blood.

The waterscape shimmered, the sun's rays reflecting back off the surface of the water. Shards of light danced in front of me, piercing my brain like hand-cut diamonds. Pain knifed through the back of my skull and radiated forward, serrating thought and movement.

The dappled shade inside the cypress darkened. The shrieks of the children on the play structure behind me peaked in volume and began to fade. They were moving away to some distant place and the thought of their leaving filled me with panic. I struggled to run, to call out to them, but my limbs hung heavy and useless, my tongue flaccid against my teeth. An icy hand compressed my shoulder.

I screamed.

"Jesus, Mary and Joseph. Are you tryin' to give me a heart attack!"

My field of vision sharpened, expanded. It was Tessa, my building manager; one hand gripping her metal water bottle, the other one covering her heart.

"I saw you step into the trees, and I thought that you must be searchin' for something, all bent over and the like." She peered into my face. "You're looking a mite peaked."

Beads of sweat pooled on my forehead and dampened the back of my neck. "I think I need to sit d . . . down." I steered myself to the edge of the grass and found the ground under me with a thud.

Tessa pushed her water at me. "You'd better have some of this."

I accepted the bottle and took a big swallow. The cold

water rushed past my throat, making it spasm. I coughed and my eyes watered.

"What were you doing in there, if you don't mind me askin'?"

I hesitated. Tessa was well aware of how I earned my living and took a dim view of my "meddlin' with spirits". She held the opinion that frequent communication with the dead was simply asking for trouble; a point, I seemed to be going out of my way to corroborate, this afternoon.

I wiped at my eyes with the back of my hand. "A friend of mine lost something out there by the cypress. I was checking around to see if I could find it."

"Using your talents to locate missin' articles, are you?" She winked at me and threw back her head, laughing at her own joke.

Although she'd been out of Ireland for more years than I'd been on the planet, her Hibernian lilt lingered. Sitting here next to her, it felt strangely comforting. The throbbing in the back of my head slowed to a mere pulsing.

A curly strand of grey hair poked out from under the sunhat that restricted the rest of her unruly mane. To be sure, it was the only part of her that was—unruly, I mean. She'd been a nurse when starched hats and uniforms and stockings with white lace-up shoes were the order of the day and, even in her blue jeans and cotton blouse, there was a nun-like air about her that seemed to make wrinkles and dirt turn tail and run before her prim countenance. To put it simply, when we stood up again, it wouldn't be her backside that would be covered with grass stains and goose feathers.

I managed a weak smile and attempted another sip of

water. I needed to steer the conversation in a different direction. She smoothed the worn, brown strap around her neck and I grasped at the obvious.

"Were you bird watching today?" I asked.

"Yes. And a finer day for it, there's never been." She gestured toward a small white-and-grey bird perched on the top of the green lamppost directly across from us. It stood guard on the amber lampshade, twenty feet in the air, casually observing a couple pushing a baby stroller beneath it.

"Take a look at that fella up there." She handed me her binoculars. "See the black tail feathers and the ring around his bill?

I peered through the glasses.

"He's a ring-billed land gull, not usually seen around these parts except in the winter months. I'm not sure what he's doing here this time of year, but he seems quite content."

"And you see those birds sittin' on the boom with their wings outstretched?"

I flipped the zoom lever on the binoculars. A group of large, dark, wet birds with hooked bills came into view, standing eight abreast with their wings spread open like bats in flight. With the exception of one lone seagull hopping from foot to foot between two of them, they were monopolizing the entire length of the boom.

"Those are double-breasted cormorants. They're some of the finest divers you'll ever be privileged to see. They hang about the fresh water inlets to do their fishin'. Unlike most of the other wildlife around here, they don't have any water repellant in their feathers, so they have to dry out their wings after a feeding."

As if to illustrate her statement, one of the creatures drew his wings down around his body and began to flap them in earnest. Apparently satisfied that he was flight worthy, he took to the air, flying level with the water for a few seconds. Like a vampire on the prowl, he disappeared from view behind the trees of the largest man-made island that occupied the middle of the lake. A stocky grey-and-white bird with plumes of white streaming from the back of his neck circled behind him.

"Is that a heron?" I asked.

"Right you are. A black-crowned heron to be exact. He and his kind are a bit lazier than the cormorants and they're not above takin' handouts from the nature center. When they do go fishin', they like to do it on the channel at the 12th Street Bridge around nightfall." She pointed toward the south end of the lake.

I handed the binoculars back to her. A few yards away, a small white bird with a thin black bill swished his yellow feet in the shallow water. He focused on his toes with fierce concentration.

I pointed him out to Tessa. "He looks like he got dressed for an evening out and is fretting over getting his spats muddy."

"That is a snowy egret. If he's worried about anything, it's whether or not he'll be gettin' any dinner. He's stirrin' the water, trying to bring a crustacean or two his way."

She gave me the once over. "Speaking of which, you look like you could stand to put a little meat on your bones. I'll bet you got nothin' in your cupboards but cat food for that mangy beast."

Tessa never missed an opportunity to cast aspersions upon her beloved birds' natural predators. But, for all her bad-mouthing of felines, I would, from time to time, find a chicken skin or shred of roast fish on a paper towel next to Audie's water bowl on the stoop. Tessa would insist it was there because she couldn't stand to see perfectly good food scraps go to waste—a philosophy Audie enthusiastically shared.

"I'll bet that cat will be dining on some gourmet thing or another while you scrounge around for something to stick in the microwave, or one of those God-awful protein bars of yours." She scrunched up her nose.

"Is this your way of asking me to dinner?"

She stood and brushed the non-existent dirt from her pants. "Well, someone's got to feed you. You look like a good stiff wind could blow you over."

"What's on the menu?" I asked, as if there was any real possibility I'd turn down an invitation to her table.

"Shepherd's pie with organic vegetables and grass-fed lamb." She paused for effect. "With iced tea and fresh blueberry cobbler."

Like I said, a slice of heaven.

The sun had descended to the horizon by the time I headed back, visions of Tessa's cobbler making my stomach growl. On my way out of the park, I passed by the lamppost where we'd spotted the land gull earlier in the day. It stood unlit: one of a hundred and twenty-six lamps that ringed the lake—each one donated, each one waiting to lend its incandescence to the string of lights city promoters called

The Jewel of Oakland. Many evenings I'd driven that route home, after work, for the pleasure of seeing the reflection of the pearly light off the shimmering water and the trees of Lakeside Park, verdant, along the shore even at night. To me, it was magic.

But the lake had a dark side, as well: rape, robbery, drug dealing, prostitution, and a history of rioting and sporadic violence that brought an end to the annual summer festivals I'd once enjoyed there. Up until now it'd been hard for me to reconcile that Lake Merritt with the one I loved, like a friend with a hidden life I preferred not to know about. Because once you saw the whole of things, your relationship would change forever.

A cool breeze ruffled the calm indigo of the water and the lamp flickered and came alive. The bulb glowed saffron in the twilight, a beacon against the oncoming night. Its light had probably been Laura's last glimpse of this world; a silent witness to her final moments before the lake claimed her—and to the face of her killer, hidden in the shadows.

Water lapped against the boom and the stained segment bobbed in the shallow depths. I rubbed my arms. It was time to get home to Casa Mariposa and Tessa's kitchen and what I hoped would be a night of dreamless sleep. I needed my psyche well rested for tomorrow.

And my first meeting with FoZ.

Chapter Eight

FoZ, aka Paul Fotakis, stroked the soul patch between his thumb and tattooed index finger and slouched back against the ivory leather sofa in his spacious living room.

"Yeah, I was tryin' to get back with her. Who wouldn't? You ever seen her, man? She was all that."

Behind the ink-work, rapper moniker, and multiple piercings, Mr. Fotakis' Mediterranean roots were showing. With his black curly hair, olive skin, amber eyes, and a physique that must have required some serious gym time to maintain, it wasn't difficult to imagine his effect on the ladies. Or why Laura had been attracted to him. After those redneck boys she'd grown up with, FoZ must have seemed downright exotic. For a split second, I caught myself wondering what their children would have looked like . . . had he or someone else not killed her.

"So, how did you and Laura meet?" Atticus asked.

FoZ eyed the two of us as if he were seriously considering the question, or getting ready to show us the door—I couldn't tell which. Atticus had introduced himself as a professional investigator who'd been hired by the family to inquire into Laura's death and, me, as his assistant. I wasn't convinced that he'd bought either story; that is, that Laura's family had the means to afford a P.I., or that it would take two people to conduct an inquiry as straightforward as this one. He must have been questioned by the police enough times to know when he was being played. I only hoped that Atticus' strange mix of obsequiousness and urban slang could keep us in the penthouse long enough for me to get a bead on the substance emanating from FoZ's solar plexus: a clinging, grimy energy that put me in mind of smoke hanging in the air on a wet day. Grief?

Or guilt?

He inclined his head in the direction of San Francisco. "We hooked up at a club, in the city. She was different, you know, not dressed all trashy like most of the bitches there."

He exchanged a knowing look with Atticus. What a relief to know the double standard was alive and thriving in the generation nexters. I stifled the urge to roll my eyes and pretended to scribble something on the notepad Atticus had given me to look the part.

"She was fresh, ya know." FoZ picked up a pack of cigarettes from the marble and glass coffee table and lit up. The sickly sweet smell of clove drifted in my direction.

He sat forward on the couch and inhaled deeply. "In my business, everybody wants somethin'. Everybody got their hand out or they're running some kind of game up behind you. It's all about take and take." He rubbed his thumb over the fingers of his left hand to demonstrate. "You gotta have somebody watchin' your back twenty-four seven."

He exhaled a twin stream of smoke from each nostril.

"Laura wasn't like that. She wasn't looking to take nothin' from nobody." He raked long, conical fingers through his tousled hair. "Hell, hyphy wasn't even her thing. She was more like a trance chick, you know, without the thizzle."

Hyp-ee? Thistle? I scrawled the words onto the notepad. Atticus was right, I was old school. I glanced over to see if the gangsta rap was throwing him. The expression on his face was oddly serene. And impenetrable.

The film around FoZ's midsection began to deepen in color and spread, growing more solid and easier to visualize. A matrix of charcoal grey threads floated upwards and adhered to his chest. They fluttered there, clinging to the front of his torso.

"She was so pretty, man, inside and out." He released a smoke ring from his fleshy lips. "When we'd go clubbin', ya know, she'd chill 'till I got done with my business. No drama. No tryin' to get wit other guys." He stamped out the cigarette in a cut crystal ashtray. "Not my girl."

His use of the possessive was creeping me out. Big Time. But the sadness in his extraordinary eyes told me that he was sincere and that, at least in the moment, he was buying his own story. Which means that he was either telling the truth or was a complete sociopath.

So his feelings for Laura were genuine. He was still a neanderthal . . . a neanderthal with a business to protect. And a bad-boy reputation that wouldn't likely allow for his woman choosing another lover over him. I took a cautious breath of nearly clove-free air.

"So, why did you split up?" Atticus asked.

FoZ picked up the cigarette pack and squeezed it. "Same

ol', same ol'." He shook his head. "Some freak got jealous, started turnin' her head, fillin' it with lies about how I was makin' my money. Made her think I was dealin'."

He extracted another cigarette from the crumpled pack and lit up. "Somebody who knew she didn't want nothin' to do with drugs, no kinda way." He stared at the glowing end between his fingers. "Hell, she's the one that got me started on these nasty things. Thought they'd be better for me than my smokes." He inhaled and gazed out the plate glass window at the bay, thirty stories below.

The morning fog had burned away, revealing a broad expanse of water that extended from the Bay Bridge to the Marin Headlands and encompassed an impressive view of San Francisco's skyline. Half-naked twenty-somethings undulated on the fifty-inch flat screen behind the couch, next to a fully stocked bar with recessed lighting and rows of what I took to be Baccarat crystal. The cream-colored carpet—so deep I could see my footprints—matched the calfskin recliners Atticus and I were sitting in. So much bling and so little happiness.

"Do you know anyone who might have wanted Laura out of the picture?"

FoZ shook his head. "No way, man, not her."

"How 'bout some of your friends? It sounds like she was something special. Maybe one of your boys wanted a taste? Got a little jealous?"

"No way."

"So, maybe you got jealous."

FoZ raised his eyes to meet Atticus and all that his statement implied. Their gazes fused like two rams locking horns; amber versus blue in a full blown stare down. According to Atticus' book, the initial interview was supposed to be an exercise in building the suspect's trust, which he'd now effectively blown out of the water. What was he up to?

My empathic sensors shot into overdrive. I didn't know which was worse; the smell of testosterone or the stench of clove. I squirmed in the recliner. For one awful moment, I thought I felt the building shake. I could picture myself on 80 East: smashed like a gnat, under the rubble of the Christie Towers. It would serve me right for getting myself involved in this. Damn Atticus and his interviewing techniques.

Out on the water, a tanker blew it's horn and drifted toward The Gate. FoZ cocked his head to the side. "You askin' me to do your job for you, Mr. Dee-tect-ive?" He drew out the last word with a air of practiced insolence.

Atticus shrugged. "Just keepin' it real, Mr. Fotakis."

"Yeah, well." FoZ fondled the tuft of hair on his chin. "If I were in your, uh, shoes…" he paused, propping his bare feet on the edge of the coffee table and giving Atticus' cowboy boots the once over, " … I'd be askin' myself who Laura had plans to hook up with at the lake. Yeah, that's what I'd do." He smiled broadly and took another drag.

I glanced at his solar plexus and got nothing. Just a black tee shirt stretched over an impressive set of pecs and the air brushed image of a white-faced, eyeless dog. And a smirk so patently calculated I wanted to wipe it off his face. Which was, I'd be willing to bet, the reaction he was aiming for.

A chorus of deafening ringtones cut through the silence.

He laid the cigarette in the ashtray and picked up his razor thin phone.

"Thistle?" Atticus roared with laughter, "Thiz-zle, grandma, thizzle." He banged his hand on the steering wheel.

"All right, thizzle. What does it mean?"

"Girl, ain't you never felt yourself?"

"Excuse me?"

He merged onto 80 West, squeezing his Honda CRX between a big rig and a mud-splattered Ford F-150. "It's an expression that clubbers use to describe how they feel when they're high. They say they're thizzin' or feeling themselves."

"And hy-pee?"

Atticus glanced in his rearview mirror at the four lanes of traffic creeping toward the intersection of 580, 880, and 80, then maneuvered into the Oakland-bound lane. "That's H-Y-P-H-Y. It's a kind of music that came of the hip-hop scene in the Bay Area. In Southern California, they call it crunk. Around these parts, it's hyphe. It means to get way crazy or hyper. Kinda like a Pentecostal revival with DJs instead of preachers—minus the snakes, of course." He chuckled to himself as we accelerated through the MacArthur Maze.

"So let me guess, trance is when ravers space out and swirl about the dance floor like their grandparents did at Woodstock."

"Very good." He nodded his approval. "It can get kind of dark, but it's generally floaty, in a visceral sort of way. Trance fans are usually pretty young things with pacifiers and glow sticks."

"Pacifiers?"

"You don't want to know. But, what's worth noticing, here, is the common thread." We exited left on MacArthur Boulevard.

"You mean other than people feeling themselves?"

"Besides that, yeah."

I'd read enough Bay Area weeklies to know what the drug of choice was for clubbing. "Ecstasy?"

"Yup."

"Do you think FoZ might have tricked Laura into doing some?"

"Maybe. He loves him some bad behavior and he thrives on negative press. He recently got some buzz for permitting a side show in the parking lot at one of his events."

"You mean the car spinning thing?"

"Yeah. Unfortunately, when it happens out on the street, it can involve blocked intersections and attracting the kind of crowds where things have, historically, gotten nasty, as in fist fights, gang rapes, etc. At one side show, a few years back, a rope was tied around the steering wheel of a car that had a brick planted on the accelerator, and aimed into a patrol car. The officer inside ended up seriously hurt. In FoZ's case, there was no damage, but not keeping a tighter reign on his security didn't win him any points with the OPD."

"Do you think that was an attempt to attract more media? Show how edgy his events are?"

"I think it's more likely that it turned into a situation he didn't intend with a bunch of hyped-up kids outta control. From what I heard, he didn't let things get too far outta hand. What makes him really interesting to local law enforcement is the question of how he's financing his various business ventures. It's generally assumed that he's using his connections within the music industry to buy, distribute, and sell drugs, but no one's been able to catch him at anything more incriminating than using bad judgment. Which still doesn't make him a murderer."

He squeezed the yellow light onto Piedmont Avenue. "What do your spidey-senses say?"

"I'm not sure. Despite that bit of theatre at the end of the interview, I think he's honestly sorry Laura's not in this world anymore. But that doesn't make him innocent. And speaking of theatre, what's with the accusation flinging? I thought the interview process was about winning over the suspect and getting them to confide in you."

The brakes squeaked as we eased up to the curb in front of Casa Mariposa. Atticus left the car idling. "It's all about timing, my eager apprentice. Besides, you didn't expect me to give away all my trade secrets, didya? I have to save something back for volume two."

I lifted my shoulder bag out of the nest of discarded burrito wrappers and Slurpee cups that littered the bottom of the car. The passenger door creaked in annoyance as I pushed past it. I looked down at Atticus, pretzeled around the steering wheel with the front seat pushed back as far as it could go.

"Why do you drive around in this thing?" I asked, slamming the door on the rust bucket. "Wouldn't an Escalade or a Hummer be more appropriate for a mack daddy like you?"

"Oh baby, this is my scrapper. You know, keeps my

M.O. on the down-low." He made a pop-locking gesture with his right arm.

"Alright, A-man, what's next?"

"Give me a call in a couple of days and we'll figure out the game plan."

Sounded good to me. I was hungry and tired and had a reading scheduled in a couple of hours. Plus, I needed a little down time to sort out what I'd sensed during the interview. I waved goodbye and started up the steps to the front door. I'd just fished my key card out of my purse when Atticus honked.

"You might want to take a look at this," he shouted.

I turned to see his pale, freckled arm stuck out of the window, waving a small, green piece of paper. I walked back to the curb and took it from him. It was a postcard; bulk mailed on flimsy card stock with smeared ink, partially illegible, and printed in English and Spanish. As best as I could tell, the card offered high interest auto loans to those with less than pristine credit histories.

I held it out to him. "From the looks of things, I'd say you need this more than I do."

He motioned for me to flip it. "Read the backside," he said.

I turned the postcard over. It had been mailed to Christie Drive, #301; FoZ's place in Emeryville. And it was addressed to Paul Aristotle Fotakis.

Aristotle . . . Ari.

Chapter Nine

"Bout the time the day goes down,
  devil whispers in my ear."
"Asks me why you're not around
  and who's holdin' you, my dear."

"Try to put you out my mind,
  like so many nights before."
"Too much whiskey, too much wine,
  only makes me want you more."

The melody drifted across the empty dance floor of Ruby's Place, its bittersweet chords hushing the racket at the bar. It was a pretty good crowd for a Monday night and everyone's attention was on the burly pianist seated at the mahogany Yamaha upright: eyelids closed, shaved head gleaming as his thick shoulders, hunched in navy pinstripe, swayed over the keyboard. His whiskey baritone bent the notes, sliding in and out of the cracks between the keys—vibrato punctuating the age-old themes of love and loss. His voice embraced the mellow tones of the old piano and mated with them, rendering them silky and deep like a fine piece of chocolate . . . the kind of confection that leaves you temporarily sated and then longing for more. Like the elusive lover in the song.

"Never thought I'd be the one
  left drinking, on this stool."
"Never thought I'd be the one
  to play your green-eyed fool."

"Got to take myself away,
  get me out of this place."
"Forget your talk, your sweet sashay,
  forget that angel face."

"Can't quit your angel face."

The vocalist and the sax player drew out the last note, synchronizing a perfect A minor chord fade. Atticus stamped his feet and whistled between his teeth as the band took a bow.

We were seated at a table not far from the stage at the club that Jessame managed. She looked particularly sultry this evening in a low cut, magenta sheath dress and filigree chandelier earrings. She was in her element; greeting customers, gossiping with the patrons at the bar, and eying Atticus with all the subtlety of a hungry fox who'd just been let into the hen house.

Inviting him to Ruby's Place had seemed like a good idea. The four musicians on stage were part of a larger blues band, the West Coast Rhythm Review, and did weeknight gigs at small venues. Atticus was a fan of the full band and I thought this would be a way to thank him for the help he'd given me with the investigation. What I hadn't counted on was Jessamae's inherent love of flirting.

"How are you two doing?" she cooed and leaned her zaftig self across the table. She set a freshly drawn mug of ale in front of Atticus and wagged one of her talons in my direction. "That girl is so tricky, keeping a good looking man like you all to herself."

She slid a chair up next to Atticus. "How come I've never see you around before?"

He stared at the head on his beer as if it were a substance he couldn't quite identify.

I took up the introductions. "Jessamae, this is Atticus Spencer, the private investigator who's helping me out with the client I told you about."

"Oh, smart as well as handsome," she purred. "How's that going?"

Atticus didn't respond, just raised the mug to his lips and gulped. A few drops dribbled down his chin onto his shirt and one of the dolphins doing laps on the front of it. Even in the dim light, I could see him pinking up.

"The lab reports Atticus got from the police showed that Laura had taken Ecstasy on the evening she drowned," I said. "We're in the process of trying to figure out what that's about."

"Um, Um, Um." Jessamae shook her head, making her earrings dance. "That stuff is messin' up our young people bad."

"It sure seems to be everywhere." I paused, waiting for Atticus to jump in about government conspiracies and the planting of drugs among minority youth; precisely the kind of thing he loved to go on about. But the A-man seemed to have temporarily lost the power of speech. And his face was now as red as his hair.

Jessamae wrinkled her brow. "I had a nephew who was into the whole rap scene and he was telling me that you never know what you're getting when you buy that stuff. He said each new batch that hits the streets looks different. Maybe that poor baby didn't know what she was taking."

She had a point. Except that I couldn't really see Laura taking drugs of any kind. Or how the Ecstasy played directly into her death. I could envision her hallucinating, or becoming anxious or faint due to changes in heart and blood pressure, or any number of side effects that might have contributed to a loss of coordination. But it was unlikely that a one-time dose would have killed her.

Unless she had a hypersensitivity to one of the chemicals in the drug . . . a sensitivity her killer knew about? Someone who was aware of her hatred of drugs? Someone who wanted to make a statement?

From across the room, the bartender signaled. Jessamae stood, discreetly adjusted her knee-length hemline and draped her arm around my red-faced friend. "It was so nice to meet you," she said and extended a hand sporting a large, radiant-cut diamond.

Atticus took her hand and shook it. He kept pumping and pumping until Jessamae, giggling, gently extracted it. She waved a demure goodbye and turned toward the bar.

Atticus took another gulp of beer, nearly strangling himself in the process.

I patted him on the back as Jessamae cut a shapely swath through the crowd. "Are you okay?"

"Fine," he wheezed. He set his mug down—half on, half off the coaster. "Just thinking how much this place has changed."

"Changed?"

"Yeah, it's more upscale than it used to be." His eyes swept the spot where Jessamae was holding court at the bar.

"You used to hang out here?"

He nodded. "When I was with the department, we used to chill after work. It was more of a blues joint, in those days . . . sawdust on the floor, Sonny Boy Willamson on the jukebox." He took another sip of ale. "Burnette would come around from time to time."

"It's kind of hard for me to get him as a blues and beer kind of guy."

"Well, whiskey was more his thing, but he managed to have a good time."

I was not in the mood for further Burnette-centric conversation. I'd just begun to allow for the possibility that, with Atticus' help, I might come across evidence viable enough to make the OPD take a second look at Laura's case. And I didn't feel like being reminded of how ineffectual my last visit to the police station had been.

"Look, I don't want to spoil a perfectly good evening by talking about that man. It's clear that he and I are not going to be able to communicate in any way that's useful to either of us." I surveyed the Margarita dregs at the bottom of my rocks glass. "I am genuinely sorry that he lost his child, but that doesn't excuse his behavior."

Atticus shifted his considerable weight on the small wooden chair. "I know how he can come off sometimes, but there are a couple of things I think you ought to know."

"Like what?"

"Like there might be some mitigating circumstances about him and this case."

"Such as?"

"Such as the fact that his daughter died in an accidental drowning. And that she had a passing resemblance to your client."

"I don't see what that's got to do with—"

"She'd been sneaking out, swimming in a neighbor's pool while the family was on vacation. She was a pretty good little swimmer for a nine-year-old, but something went wrong and she drowned. The house was at the other end of the development and the pool hidden from the street, so she wasn't found until the family got home—nearly a week after she came up missing. His wife consulted a psychic, after she disappeared, and was told she was still alive. She held out hope for days. Long after the kid was dead."

He paused. "Are you beginning to get the picture here?"

I was getting it alright, in HD. I didn't want to but I was. Not ever having had a child, I could only guess at how awful the loss must have been for Burnette and his wife. It didn't make me like him any more, but it certainly did explain his reaction to me.

"So, if I hadn't been a psychic, do you think he might have been willing to put a little more into the case?"

"Possibly. I don't know if it's that cut and dried. I'm just saying that I could see that this might have stirred up some stuff for him. As it was, he did everything by the book. Even followed up your lead about FoZ."

"And you know this how?"

"I called him a couple of days ago and told him you'd hired me. We discussed what he'd turned up, off the record." Atticus polished off the last of his drink. "For what its worth, I told him I thought you might be onto something."

A trace of foam still clung to his upper lip and I found myself resisting the urge to brush it away. He really was a good man, going to bat for Burnette—and me. Big and funny and smart and loyal. All and all, it was a pretty appealing package.

"Is that your way of telling me that you don't think I'm a complete whack job?"

He closed one eye and leaned back in his chair. "A little height challenged, maybe, but definitely not whack." He grinned.

"So, you're okay with my Ari/Aristotle theory?"

"Yeah, I think it's worth keeping in mind. But even if his name was the last word out of the vic's mouth, it doesn't prove FoZ killed her. Maybe she didn't like how they ended things. Or maybe she still loved him. We need more to go on."

"From whom?"

"If I were you, I'd question the roommate. She doesn't have much of an alibi for the evening Laura drowned. Could be interesting."

Interesting? Not exactly the word I'd use. But I couldn't

expect Atticus to devote all his time to Laura's investigation. He had a living to earn, too. It was time for me to put on my big girl pants and take this thing on, ready or not. I was scheduled at the salon the next couple of days, so maybe Thursday, early in the day. Before I could give myself a chance to chicken out.

"Nice to know you think I'm up to it."

He slapped the table. "No sweat, Big Ron, you were trained by the best."

"Yeah, but you left out the part about petty thievery." I still hadn't figure out how he got his hands on FoZ's postcard. We'd both been in the living room throughout the entire interview and I hadn't seen him palm anything.

His reply was drowned by the opening chords of a scorching blues riff. The guitarist moved to the front and center of the stage and the energy in the room shifted instantly. The woman at the table in front of us jumped to her feet and began swaying to the sultry backbeat the drummer was laying down behind the pianist's eight-to-the-bar rhythms, the rolling motion of her ample hips telegraphing an invitation for her partner to take her to the dance floor. Couples brushed past us and crowded onto the hardwood.

Atticus shrugged out of his leather jacket and mouthed the word, "Dance?"

I hesitated. I didn't know if mixing business with too much pleasure would be a smart move right now. Or how far I wanted this evening to go.

Over Atticus' shoulder, I spied Jessamae pushing her way through the crowd toward our table. As enjoyable as it would be to watch her weave her spell, I should probably spare him another estrogen-induced coma. Besides, I was seriously overdo for some fun.

I grabbed his big mitt of a hand and pulled him onto the floor.

Chapter Ten

Laura's roommate opened the door. She was short and stocky with greasy dishwater blonde hair and an oily complexion the color of pizza dough. Her pierced navel and a paunch of pale, puffy flesh hung over the top of a painfully tight pair of low rise white jeans. A skimpy, ribbed, white tank top and a red rollup cap, combined with her other physical attributes, brought to mind a human fireplug: an unhappy little fireplug, named Ravenwaif.

I stepped inside and she closed the door, shutting out the constant hum of traffic on San Pablo Avenue. The apartment reeked of scorched popcorn, and was as dumpy as its inhabitant. Everything in the living room wore the same depressing shade of beige, from the carpets up— furniture, peeling wall paper, and curtains. The blades on the blinds that covered the one window in the room were folded tight against the morning sun, but so badly bent that a few rays of light still managed to penetrate the gloom. A glimpse between them revealed the water-stained retaining wall at the back of the building.

But the living room held one blast of color. On the

purple computer hutch, next to the front door, sat a sleek and sexy desktop with a Chameleon green skin and lights pulsating from its innards: techno blue from the side vents, teal from the ports in the middle of the chassis, and a violet glow from the skull shaped logo. It was the mother of all gaming gear, the kind of toy your average teenage male would give up an appendage to own. And the perfect entrée for Atticus' first rule of interviewing: *Create a rapport with the client.*

"Check out that system!" I said. "You must be a serious gamer."

A guarded enthusiasm lit up her pudgy face. "You could say that," she said, in a loud, adenoidal tone.

"MMO?"

"Of course."

"PVP or PVE?"

"RP realms, mainly."

"Cool," I said, nodding my approval. "You don't find it hard to stay IC?"

"Not really."

"Do any RPPvP?"

"Yeah, I'm starting to get into it with my sorceress." She eyed me with open curiosity. It had apparently not occurred to her that one of the people she'd engaged in role play with on her favorite massively multiplayer game might be me. Which, as it happens, was not the case. But she didn't need to know that.

"Favorite race?"

"Elf."

"Class?"

"Priestess."

"Level?"

"Eighty."

I whistled appreciatively. "You must be pretty hardcore."

"I play some." She shrugged.

From the look of the dried tomato sauce and cheese on her pants and her bloodshot eyes, I'd guess she played more than some. I would, in fact, be willing to bet that, barring an occasional trip to the microwave, her life revolved around the 24" monitor in front of us. A monitor presently displaying a post:

> *"She raised the sword of Ilnore and plunged it into the screeching wyvrn, the edges of the blade glittering as the creature's foul, black blood spewed across her burgundy robes. The mists of the Tainted Wood swirled around her as she pulled the arcane crystal from beneath the corruption that was now its writhing carcass. Holding the glowing stone aloft, she summoned her griffin, mounted, and began the journey back to the Veiled Lands. She would be honored there by the nightkeepers, in their homeland. She would return a Lightbearer and finally free the heart of Cerberus."*

So our little geek girl had a romantic side. And an impossibly beautiful and hard-bodied avatar who roamed the virtual world in search of experience points, epic quests, and the heart of a fallen hero. An avatar named Ravenwaif?

"Fan fiction?"

"Uh huh." She stepped between me and the monitor, effectively blocking the screen. Never mind her thousands of online "friends"; guess I'd read more than I was intended to see. Go figure.

"May I sit down?" I asked.

"Whatever." She shrugged and plopped down on the chenille-covered sofa.

I seated myself on the opposite end of the couch in an attempt to create some physical distance between us, for her sake as well as mine. I sensed that she wasn't too comfortable with people, in general, and I wasn't too comfortable with the current state of her personal hygiene which, at the moment, was pretty ripe.

"How long did you know Laura?" I asked.

"About six months."

"How did you meet?"

She flopped back against the threadbare cushions. "She answered my Craigslist ad."

"Why El Cerrito?"

"The rent, I guess." She shrugged, again. "Or maybe the commute."

"Did she talk to you about her job?"

"Not really. She was kind of a workbot."

"Long hours, you mean?"

Ravenwaif yawned. "I don't know," she said irritably. "After she dumped FoZ, she started spending most of her time in Marin."

"Did she talk about why?"

"Nope."

"Did she ever mention her co-workers?"

"Nope."

It was clear any cred I might have earned for my

knowledge of gaming was swiftly evaporating. And that I was losing control of the interview—something Atticus' book had warned against. Ravenwaif's puffy eyelids drooped.

I refocused on my mental list of questions. "Did FoZ come around?"

"Yeah, he came by a few times."

"Do you think he might be connected to her death?"

"Nope."

"Not even to get back at her for breaking things off?"

Her eyes snapped open. "No."

"You seem pretty sure about that."

Ravenwaif sneered. "He was a player. Laura wasn't anything special to him."

"That's not what he says."

Her mud-colored irises lit up with unguarded hostility. This was the most lively I'd seen her all day. I'd obviously hit a nerve.

She glared at me. "Gossip is not my thing, okay. I'm giving you my opinion."

"Okay. Are you of the opinion that Laura was into drugs?"

She heaved an exaggerated sigh. "You mean like getting high?"

"Yes."

"That's not what she did for shits and giggles."

I waited for her to extrapolate further on Laura's idea of a good time, but none was forthcoming. Her ephemeral body, however, was speaking volumes. Waves of spikey, multicolored energy emanated from Ravenwaif and shimmered around her like a host of angry wraiths; pulsating emotion as visible to the inner eye as the Northern Lights. Her posture and facial expression implied profound boredom, but her ego and armpits were doing a core meltdown.

I'd had about enough snarkiness for one day. And B.O. But I needed one last thing.

I stood up. "I appreciate your time. I'd like to take a look at Laura's room, before I go."

She flicked a wrist in the general direction of the hallway to my right.

I crossed the living room in four steps and turned down the short hall to what I hoped was Laura's bedroom. As I reached for the door knob, I heard the sound of a PC being awakened from its slumber. Dungeons to raid, trolls to kill: a Lightbearer's work is never done.

I opened the door and involuntarily shielded my eyes. In contrast to the gloom in the rest of the apartment, the sunlight pouring through the yellow sheers was blinding. It took a couple of seconds for my pupils to adjust.

The room was a ten-by-twelve, probably the smaller of the two bedrooms in the apartment. The predominant piece of furniture was a twin bed, covered by a quilt with a star pattern of gently-hued blue, yellow, and white patches of fabric. The coverlet had been hand-stitched and closer inspection showed Laura's first name embroidered in one corner of it. Given its size, I would imagine it had been made for her when she was a child; a legacy from her days in Tennessee.

There were two other pieces of furniture in the room: a

bookcase and a chest of drawers made of white particle board. A romance novel, a community college catalogue, an art text, and a seahorse-shaped, mother-of-pearl box sat on the top shelf of the bookcase. A peek inside the pink velvet-lined box revealed a pair of thin, gold hoop earrings and a tiny pair of gold studs.

I sat down on her bed. With the exception of an alarm clock and an IPOD docked on the chest of drawers, the space was free of electronic gadgetry. The closet was open and about half-full of neatly organized jeans, skirts, dresses, and shoes.

A hint of citrus clung to the air; the fragrance she'd worn the night of her reading. It was the kind of scent that most women Laura's age wear too much of—only in her case it came across as clean and light and welcoming, like this room. The exact opposite of the hermit's den next door.

The Hermit, the Ascetic, the ninth card of the Major Arcana. A squat friar in a rough-hewn cloak chasing after a three-headed dog. A dog that had always reminded me of Cerberus, the Greek guardian of the underworld. As in, Cerberus, the sightless dog. As in the image on FoZ's shirt. The light show I'd witnessed in the living room; it was all about Ravenwaif and FoZ . . . and the biggest boss monster of all: Desire.

Chapter Eleven

"There's a cat named Audie
 who lives in my house."
"She don't pay rent,
 never caught me a mouse."

Audie loved it when I sang to her. The content of the lyrics were unimportant as long as there were frequent references to cats, kitties, or, best of all, her own name. She sighed and scrunched deeper into my lap.

"That kitty sleeps in late,
 never misses a meal."
"Like to know how she sold me on
 such a purr-fect deal."

Two neighborhood squirrels—one hot on the bushy tail of the other—scampered up the trunk of the yellow maple next door and rustled the thick-leaved branch just inches beyond the living room window. Normally their antics would have her diving for the window sill, but not this evening. Between work, private readings, and my attempts at sleuthing, I hadn't had much time to hang out with her this week. Now that the proper balance of the universe had been restored, she was staying put, which was okay by me. There were worst places to pass a sultry Friday night.

I'd been mulling over my suspicions about Ravenwaif and trying to position her on my list of suspects which, at this point, was a pretty short one. That she was infatuated with FoZ, I knew, but how likely her feelings were reciprocated was questionable. I really didn't think any physical relationship had occurred between them and, at the risk of sounding cruel, I was pretty sure he wouldn't have pursued her had she made it known she was willing.

Her demeanor and near total disregard for her appearance told me she'd probably missed out on the social experimentation many of us devote countless hours to in our youth. Being so in her head, she probably hadn't had the chance to learn how to attract much in the way of close relationships. So what's a woman of superior intellect and limited social skill to do when faced with the intensely attractive and utterly unobtainable object of her desire? Knowing full-well that if her wants were revealed, she'd be rejected? She retreats to a safe haven where the relationship can be lived out in her fantasies or, in this case, on the internet—an impossible romance hidden in plain view.

And, best of all, a romance with a dark and tragically flawed anti-hero; a mythological creature with three heads, one of them canine and the servant of Hades. A watchdog charged with keeping the living from passing through the gates of the underworld and devouring any spirits that might try to escape. A monster with a weakness for music. It wouldn't take much of a leap for Ravenwaif to connect the myth of Cerberus with FoZ's shady persona and logo and exploit it in her heart and fan fiction.

The ethereal pyrotechnics she displayed when I brought up FoZ's attachment to Laura revealed, in technicolor, the depth of her jealousy. But was it enough for her to have offed Laura? Unlike FoZ, who had corroboration from his posse at the time of Laura's drowning, Ravenwaif had told the police that she was at home by herself on the night of July 5th. That was the problem with being a loner: no backup. Even though I'd be willing to bet that FoZ's peeps were far from credible witnesses.

All this thinking had left me parched. I reached for the ice tea on the side table and unsettled Audie in the process. She gave a grunt of protest and stretched a chubby paw across my thigh, hooking her claw lightly into the worn denim of my cut-offs. Possession is, after all, nine-tenths of the law.

I savored the cooling effects of the honeyed amber liquid on the back of my throat and thought about how stifling it must be in Ravenwaif's apartment. I couldn't imagine being shut up in that dump. Although, in some ways she and I were not so different.

Granted, I curried the favor of the thirteen-pound feline snoozing on my lap on a daily basis, but—Audie aside— hadn't had a significant relationship in years. Nor was I sure I wanted one. Dancing with Atticus the other night had felt good, I had to admit; I had almost forgotten the sensation of being held in the arms of someone you genuinely liked.

But, if memory served, the price of attachment could be exorbitant.

And I was pretty sure it had cost Laura her life.

Chapter Twelve

The plump, pink salmon gave off a tangy aroma, sizzling on the grill. I'd marinated the filet for several hours this morning, and the mouthwatering bouquet of olive oil, garlic, lemon juice, Worcestershire sauce, and mesquite served as a fragrant reminder that I'd skipped breakfast. Wild coho was a dish that Audie and I both loved, and it had taken considerable machinations to get it in and out of the apartment without her noticing. I was feeling only slightly guilty for not having left her a piece.

I'd been looking forward to Saturday all week. A few months back, Atticus had purchased a two-bedroom Craftsman bungalow in the Rockridge area of Oakland, and had finally accumulated enough household goods to throw an impromptu barbeque. His house had been built around the turn of the twentieth-century, at a time when the Arts and Crafts movement was in full flower in the Bay Area. The movement had come about as a reaction to the excess of Victorian design, he'd informed me, and emphasized the importance of using simple elements and locally derived, natural materials in home construction.

His one-and-a-half story house resembled every other home on the tree-lined street: low pitched roof, horizontal lines, stained wood shingles, and an expansive front porch. It was a hot afternoon and the opened casement windows captured the breeze blowing in off the bay, providing natural air conditioning to the redwood-paneled interior. The house itself blended into the surroundings, so much so that the boundaries between the interior and exterior blurred—an effect, I really liked.

A dozen of Atticus' neighbors milled around the backyard, dissecting the A's game in progress on the ginormous flat screen in the living room and sipping on beer and wine coolers. Our host was on the deck, in full possession of the grill. He was wearing his dress shirt today: a hot pink hibiscus and teal plumeria print, which clashed with the red stripes in his apron. He poked at the salmon with his tongs.

"Tell me again, what's so good about this stuff?"

"The omega-three fats."

"As opposed to?"

"Omega-six fats."

"What's the difference?"

"The omega-three's have two kinds of fatty acids in them—DHA and EPA—that help to prevent and treat everything from heart disease to Alzheimers. They also have antioxidant and anti-inflammatory properties. When I hurt my back, the fish oil really helped me to reduce pain and increase mobility."

Atticus raised an eyebrow. "I thought Americans eat too much fat."

"We do. But we eat diets high in the omega-six fats; the oils that come from sources like corn, canola, safflower, etc. Ideally, we should have a one-to-one ratio between the sixes and the threes. Lots of people have ratios as high as fifty-to-one."

"So, what should we be eating?"

"Wild salmon, grass-fed beef, free-range chicken. And cut out the junk food." I pointed at the bag of potato chips he'd been noshing from.

"Are you insane?" He grabbed the bag and cradled it against his chest.

"No, I just care enough about my body to do a little research."

He flipped the filet over and narrowed his eyes.

"So what are you, the Queen of the Food Nazis? I'm not giving up my fried spuds. No way!"

"Have you ever tried roasting them in the oven? With a little olive oil and sea salt, they're really quite tasty."

He winced. "But that's so inconvenient."

"So is a heart attack."

"So is a tong attack."

He advanced, making a pincer motion with the end of the tongs. For a second, I stood my ground. Then it dawned on me he had no compunction about smearing my one good sundress with grease. I shrieked and ran for the kitchen.

Just past the opened door I collided with something solid. And amber scented. The force of the impact pushed the air out of my lungs and I staggered back into Atticus.

"Daniel!"

Dazed, I watched as Atticus extended his hand to Burnette.

"What's up, man?"

"Looks like you are." Burnette shook Atticus' hand and his eyes swept the deck. "Nice place," he said, nodding.

"Well, it's not the Hiller Highlands, but I like it."

So, Burnette lived in the highlands. Probably in one of those pricey condos that was all but guaranteed to come crashing down the Oakland hills when the Big One comes. Nothing like trading the threat of daily extinction for a great view. How appropriate.

"A gift for the house." Burnette lifted a bottle from the paper bag he was holding: a twelve-year-old bottle of single malt whiskey.

"It's from my private stock. From Galway."

I was pretty sure he wasn't talking about Galway, Nebraska. Well, at least he wasn't a cheap gifter. Pretentious, but not cheap.

Atticus' face lit up like a hundred-watt incandescent. He genuinely liked the man. Go figure. There really was no accounting for taste. Or smell.

"The salmon!" I grabbed the tongs from Atticus and sprinted to the grill. I yanked the filet off the grill and plunked it on the platter. It was blackened and smoking, the flesh charred beyond repair—the meaty side, not the skin side. I could scrape off the scorched portion, but there wouldn't be enough left for the guests.

Burnette whistled long and low. "What did you do to that fish, man?"

"Is it ruined?" Atticus asked.

"Well, not all of it," I sighed. "But what's left won't go very far."

I turned to find both of them staring at the incinerated mass on the platter. Atticus' hangdog expression echoed the disappointment I felt. I didn't know who I was the most sorry for: me, him, or the salmon.

Burnette squared his shoulders. "You have any honey?" he asked Atticus.

"By the grill."

"Pasta?"

"Yeah, somewhere."

"I think this fish can be resuscitated."

He picked up the platter, honey, and a bottle of Dijon mustard sitting on the deck railing and disappeared into the kitchen.

I wasn't sure I was liking this; that is, Burnette taking charge of the salmon. It was, after all, my fish. I followed after him.

He was already mixing the honey and mustard at the sink, whisking the frothy concoction against the insides of a glass bowl with efficient strokes. The sleeves of his white, collarless shirt were rolled up and he'd tucked a towel into the waist of his jeans.

He glanced up, then returned to the task at hand. "Do you know where he keeps the pasta?" he asked over his shoulder.

"I think I can find it," I said a bit tersely.

A survey of the cabinets between the sink and stove turned up a bag of rotini. Ditto for a saucepan in the drawer under the stove and bottled water in the refrigerator. I emptied most of the liter into the pan with the pasta and placed the contents on the stove to boil.

"Kind of expensive, isn't it, using bottled water for pasta?"

His eyebrows and forehead were doing that inverted "V" thing. Like he was really puzzling over my choice of cooking liquids. Like it was any of his business. Well, we weren't going there. If I didn't want chloramines in the salmon salad, it was my call.

I leaned back against the stove and crossed my arms in front of me. "Not as expensive as a twelve-year-old bottle of Irish whiskey."

The corners of his mouth twitched. He finished the dressing and began scraping burned bits of fish into the sink.

"How long have you known the A-Man?" he asked, his eyes focused on the salmon.

"For about a year."

"How did you meet?"

I couldn't tell if this was an attempt to turn the conversation in a polite direction or was another police inquiry. Since he and politeness didn't seem to spend much time in each other's company, I surmised he was sizing up my intentions. Which was reasonable, I suppose. Only I wasn't sure what kind of relationship Atticus and I were having right now. And I wasn't about to confide in Burnette. I tightened my arms.

"I feel like I'm being cross-examined here."

Burnette looked up. "Sorry. Do you know if there are any vegetables around here? Something to fill this out?"

I opened the refrigerator. It was devoid of anything but the water and some soda and beer. I pulled open the drawer to the crisper. There was a crookneck squash, one small zucchini, and a red bell pepper; undoubtedly contributions from one of Atticus' neighbors.

I presented them for approval. "Will these do?"

"Excellent," he said. "Chop them up."

Boy, he sure liked to be the boss of things. Okay. For Atticus sake, I'd play nice. I ferreted out a chopping board, a knife, and some vegetable wash.

Burnette had located a large bowl and was tearing bite-size pieces of salmon into it. The bright yellow color of the china complemented the pigment in the fish and the dressing like it'd been custom made for it. The man obviously knew a thing or two about presentation.

"I have the impression you've done this before."

"I've given a few dinner parties," he said.

Silence settled over the kitchen. I cleaned and dried the veggies and cut the zucchini and squash into paper thin slices. I'd nearly finished chopping the peppers when he spoke again.

"How is the Neff investigation going?"

I focused on the knife's edge. Anything I said would only draw more questions, which I wanted to avoid. What I had intuited so far—FoZ's possessiveness toward Laura and Ravenwaif's infatuation with him—weren't suitable subjects to discuss with Burnette. The only tangible piece of evidence we had was the postcard with FoZ's full name on it and I couldn't see explaining the significance of that without telling him about the dream, which he would lend no credence to.

"I guess you could say we're still in the information gathering stage."

"Atticus is very good at that," he said, shredding the last bits of salmon. "When he was on the force, he was one of the best investigators we had."

I wasn't sure how to follow that up. Or why he was bringing the case up at all, now that he'd washed his hands of it. I finished the pepper and went to check the pasta. It was *al dente*. I pulled it off the stovetop and drained the hot water into the sink.

Burnette tossed the noodles into the bowl with the fish. He retrieved the saucepan from the sink, added a dollop of olive oil, and placed it back on the burner. When it hissed, he reduced the flame and slid the veggies into the pan for sautéing.

"What do you hope to get out of this?" he asked.

It took me a minute to realize he wasn't talking about the salad. Truthfully, I wanted a lot of things. Like a good night's sleep. And the ability to know that the information I gave my clients would serve them. To put a face to whoever was hiding in the cypress trees that night by the lake, and see them standing, exposed, before judge and jury. And to be able to picture Laura, in my mind, the way she'd been that evening in my apartment, instead of floating on her back in a pool of shadows.

"I guess you could say that I'd like to clear my conscience," I said, as much to myself as Burnette.

He removed the pan from the stovetop. Adding the contents to the bowl, he set the pan in the sink and rinsed it, simultaneously dodging the steam rising from the hot cookware. He drizzled the honey mustard dressing over the salmon and folded the ingredients together.

"You do realize that you and Atticus have a tough way to go on this one?" he said. "There is no evidence of a crime. *No* injuries inconsistent with the head trauma Miss Neff suffered when her head hit the boom. *No* witnesses to the drowning. The only real suspect you have is someone who's made a career out of being untraceable. What do you think you'll accomplish by going through with this?"

Good question. For the first time since I'd meant him, we were in a conversation that didn't leave me completely on the defensive. He thought I was engaging his friend in a fool's errand and he wanted me to know he didn't like it. I could understand that.

We were two individuals with separate sets of concerns, considering the same situation from different perspectives. From his citadel of logic, I did appear foolish. But, from my viewpoint, The Fool represented fearlessness: the kind of courage that it takes to believe in yourself and whatever you've been called to do, even if you're clueless as to how you're going to get there.

I smiled. Not at Burnette, but at the memory of a slight blonde teenager, one flip-flop dangling from metallic pink toenails, her face lit with the promise of her tomorrows.

"Laura was alive with possibility," I said. "She had a shine about her that made this world seem less jaded and gentler somehow because she was in it. I won't have that memory diminished by a lie. Or a mistake."

He wiped the edge of the bowl with the towel he'd tucked at his waistband. I stole a peek at the salad. The reds and greens and oranges popped. Thanks to him, no one at the barbecue would mistake the dish for the blackened ruin it had been fifteen minutes ago.

I pinched off a bite. It was delicious.

A cheer went up from the living room. The Athletics' pinch hitter had just homered with the bases loaded. Burnette picked up the salad and carried it out onto the deck. I started after him and then checked myself. Maybe I'd go into the living room and mingle with the faithful, sip a Blue Moon, savor the victory. As grateful as I was for his culinary prowess, I was ready to hang with more relaxed company.

And get my mind off the case for a while.

Chapter Thirteen

My triceps burned. It'd been a while since I'd been on a mountain bike and even longer since I'd ridden without the benefit of fingertips shifters. Synchronizing pedaling and shifting from the crossbar required more focus than I remembered, and a lot more coordination, but if a decrease in gear scraping was any indication, I was emerging from the learning curve. And my back seemed unaffected by the activity. Maybe it was time to rethink buying a bike—a later model then the rented clunker under me.

Still, it was a beautiful afternoon to be out in the woods. It was a bit humid for this time of year, but the extra moisture in the air had brought with it the scent of damp earth and ripe blossoms. A breeze wafted through the dense foliage that projected out over the trail and stirred the tree limbs, ferns, and thick brush. Except for the asphalt road, it was uncleared forest: one layer of green draped over another with an occasional red leaf spear or fluted yellow blossom peeking out from ground level.

The hill beyond the next curve towered up ahead; not exactly Kilimanjaro, but a good forty degrees straight up and a bit prodigious for my fitness level. I took a deep breath, relaxed my shoulders, and began to weave back and forth across the surface of the hardtop. It was the wimp's way to take the incline, but there was no one else around, so what did it matter?

I reached the summit no worse for the wear; in fact, I'd barely broken a sweat. I must be in better shape than I thought. And the vista below was well worth it. To the west, terraced rocks reached for the clouds, their faces smoothed by eons of wind and water. Rivulets sprang from the slabs of stone and flowed past frilly shoots of wet greenery, tumbling to the pool below.

At the bottom of the hill, the road bent left in a hairpin curve that swerved past a turnout then veered back to the right. The turnout was heavily graveled and, unlike the rest of the trail, there were no trees to block the view. Swift water rippled past, a sheer thirty-foot drop from the lip of the shoulder, murmuring and crystalline in the summer heat.

I dropped low over the handlebars and leaned into the turn. Cool wind brushed my face, pushing my hair back from my forehead. The wheels hummed in perfect cadence and something small and hard ricocheted between the spokes of the front one and broke free, flying out at such a velocity it became unrecognizable in its bid for freedom. Heavy wings rustled in the branches overhead.

The crank set rattled as I repositioned my hips and the saddle tipped backward, nearly unseating me. The frame began to shake in earnest and I compressed the brakes gently and got no response. Centering my hips, I eased off and squeezed again, this time with more pressure. The bike continued to pick up speed and I stood up in the stirrups in an attempt to create wind resistance. It was then I realized I wasn't wearing a helmet.

I was racing downhill now; handlebars vibrating so hard, my teeth chattered. It was taking all my concentration not to bite my tongue. I really didn't need another back injury. Or a head trauma. The turnout loomed ahead with the long drop below.

Above me, feathered scarlet arched against a cloudless sky, its shrill cry, a warning: "KA-WALK, KA-WALK, WAK-WAK-WAK." The tires jounced across the uneven hardtop and spun out, full speed, into a pile of gravel. I leaped off, shaking but intact. Only my left toe remained tethered to the dented toe clip. I heaved a sigh of relief and pulled it free.

Then I stumbled and fell backward over the edge of the precipice.

The icy wet jolted me awake. The sheet was wound around me, covered in sweat. The bedspread and Audie were nowhere to be found. Maybe she'd taken it and headed for higher ground.

The first fingers of morning light reached through the curtains. I propped up the pillows and eased my back against them. I hadn't been this restless in years ... not since the worker's comp injury. And then it was because of physical pain—my pain. Now I was operating as a fully functioning receiver for someone else's.

The empath's curse: a phenomenon with which I was well acquainted. And not a particularly useful sensitivity when your chosen profession involved working with sick people. Many was the time I'd "caught" my patient's symptoms. And if I let myself get emotionally involved, I'd have to make a concerted effort to detach or I'd take on their full-blown illnesses as well. Visualization or Tai Chi would usually get me past the worst of it, but there were times I needed massage or acupuncture to move the stuck energy out of my body.

In this case, I was disinclined to believe that any amount of bodywork would close down the connection. Laura was very much in communication and broadcasting from a new location. So, why the change in venue? She couldn't have drowned in two places.

The terrain and the woods had a familiarity. Maybe a scene from the south? The mountain trails of Virginia and Tennessee were practically identical. I could be picking up on a memory from her life there: a biking accident that involved falling into a lake or stream.

So what did this have to do with her drowning here, in California? Was she showing me a childhood trauma? Or trying to convey that the person who killed her knew she had a fear of water?

I pulled the blanket up over me. It was too early in the morning for this kind of guesswork. Any secrets hidden in the dream could wait till later in the day for consideration. Much later.

Chapter Fourteen

A barefooted man in torn chinos with sun-bleached, matted dreadlocks that fell well past his waist paced up and down in front of the Berkeley BART Station, punching the air and laughing to himself. He threw a few jabs at an invisible opponent, then dropped his emaciated torso onto a nearby bench. Pedestrians streamed out of the station and he watched them intently, pouring over their faces as if searching for one that was familiar. The crowd thinned and his head dropped to his chest and lolled to one shoulder.

Out on Shattuck Avenue, a car horn blared. He jumped awake and off the bench, suddenly executing a remarkably graceful pirouette in midair. In a language decipherable only to himself, he barked out what I took to be a command and resumed pacing.

I tossed the remains of my tepid soy latte into the bin of stained cups by my table. In the twenty odd minutes I'd been sitting outside of the coffee shop by the station, I'd seen him repeat the scenario twice and, with the exception of an occasional glance from the pigeons scuttling around his feet and myself, no other bystanders paid him any attention.

Sights like this were so common in many Bay Area cities that they failed to register any measurable response from most of us. Perceived as too insignificant, pathetic, or unsettling to retain, the images of those who'd fallen through society's cracks got automatically deleted from our busy, important lives.

I was waiting for Kalie, Tessa's niece and a grad student at Cal. She'd recently rescued a mixed breed dog and hadn't been able to locate its owner. Her inquiries at the local animal shelters had gone unanswered and with the majority of the salon patrons on vacation and Atticus in Marin interviewing Laura's employer, I had a few hours to spare—all the rest of Monday afternoon, for that matter. Maybe I'd be better at animal communication than I was at interpreting my own dreams.

I spotted her tendrils of shoulder-length, flame-tinted hair, about half of a block down Shattuck Avenue and the ripple of activity from people turning to stare as she passed by. She was striking—not just because of the hair and the porcelain complexion that accompanied it—but also for the way she carried her 5'11" frame, in a more relaxed version of her aunt's steely posture. Kalie stepped up to the traffic light at the crosswalk and my mouth dropped open. Beside her, on a leather leash, stood a copper-colored animal roughly the size of a mountain lion.

My mouth was still open when she reached me. "Good lord, where did you find this creature?" I said.

She threw her arms around me for a quick hug. "He was running down the street. On Fruitvale Avenue," she said, releasing me.

Her companion examined me with almond-shaped, gold eyes. His coat hung long with the color and thickness of a cocker spaniel's, but his face was broad like a husky's, only with a shorter muzzle. Stranger still, he showed none of the need for constant motion that I'd seen in both breeds. He displayed a quiet nobility standing next to Kalie, a nobility accented by his most curious feature: a thick mane that gave him the appearance of being almost as leonine as he was canine.

She reached down to stroke the top of his head. His jaws parted in an expression of contentment and I gasped. His front teeth were horribly mangled with six incisors and one canine tooth jagged and uneven, as if they'd been sawed.

"What happened to his teeth?" I asked.

"I'm not sure. When I found him he was dragging a chain. There were marks on it that made me think he might have chewed through it to get free."

So this animal had the heart of a lion as well as the bearing. I offered him the back of my hand. He sniffed it briefly and then took a step forward, pressing his one hundred-odd pounds against the side of my legs. I petted the top of his head and he panted contentedly. He nuzzled me with a scarred, pink-and-brown speckled nose.

"What a big sweetie," I said, enjoying the wet of doggie nose on my palm. "Does he have a name?"

"I've been calling him Mara." She laughed. "It's the only region in Tanzania I can remember and he looks like he's fresh off the Serengeti." She ran her hand down his spine, drawing my eye to the clumps of fur missing from his back and withers.

The foot traffic at the light had formed a bottleneck, with every pedestrian stopping to check out Mara. Reluctantly, I quit petting him and we started up the street toward Hearst Avenue, Kalie and Mara walking a few feet in front of me on the crowded sidewalk. Passersby continued to turn and, from my vantage point, I could see why.

Together, they embodied the beauty and the beast myth. And the Fortitude card: a lion, leaping from his cage, released from imprisonment by an angel with wild, curly red hair—modeling the inherent strength and creativity needed to free ourselves from limitation, self-imposed or otherwise. Clearly, Mara was a living testament to that spirit.

We rounded the corner of Hearst and walked half of a block to her apartment building, a three-story, pink stucco. At Kalie's suggestion, we sat down on the postage stamp of a lawn and Mara settled in between us. Thus far he'd shown no signs of skittishness or anxiety. I was taking that as a good sign.

"So, how do we do this?" she asked.

"Well, you don't have to do anything," I said. "In my experience, animals are usually quite open in their communications. I'm going to ask Mara some specific questions and we'll take it from there. But I want you to understand that I won't try to force him to remember. If he becomes uncomfortable in any way, I'll stop the reading."

Kalie shook her head in agreement.

I positioned myself so that I was facing the dog. *"Where did you come from?"* I asked.

Mara looked up at me, back at Kalie, and then up at me again. He settled his haunches deeper into the grass and placed a paw the size of my fist on my right foot. Images flooded into my brain. A masculine voice began to narrate the scene before me.

I interpreted what I was seeing for Kalie. "He's showing me a picture of two smaller dogs, about half his size, jumping up and down, barking. They're kind of frenetic. Does that mean anything to you?"

"They're probably my roommate's dogs; she has a Jack Russell and a Corgi. They're pretty hyper." She grinned.

"He's saying, that even though he knows they're silly and annoying at times, he's glad to have them around. He says they help him to forget the sad times."

"Sad times?"

"Yeah, let me see if he'll elaborate on that."

What makes you sad?" I asked. The two dogs vanished and new pictures began to form in my mind.

"He's showing me a place with rusting metal, car parts, trash. I think it's a junkyard or some kind of garage. His paw is in a bowl of spilled water and a man is yelling at him. He wants to get away." My heart began to thud against my chest.

"The man is shouting and he doesn't understand why. I think he's showing me a memory from when he was a puppy. He's very confused and frightened . . . he doesn't like the way the man smells, or the way he touches him."

The odor of sweat and rancid grease filled my head. "He says he was very lonely there. He's showing me children running by a chain link fence laughing and stopping to look at him and he is telling me sometimes they threw rocks. He says he used to sit and watch and hope they'd stop and play."

My chest ached. The longing in this animal was palpable; so much so, I could hardly bear it. Sadness welled up inside of me. My psyche strained to pull back, but I wanted to get Mara's story.

"Is there anything else you want me to know?" I asked. The dog seemed to sense I'd seen enough of that part of his life because, once again, the scene changed.

"I think he's remembering his litter," I told Kalie. "There's a tan, brindled puppy next to him . . . I can feel its fur and body warmth. He says the first two dogs he showed me remind him of his family and that his life was hard after he was taken away. But he's happy now, with you."

A feeling of contentment bubbled up inside of me as he showed me a picture of Kalie grooming him. "He says he really likes it when you brush his coat. He thinks that means you will let him stay."

Kalie took his enormous head in her hands and blinked back tears. "Of course, I'm going to let you stay, you big goof." She buried her face in his thick ruff.

I reached out to pat Mara. "At the risk of pointing out the obvious, I wouldn't spend any more time searching for the previous owner. I think he wanted a far more aggressive canine than our gentle giant here. I would give this one all the love I could and not look back."

Mara thumped his tail in agreement.

Swaying back and forth in the BART car, I thought about the man at the station and Mara and how easy it is to write off those we consider to be lesser beings. Like Burnette with Laura. And, most of the rest of us, when we see people dirty and begging for money or food on the street. Yet Mara, guided by an intelligence and courage I couldn't begin to gauge, had found Kalie and begun a new life for himself, against impressive odds. I wanted to believe the same opportunity existed for the homeless man. I wanted to think that because deep down I knew that, short a few paychecks and a handful of friends, I could be that man. And the thought terrified me.

I was pushing through the turnstile at the MacArthur station when my cell phone rang. On the other end, I could hear Atticus, or at least every other syllable of what he was saying.

"Can you repeat that?" I yelled over the accelerations of an AC Transit bus.

"I said . . . have you ever worked in a doctor's office?"

"On occasion, why?"

"I think it's time you got some cosmetic surgery experience."

Chapter Fifteen

Janis Keene looked like she'd collided with something massive. And angry. Her pupils were barely visible behind the bruised and edematous flesh that disguised her eyelids and blood droplets oozed through the white ointment that glistened on her raw, scraped cheeks. She winced as I gently peeled back the bloody gauze partially adhered to her face. Beneath it, her skin had taken on the shadings of a cheap red wine spilled across a white tablecloth with serosanguineous fluid crusting her nose and chin. This was the kind of facial trauma I would expect to see coming out of the ER, but Ms. Keene had paid for the privilege. She was a seventy-two hour post-op blepharoplasty/chemical peel. Now I knew why there were no mirrors in exam room one.

Further assessment showed no hematoma or signs of infection. Her radial pulse was a jumpy ninety but her other vital signs were within normal range. When I asked her to describe her pain level on a scale of one to ten, she said it was a twelve and instinctively smiled at her joke; a decision, I could see, she immediately regretted. I patted her hand and reminded her not to engage her facial muscles right now.

Becoming a medical assistant for Laura's employer had been easier than I'd anticipated. I'd emailed my resume on Tuesday, got called in for an interview the next day and pretty much hired on the spot. As luck would have it, the practice only needed someone with patient care experience to fill in three days a week until the new grad they'd lined up became available at the end of August. They were willing to overlook the fact that I was overqualified as long as I was willing to overlook being paid fifteen dollars an hour, which pretty much explained why the position was still open.

No more clients than I was seeing right now, even a trickle of steady money would come in hand. On the drive home from Marin, I negotiated my way into on-call status at Paul Roberts until the end of summer. Then I dusted off and ironed my two remaining pair of scrubs, and spent the evening reviewing Atticus' interview techniques. With only four weeks to play detective, I needed to hit the ground running.

It was Friday, my second day on the job. With the exception of the handshake that'd followed my interview, my contact with Dr. Neil Landon had, thus far, been minimal. He was not yet forty, tall and gawky, with hazel eyes and scraggly light brown hair that had a habit of looking perpetually windblown. And he was reserved to the point of being monosyllabic. The past two mornings he'd shown up with a SF Giants' hoodie thrown over rumpled scrubs and a scratched and dented silver Bianchi on his shoulder. Between his diffidence and appearance, it was difficult for me to imagine how he competed against the heavy concentration of cosmetic surgeons in the Bay Area sporting slick, aggressive marketing techniques and personas. But his patients seemed to genuinely like him and there appeared to be no shortage of people in want of cosmetic enhancement or reduction.

In addition to him, there were two female staffers and I'd been working at not being overly inquisitive in front of any of them. I'd done my best to be professional and friendly and get up to speed with my job description which basically consisted of taking vitals, assessing patients with an eye to pain control, reinforcing post-operative instructions, and changing an occasional dressing. After years of working the floors, it felt like a cakewalk.

The office manager, Marina, was a chunky middle-aged lady who ran the office like a well-oiled machine. She was fastidious in both her appearance and work ethic and leaned heavily in the direction of micromanagement. She had a penchant for pastel-colored scrubs with flower motifs and seemed utterly devoted to Dr. Landon, who appeared to leave all management decisions up to her.

The other employee, Karin, was a pretty blonde about my age and the part-time biller. She was the mother of two teenage girls and loved to talk about their antics. Family came first with Karin, and she was considerably more laid back than Marina in her approach to work—an obvious source of friction between them.

Atticus had suggested that I focus my attention on the staff, initially. He felt that if anyone in the office would be forthcoming about Laura, it would be them. "Them" meaning people who were female; that is, people who liked to talk. He stopped short of using the G-word, but I knew what he was getting at. And I fully intended to exploit that predisposition.

I assured Mrs. Keene that the doctor would be in soon, reviewed my assessment, placed her chart in the plastic holder on the door, and closed it behind me. The clock over the front desk read 4:00 p.m., just one more hour until the day was done. I slipped into the tiny kitchen that passed for the employee break room and located a packet of green tea.

Marina stepped through the door as I poured hot water over the bag in my cup. "Do you like that stuff?" she asked, pointing at the sencha tea.

I watched the steaming water turn golden and considered her question. Truthfully, I preferred black tea, but couldn't find anything else but this and coffee on the premises. And I didn't want to sound ungracious, being the new kid on the block.

"I drink it sometimes," I said.

"It tastes like grass to me. I was going to throw it out since no one else drinks it. But if you like it, I'll keep it around."

"What's it doing here, if no one drinks it?" I laughed.

"It belonged to someone who used to work here." She peeled a filter off the stack and placed it in the basket.

"The girl whose place I took?"

"Yes," she said, focusing on the task at hand.

"I heard she died unexpectedly."

"Yes, it was really sad, God bless her. She was a sweet girl." Marina measured out a few tablespoons of ground Columbian.

"Did she work here for very long?"

"About a year. Came here fresh from technical school." She poured a half-carafe of water into the coffee maker, then set it on the burner.

"I heard that she drowned."

"At Lake Merritt, of all places." She shook her head. "I can't imagine what she was doing there, after dark. She wasn't like the kids nowadays, running wild."

"Well, sometimes young people use bad judgment."

Marina swept a speck of ground coffee bean into the trash. "If she used bad judgment, it was in her choice of boyfriends." The corners of her mouth drew down in a display of disapproval.

"What do you mean?"

"She was going out with one of those rappers for a while. After she stopped seeing him, he kept bothering her. Even called her at work, if you could imagine."

Knowing FoZ, I could imagine that and far more. But, per Atticus' handbook, I was working at not jumping to conclusions.

She poured some hot coffee into a mug painted with geraniums and stirred in a packet of artificial sugar. "I thought she had finally gotten rid of him, since he hadn't called here for a bit. Then when I heard about what happened, well . . . it gave me the willies." She gave off a little shiver.

"Do you think he was stalking her?" I asked, striving for a tone of polite concern.

She glanced around the ten-by-seven-foot space as if to assure herself that no one was hiding in the cupboards, then lowered her voice. "The last day she was here, she got a phone call. She rushed into the bathroom right after she hung up and when she came back, I could see her face was flushed. So I asked her if she was alright. She said she was, but then she did the strangest thing."

A sharp ring cut through the quiet of the front office. The phone at the desk. *Damn.* I really didn't want to loose the thread of this conversation. And Marina would never let it go to voicemail.

Time for a little show of impertinence.

"Finish your coffee, I'll get it." Before she could protest, I sprinted to the front desk and picked it up.

"Neil Landon's office. This is Eileen. How may I help you?"

"Hello?"

"This is Eileen, may I help you?"

"I can hardly hear you," the woman on the other end shouted. "We must have a bad connection. Dr. Landon please."

"He's with a patient. May I take a message?"

"Tell him his sister called," she enunciated carefully. "I need to speak to him as soon as possible."

"Of course. Would you like to leave a number?"

Her voice faded and the connection dropped.

I noted the number on the caller ID and wrote it on the memo pad. When I got back to the kitchen, Marina was industriously scrubbing out her coffee cup, with a long handled sponge. The smell of lemon-scented soap permeated the kitchen.

"That was Dr. Landon's sister; she wants him to call her ASAP."

She nodded and said nothing. I hoped she hadn't interpreted my answering the phone as an infringement on her core authority. I couldn't afford to be generating hard feelings so early in the game.

I leaned against the counter and swallowed some tea. "You were saying that Laura had done something strange." *Oh, crap.*

Marina turned from the sink and eyed me with open curiosity. I could see the wheels turning; her brain trying to download when she'd used Laura's name in my presence. She studied me for a full minute, then reached for a hand towel that was hanging from one of the cabinet handles. She began to dry the cup methodically.

"Oh, yes," she said finally. "She asked if she could get off work early. Which was not at all like her. She was always willing to work late or come in on Saturdays if she was needed. And she never took off for personal time."

That was the big reveal? A nineteen-year-old girl putting her personal interests above work? Most women her age were ruled by their social lives.

"Did she say why?" I asked.

"Yes, that was the oddest thing of all. She said she needed to go home and change—that she had to look her best. And she said it with real conviction, like it was a matter of life or death. Poor thing." She examined the cup for a moment, then set it up on the shelf and aligned it with the mug next to it.

She turned to face me. "Well, I guess that's enough chit chat. Time to get back to work." She gave me a pointed look and pushed through the door.

I went over to the sink and dutifully washed my cup. I wanted a quiet place to put her disclosure into perspective, but Marina would surely object to me extending my break. Dr. Landon's one remaining patient for the day was a rhinoplasty coming in for her four-week follow up and wasn't due for fifteen minutes. Maybe I could put that time to good use.

I slipped back into the front office and paused by the desk. "Marina, is it okay if I re-familiarize myself with the stock room? While we're waiting for the next patient?"

She glanced up from inputting tomorrow's schedule into the computer and gave me a nod.

I walked down the hall and pushed the door next to the first exam room open. Flicking on the overhead light, I closed the door behind me. The room was half-full with metal stacking units filled floor-to-ceiling with medical supplies. The items were arranged methodically: rows of bandages and dressings, bandage scissors and scalpels, suture removal trays, thermometer probe covers, antibacterial ointment and soaps, Betadine, hydrogen peroxide, normal saline, latex gloves, tongue blades, tissues and exam table covers . . . even IV supplies in case of a patient emergency. Almost everything was unit packaged and neatly labeled.

I sat down on the exam table in the middle of the room and admired Marina's handiwork. She was precise, I had to give her that. I only hoped she was equally pristine in her recollections about Laura. If she was right, then Laura left work to meet a person she considered important enough to try and impress; someone who was probably not FoZ. A person she felt the need to freshen up for. A new boyfriend?

So, why the urgency—and the secrecy?

If I could only remember the details of her last reading, it might give me a clue. I breathed into my gut and focused on the layout. The muscles in my body started to relax.

I could see her sitting on the futon across from me, the cards spread out in front of us. The overall feeling was positive and expansive and indicated her using good judgment in regards to letting go of people and situations that were no longer in harmony with her nature. I could also see forward movement; the kind of movement associated with relocating. Having seen the inside of Ravenwaif's lair, I could understand the need for that.

Now, what about the relationship card? The odds of me remembering were pretty slim, but it was worth a shot, if I could get out of workhead. I took another breath and closed my eyes, picturing the positions of the Celtic cross. What were the last four cards? Partial images began to coalesce in my brain and become more distinct, drifting into place in front of me.

Then the room went silent. Dead quiet.

I opened my eyes. The electricity had gone out. I sat for a moment and waited for the power to come back on. I could hear Dr. Landon reassuring the patient in the room beside me in a quiet, calm voice. With the door closed, it was pitch black. I got off the table and groped for the shelving units. The front of my clog caught on the table pedestal and sent me sprawling. My hand brushed against a hard plastic container and knocked it to the floor.

It was freaky how disorienting the dark could be. I made my way along the shelves with my right hand extended out in front of me until I felt the wooden surface of the door. The emergency generator kicked in as I grasped the handle and pulled it open.

My breath caught in my chest. I was seeing, really *seeing* what I should have recognized a day ago. There, in front of me, in the dim light shed by the single fluorescent bulb lay the eerie hallway of Laura's dream. There were no stones underfoot, or vegetation clawing at my ankles, or bubbling muck to impede my progress. But there was a woman sobbing at the end of the corridor.

Mrs. Keene.

Chapter Sixteen

I took a hefty bite of lemon square and congratulated myself on my timely arrival. Saturday mornings at Uncle Gaylord's generally meant thin pickings, seating-wise, and today was no exception. The line of customers wound itself around the counter and past the wooden bench and scattered tables and chairs, spilling out onto Piedmont Avenue—a street not located in the city of Piedmont, two blocks away, but in Oakland.

Situated along the infamous Hayward fault west of the Oakland Hills, Piedmont was known for its sweeping views, tree-lined streets, outstanding architecture, and seven-figure real estate. Originally a place for San Francisco's rich and indolent to summer, it had at times been home to such famous residents as Jack London, Robert McNamara, and Charles Schwab. Since little in the way of commercial zoning was permitted within its densely developed and tony confines, Piedmont Avenue served as a retail arm for both Piedmont and North Oakland: a bustling strip made up of gourmet eateries, boutiques, antique and book stores, a spa, an art house, a tea shop, and no less than five cafes.

A kid with a grown out buzz cut, in a wrinkled *I Hella Luv Oaktown* tee shirt, juggled his laptop and mocha as he squeezed past. He excused himself, slid onto a stool, and plugged into the last remaining electrical outlet. Which reminded me of what I'd come here to do.

While yesterday's attempt at visualizing Laura's reading had been a bust, it had served to remind me I might have a written summary. In the confusion of switching to Ravenwaif's car, Laura had left her cell phone behind and, with no way to record her session, she'd paid me a few extra bucks to email her a synopsis. When I checked my sent folder, it was sitting there waiting to be deleted. For once, my sloppy file maintenance had paid off.

I'd also brought a mini-version of the deck I'd used during her last session. The cards were so small they were unlikely to attract much in the way of attention, but enough of a visual stimulus to keep me on track. With any luck, I could, at least, identify the influences surrounding Laura in the weeks before her death.

I began to review the synopsis.

Position One: Moonset – *You, in regards to your question.* A barefoot country girl in a chemise, laced bodice, gathered yellow skirt, and with a muslin bundle slung over her shoulder bends to touch the dirt road she travels. A crescent moon dips toward the horizon, illuminating her way and making the pebbles in her path sparkle like diamonds. Like the young woman who has risen early to make her journey, the querent is reminded that while reaching her goals requires planning, her ability to manifest her dreams lies within reach as long as she stays true to her authentic self.

Position Two: The Cygnet – *General influences.* A young swan with white-and-grey plumage swims across the face of a pond, cygnet feathers floating in its wake. In the background, a small isle of barren, stunted trees casts a shadow across the surface of the water, but the bird's attention is trained toward the teeming fish and lush greenery along the distant shoreline. This is the card of transformation: the inherent potential for change that lies within, if we commit to let go of the past and move forward. Can also refer to a desire to relocate.

Position Three: Eight of Pentacles, reversed – *Opportunities or obstacles.* A knight in a breastplate stamped with pentacles stands next to a sleek war horse, its saddlebags bulging with the spoils of battle. The figure is lean and bareheaded, one muscled hand raised to shield the sun's rays, a helmet dangling from the gauntlet of the other. Upright, this represents the warrior crusader: the soldier who offers up body and prowess for a just cause. The reversal indicates self-delusion leading to obsession and misuse of talents. In your case, I believe this represents a misdirection of focus and energy—your own or others'—blocking your current goals.

Position Four: Queen of Chalices – *Physical concerns.* A woman in a simple white shift dangles her feet in a stream, a half-eaten apple and an overturned cup lying on the ground next to her. She drowses, resting against a tree whose branches shelter her from the heat of the day. This is the self-nurturer, who consciously supports herself through a healthy balance of diet, exercise, and relaxation: an example for you to follow. You are also reminded that engaging with nature at this time would benefit body, mind, and spirit.

Position Five: The Duel – *Emotional concerns.* Two knaves—one blonde, one dark haired—stand at the top of the world, engaged in swordplay: the fair-haired youth knocking his opponent's weapon, end-over-end, into the abyss. This card represents a choice between two relationships or ways of being. In this matter, your decision is driven by a deep need to expand your personal vision and world view. Can indicate a sharp break with people and situations that are no longer your energetic match.

Position Six: Three of Pentacles, reversed – *Career/money concerns.* A shopkeeper in breeches and waistcoat drops three gold coins into the apron pocket of his assistant: a girl in a blue kirtle, with a single braid of gold hair. The merchant's plump wife and a young man watch from behind a wooden counter and applaud the youth's good fortune. This is prosperity and promotion arising from initiative, diligence, and a willingness to work at one's craft. The reversal indicates jealousy in the workplace or with regard to career advancement.

Position Seven: The Cathedral Spire, reversed –

Present/immediate future. A carpenter, raised chisel in hand, leans off a church spire and takes in the village and movements of the townspeople below. This is the cathedral view: the world revealed from a broad perspective. Upright, this indicates the ability to see people and situations objectively. The reversal represents myopia and, as a result, the potential for disappointment and deceit.

Position Eight: The Lark - *Goal to assist you.* A grey-breasted lark sits on a patch of ground, orange crest aloft, singing in an open field of grain. She nests on three crystal eggs: the natural products of her self-expression. This is the designated card of the clear communicator, one who has confidence her message will be heard, understood, and well received.

Position Nine: May Day - *Significant other.* A tow-headed boy and girl skip around the maypole interweaving multicolored streamers. The girl wears a garland of wildflowers and the sun is at mid-day, shining on the blooming garden that surrounds the pair and the other children running to join in the dance. This represents a current romantic relationship and the abundance of love, playfulness, and joy that you share. Can also indicate you and your partner's commitment to sharing these qualities and your combined resources with your community at large.

Position Ten: Six of Staves - *Hopes and fears.* A peasant in torn rags, clutches a grimy rag and stumbles across a scorched field, his feet bare and bleeding. Dark clouds rain down pointed staves, pinning him in place as he raises his face to the sky in despair. This is imagined scarcity: a desolate view of the future, amplified by fear of an unhappy outcome to a relationship or situation one has become attached to. The message is to release the fear and subsequent overattachment that there may be room for growth and expansion.

Position Eleven: Four of Wands - *Final Outcome.* An archer with a bow and four arrows in a leather quiver squints at the center of a target. This is the bulls eye, attainable only when physical, emotional, mental, and spiritual energies are aligned and directed toward the same goal. The target is at some distance from the archer indicating a need to review his current position for any perceptual errors, before taking aim. The message of this card is to avoid impulsive action, at this time, no matter how tempting.

I sat looking at the cards spread out in front of me.

The significant elements of Laura's reading were reminders that in order to accomplish her goals she would need to have clarity, an ongoing commitment to herself and her dreams, and let go of a tendency to self-identify with the past. A choice between two lovers was indicated as well as a need for more confident communication. Caution was expressed about taking care of her body. All generally useful advice, but no red flags. If there was a harbinger, it was in the reversed cards.

The Eight of Pentacles: an individual possessing

specialized skill, ability, and the level of single-mindedness required for successful follow through. Upended, this indicates blind devotion to a given ideal resulting in actions that are misguided and, at their worst, damaging to one's self and others. Was this a lack of clarity on Laura's part . . . or the obsessive focus of another? A man or woman who viewed Laura's new expression of herself and/or choice of partners as a threat?

FoZ? Or Ravenwaif?

The Cathedral Spire, reversed: a view of life and relationships that tends toward the subjective. Given Laura's age, this was hardly surprising, but unfortunately made her more vulnerable to anyone looking to exploit that propensity and keep their true motives hidden. And the jealousy indicated in the reversed Three of Pentacles? I was getting this as an obstacle being created by someone other than Laura; maybe a co-worker who felt threatened by her presence in the office? I hadn't been there long enough to draw any conclusions, but it seemed like Karin's attachment to the practice was minimal. Which only left—

"Do you have a license for public solicitation?"

Oh joy, a little cop humor. It was Burnette, in a navy blue Henley and grey sweats and a hint of stubble on his chin.

"No, just working on the Neff case," I said, hoping the mention of her name would send him running.

He tucked a Wall Street Journal under his arm and surveyed the layout in front of me. "Is this some kind of remote viewing?" he asked.

Okay, so I was wrong. He wanted a debate. And just

when I was beginning to get somewhere. Maybe if I ignored him, he'd go away. Back to wherever arrogant cops hang when they're not making nuisances of themselves.

To my dismay, he laid the newspaper on the table and took the seat opposite me. He settled his trainers under the table and crossed his legs. "Atticus tells me that you're, um, working undercover."

I gave him a saccharine smile. "And, you, um, don't approve."

He shrugged. "I think you're wasting your time."

First, he couldn't dispense with Laura Neff fast enough. Now he couldn't stop bringing her up, every time he saw me. What was his problem?

You didn't have to be intuitively gifted to see I'd become a thorn in his side; an irritant that reminded him he wasn't quite the professional he prided himself on being. On the other hand, this could be the universe's way of letting me pick his brain—something he would never have permitted a few weeks ago. I guess I could see what he had to offer.

"Okay, if you were me, how would you best utilize your time?"

"*If* I believed an actual murder had been committed, I wouldn't focus on her coworkers. Given the kind of homicide that Ms. Neff would most likely be, *if* she'd been murdered, I'd put my attention closer to home."

Alright, the disclaimers were getting a little old, but I was willing to play.

"How close?"

"Start with significant others. If she was killed, odds are she would be classified as a domestic murder. Women are twelve times more likely to be murdered by someone they know such as a family member, husband, ex-boyfriend. And three times more likely to be killed by a man than vice-versa."

"So you're saying women are safer in the company of strangers and other women?" I laughed.

Burnette didn't smile. I guess he didn't get those kind of stats as a cause for levity.

"It's more a question of motive. I'd be asking myself which of her male acquaintances had the strongest reason for wanting her dead."

"What about FoZ? Maybe she knew more about his business activities than he felt comfortable with."

He nodded. "Possibly. But if that were the case, drowning would be an unusual method of killing."

"What if he only wanted to deliver a warning. Or get back at her for ending the relationship—force her to take Ecstasy and then have one of his minions dump her by the lake after dark? He made a point of telling Atticus and I that she would never do drugs, so he knew how strongly she felt about them. Perhaps he didn't intend to kill her, just intimidate her, and then things got out of hand."

"Could be. But force implies there'd be bruising on the body from struggling when she was given the drug, or when she was transported to the lake. Not to mention taking the risk of being seen with her in a public place. FoZ and his boys are smarter than that.

I didn't like to admit it, but he might be right. FoZ wasn't stupid. A borderline misogynist, maybe, but not stupid. And Ravenwaif? It was difficult to imagine those flabby arms lifting anything heavier than a frozen pizza. Although jealousy had been know to fuel stranger acts than this one.

"So, given what you've told me, what kind of scenario makes sense?"

Burnette leaned forward. "Think about the crime scene and the body. There was cash in her purse, and no signs of assault, sexual or otherwise, on the body. The only trauma noted by the ME was a small abrasion on her hand, a few leg scratches, and a fracture of her skull from where she hit the boom. No signs of beating or a struggle. If someone killed her, they didn't rob her, or try to inflict physical injury or make her suffer; they just wanted her gone."

"So you're saying there wasn't any rage involved?"

He raised his voice. "I'm saying that if your friend was murdered, someone took advantage of her being down by the lake, at night, when she was high. Someone who was motivated and clever enough to follow the path of least resistance. Which means they would've had to know her plans for the evening and have followed her there."

And watched and waited, in the stand of cypress.

A chill squeezed my insides. Which was my intuition's way of confirming what I was seeing in my mind's eye was correct. I pulled my fleece hoodie around my shoulders and zipped it closed.

Burnette must have taken that, and my silence, as a sign of my imminent departure. He stood up and pushed his chair in.

"What can you possibly get out of this?" He made a dismissive gesture toward the Celtic cross spread.

"Truthfully, it gives me a lot of information," I said,

pointing to The Cygnet. "This card shows me that Laura was opening to new possibilities and expanding her skill set. And that she was in a period of transition."

I picked up the The Duel and held it up so he could see it. "This represents a new man in her life; someone she was beginning to care about, with whom she shared a common vision. I also see that there was jealousy around this relationship and her work accomplishments."

I indicated the three reversed cards. "These refer to the challenges she was facing in dealing with the source of this jealousy and in seeing her relationships more realistically."

I swept my hand over the layout. "There is also information here that tells me she was planning to move from El Cerrito."

"You're guessing," he said.

"No, I'm intuiting, which is a completely different act. Look, I'll make you a bet. I'll shuffle these cards and let you pick one. If the card you select isn't pertinent to what we've discussed, I'll buy you a case of that ridiculously overpriced whiskey of yours."

He didn't respond, just glared down at the layout. He was probably wondering how I could possibly afford to make good, if I lost. And to be honest, so was I.

He leaned over, picked up the paper, and crossed his arms. His jaw tightened. "Alright," he said.

I returned the cards to the deck and shuffled. It was a little tricky given their size, but I managed. I focused my attention on the question, *"What is most important here?"*. Then I fanned all seventy-eight of them along the table's edge in a semicircle. Showtime.

Burnette pulled a card from the middle of the spread. He turned it face up and laid it on the tabletop, tapping it once with a shiny fingernail: a bloodied battlefield, littered with the bodies of the dead—the folds of a white flag unfurling on the hill above.

Conflict followed by a period of peace: The Truce card.

Chapter Seventeen

It was Monday, my third day at the office, and the constant scrutiny was beginning to wear. I hadn't been clucked over this much since I was a student nurse. My job performance had evidently failed to inspire Marina's confidence in my ability to maintain workflow and the pressing need to appear industrious was getting old. In the past five hours, I'd assessed ten patients, restocked the rooms for the day, organized the patient charts for tomorrow, and left a partial stockroom order for her review. Stuck in the front office until Dr. Landon discharged his two o'clock patient, I stole a peek over the desk.

The woman in the waiting area crossed one leg over the other and began to swing her right foot back and forth in an impatient semicircle. She flipped through the pages of an investment magazine, scanning the print too quickly to retain any of the contents. I had the impression that she had places to go, things to do. Drug rep, probably.

She certainly looked the part. The maize print faux-wrap dress fit her long torso and angular shoulders like it had been tailored for her, as did the white sling backs that accentuated her bare runner's calves. Light brown hair stopped short of her shoulders in a sharp blunt cut accented by golden streaks too uniform to have been placed there by the sun. She reeked of carefully-acquired elegance; her only adornments, a high polish gold bangle and a pendant on a long rope chain. The pendant kept pulling my attention, despite being under the watchful eye of Marina. It was multifaceted and brilliantly cut and the buttery glow of 24K was unmistakable, even from across the room.

Marina scanned the stockroom order and stood. "He should be finishing up any moment," she trilled over the contents of her inbox.

Under the fluorescents, the pendant sparkled and drew me to it once again. It was about an inch in length, flat on the bottom, and pointed at the top. The woman closed the magazine and placed it squarely back on the stack in front of her.

Dr. Landon loped down the hall, his scrubs hanging off his boney shoulders like a wrinkled coat on a scarecrow. I sometimes wondered if he slept in them. Or if he even owned a mirror. It seemed like a contradiction in terms to appear so consistently worn out and call yourself a health care provider.

"She's good to go," he said to Marina and handed her the patient chart.

The woman in the waiting room stood and, in an instant, the similarities between her and Dr. Landon became apparent. They were both tall, with the musculature of lean athletes, and the same Grecian noses and eye color. Only she looked vibrant and healthy and he looked, well, like Dr.

Landon. This must be his sister. She mouthed a silent "thank you" to Marina as she passed by the desk and out the front door which Dr. Landon had opened for her.

I walked down the hall to the second exam room. Tearing off the used paper from the table, I pulled down a new sheet and tossed the crumpled ball into the metal trashcan along with a pair of latex gloves, a suture removal tray, and the exam gown. A torn packet of Betadine ointment followed, still half-full. Nothing to wash, sterilize, recycle or reuse, just a straight shot to the medical waste facility; waste being the operative word. Never let it be said that modern medicine has any qualms about the size of its carbon footprint.

I could hear Marina making small talk with the patient. Thank God. At least I could take a moment to focus on something other than looking busy. I sat down on Dr. Landon's exam stool. I'd been revisiting the elements from Laura's nightmare in my head, all morning, without much to show for it. The only things that had surfaced, so far, were more questions; the same ones looping around and around in my brain. Was there a reason the dream was set in the office? Had someone who worked here killed her? And what did any of that have to do with her calling out FoZ's middle name?

I was used to working with sets of symbols that were familiar to me, images that my spirit guides knew I would recognize. But in this case, Laura was sending me clues whose meanings, I suspected, were more specific to her. And I was getting frustrated with my inability to re-arrange the fragments into a discernible pattern. So far, the only connection I'd made was between the light bulb in the hallway and the lamp at the lake near where her body had been found. Were they metaphors? The truth illuminated, maybe? Being betrayed in full view?

"Finding everything you need?"

I jumped to my feet. Dr. Landon stood in the doorway, his hair shaggy and windblown. He sagged against the doorframe as if he needed the support.

"Everyone treating you alright?"

"Your staff has been very helpful," I said, a little surprised at the attention.

"Good," he replied. The dark circles under his eyes stood out in harsh relief under the artificial lighting. He looked too tired to move.

I felt like I should offer him his stool before he toppled. My inner nurse took over. "Dr. Landon, are you okay?"

He scratched his head and a cowlick erupted at the back of it. "Oh, nothing that a trip to the islands wouldn't cure." He attempted a smile.

The islands: Bay Area code for Hawaii. Of course. The pendant was a pineapple, second only to the plumeria and the gecko in its predominance in the tourist shops there. I had a sterling replica from back in the day when I could afford to take vacations. No wonder it had caught my eye.

"I take it you've been there," I said.

He and the spike of hair nodded in agreement. "Many times. It was my family's favorite place to vacation."

"I've only been to Oahu, but it was fantastic, even with all the tourists."

A spark of enthusiasm warmed his bloodshot eyes.

"How long were you there?"

"Ten days. Just enough time to get me hooked."

"Sample any of the seafood?"

"As much mahi-mahi as my credit card would allow."

He threw back his head and laughed; a short, boyish laugh that invited you to join in. It was a pleasure to see him so animated.

"You must have some great memories." I said.

"Oh yeah. We spent July and August there nearly every summer. Had a condo on Waikiki. I could've given guided tours."

"So what was you favorite part of the island?"

"Besides the water you mean?" He sighed. "Probably Diamond Head. Nothing is more seductive to a ten-year-old boy than the promise of an abandoned fort inside of a crater. And a hidden underground complex left over from WWII."

"Sounds like I should have taken your tour. I never got any closer than admiring it from a catamaran."

"I used to drag my father up there at least once a week. A mile and three quarters to the summit, but worth the view with the western side of the island and the Pacific at your feet."

He shifted his weight from one side of the doorway to the other, his face alight with the memory. It was easy to picture: the sunlight glinting off the lava rock and the crowds, sunning and romping in the waters of Waikiki, growing smaller as he and his father made their way up the side of the volcano.

"How about you?"

"The Valley of Rainbows," I said, without hesitation.

He snapped his fingers. "The rainforest with the seven waterfalls and every species of orchid on the planet. My mother used to love that place."

"Wow, you weren't kidding about being a tour guide."

"It's my backup plan, in case the surgery thing doesn't work out."

I burst out laughing. This must be the part of him he saved for his patients. No wonder they liked him.

"I also thought the cliff diving at Waimea Falls was pretty spectacular," I said, catching my breath.

His eyelids fluttered. The muscles in his face went slack, and he gaped at me wordlessly. For one awful moment, I thought he'd had a stroke. Then the lines around his eyes and mouth resumed their fixed solemnity, as if a reveler's mask had been whipped away to reveal the authentic self beneath—a sad one, weighty with resignation. His cervical spine drooped forward in a curve of bone that seemed scarcely able to support its own weight.

The exam room phone beeped twice. Marina paging him. He ran his hand through his hair. "Duty calls," he said and stepped out into the hallway.

I watched him lope away, wondering what had made him flip personas like that. Maybe our conversation had made him homesick for Hawaii. Maintaining a successful practice couldn't be easy. A grind was a still a grind even if it was a lucrative one.

The phone beeped again. Dr. Landon's line was still in use, so this one must be for me. My reprieve was over.

I walked to the front desk. There was a legal-size manila

envelope sitting on the front counter. Marina looked up from the computer.

"Could you walk this out to the mailbox in front of the building? The postman has already made his pickup and it needs to go out in the late mail. Then you can take your break, if you like."

Short, dark hair softened her round face, framing it in wispy layers. The purple irises on her top complemented the amethyst studs in her ears, as did the lavender jade crucifix that hung from the rope chain she was wearing. A discreet touch of violet eye shadow in the crease of her upper eyelids brought out the cinnamon tones in her eyes, making her seem less formidable. Up until now I hadn't noticed, but she was rather pretty.

I thanked her and took the envelope from the desk. Getting out of the office for a few minutes was exactly what I needed.

I opened the door and hot wind pressed against me. My skin prickled. It was Diablo, a dry northeasterly blowing in from Contra Costa, more than a month ahead of schedule; the same wind that had fanned the flames of the Oakland firestorm. The suffocating perfume of scorched eucalyptus filled my head. More than two decades later, the memory could still make my eyes water.

The envelope flew free of my grip and tumbled end over end across the grass. I chased it down the sidewalk and managed to intercept it a few yards shy of the street that ran past the medical complex. Pushing my hair out of my eyes, I inspected it for damage. With the exception of a smudge on the right corner, it was no worse for wear.

The envelope was addressed to a real estate agency in Novato, with the office address on the return label. That could explain Dr. Landon's perpetual fatigue; Marin was one of the priciest markets in the state. Maybe he was suffering from buyer's remorse.

The handle of the postbox singed my palm, exposed as it was to the afternoon sun. I released it involuntarily and the metallic door slammed shut with a resonant clang. The wind prowled aimlessly past me, whistling low and reshaping the tops of the cedar trees that lined the sidewalk; the air hot and dusty in its wake.

Suddenly I wanted to be on the futon with Audie on my lap and the smell of Tessa's cooking drifting up the stairs. I wanted to hear the click of Jessamae's heels in the hallway and the sound of her voice, gossiping on her cell outside of my door. An emptiness had opened up inside of me; a vacuum, yawning and deep, that demanded comfort, familiarity.

It wasn't the memory of the firestorm, at least, not only that. An energy in the here and now encircled me: a broken and malevolent spirit as powerful as Diablo. One I felt completely alone in the presence of.

But I wasn't alone. Someone was watching me from behind the office's plate glass window . . . a young woman in white, with blond hair pulled back into a ponytail. A girl not yet out of her teens, if I had to guess.

I squinted up at her from the sidewalk. No one had gone past me since I'd walked outside, I was sure. Which means she would have had to access the office from the back of the building, via the employee's entrance.

Wherever she'd come from, she was following my progress up the sidewalk with great interest. I blinked against the sun's glare and the dirt kicked up by the wind. The figure behind the glass shimmered and disappeared from view.

Chapter Eighteen

A toddler in a yellow dress and a white-and-green petal-shaped hat waddled toward the incoming tide, her short, chubby arms flapping in the breeze. She lurched forward—one unsteady but determined step at a time—and, as her tiny toes reached the water's edge, lost her balance and plopped a diapered bottom into the wet sand. A seagull circling overhead watched from on high as she splashed her arms in the sea foam, squealing with joy.

"You ever thought about having one of those?" Atticus shaded his eyes from the bright light reflecting off the water.

"No, but I have put prodigious effort into not having one." I selected a seat with my back to the sun, at the picnic table closest to the water.

Atticus squinted at me. "A good Southern girl like you, you should be Grandma by now."

I stuck my tongue out at him. "You'd better watch your mouth, young man, or I won't give you any lunch." I extracted a sandwich and bottle of tea from the deli bag and placed them on the bleached wood in front of him.

He straddled the seat opposite me. "So, you're sayin' you have no maternal instincts?"

"Nope." I pulled my lunch from the bag. "My mother made it perfectly clear that parenthood was an arduous undertaking and not to be taken lightly. I guess I never felt up to the challenge."

"How did Audie rate her setup then? Sneak in the backdoor?"

I popped the top on a bottle of chilled white tea. "Let's just say she caught me at a weak moment."

Atticus inhaled a piece of mozzarella and mushroom focaccia. "This is incredible!" he murmured between bites. "Where did you say you got this?"

"From that place Jessamae suggested—Bacci's on Lincoln Avenue. It's the Italian deli owned by those three guys she's crushing on. Focaccia's the Tuesday special."

Atticus wiped a crumb from his chin. "The pep boys?" he said.

"Sort of, except that their names are Nick, Brandon, and Chris, and they're young and seriously cute. And they make killer chicken salad." I took a bite of sandwich, savoring the delicious blend of Dutch crunch and creamy filling.

Salt air filled my lungs. It was my first weekday off since I'd started at Dr. Landon's, so Atticus had suggested doing lunch at Crab Cove in Alameda. Even though it was a five-minute ride through the tunnel from downtown Oakland, I seldom made it to the beach or the little island town.

A few wispy clouds drifted out beyond the horizon, the sun hot on our backs. Local lore had it that both the snow cone and the kewpie doll were first sold here, back when it was an amusement park known as Neptune Beach. Eighty years ago, I probably couldn't have seen the water lapping at the sand for the roller coaster, Ferris wheel, carousel, and the tourists queuing up to watch Johnny Weissmuller or Jack LaLanne race in one of the outdoor swimming pools. In the days preceding the Great Depression, "The Coney Island of the West" was one of the most popular seaside attractions west of the Mississippi.

Today, the only other person sharing our section of the beach was a middle-aged man with a buzz cut and leathery skin waxing his board. A group of young women sunbathed close to the water's edge, snapping pictures of themselves with their phones and screaming with laughter in that ice-pick-in-the-ear range only teenage girls can attain or tolerate. Further down the shore, a woman in cropped pants and a sun hat typed on her laptop from the comfort of a striped, folding chair.

"What was it like growing up around here?"

Atticus crumpled his sandwich wrapper into a ball, took aim, and dunked it into the trashcan a few feet away. "Alameda? It was pretty idyllic, in an Ozzie and Harriet kind of way. Still is, as far as I know. The red, white, and blue bunting goes up in May and stays put 'till the pumpkins come out. Twenty-six miles per hour is considered speeding. And it's very family oriented—good public schools, lots of parks, not much in the way of crime. Plus, there's a real sense of community. My dad had a civilian job at the base and we were involved in lots of stuff there."

"So what made you move to the mainland?"

"They roll up the streets by nine o'clock. And the island's

pretty conservative in a lot of ways. Too buttoned down for my tastes."

He swigged his tea. "So what made you leave the Blue Ridge? One of those Hatfield and McCoy things?"

"No," I said, ignoring the inference. "It was more like what you described. I found the need to conform oppressive. In an urban area like this you can have anonymity and not so many folks invested in telling you how to live your life."

"Anonymity can get pretty lonely."

I followed his gaze. He was watching the toddler again. A man I took to be her grandfather had scooped her up and was making a slow arc over the sand, swinging her gently in his arms. A grey-haired woman in a denim jumper stood close by and clapped her hands. The little girl wiggled her toes, her face upturned, rapturous.

Atticus turned back to face me. "How's the undercover work going?"

"Okay, I think. Marina, the office manager, says that Laura was getting calls from FoZ at work, after they split up, that seemed to upset her. She also told me Laura left work early on the afternoon of the day she was killed on some kind of urgent business."

"How urgent?"

"She apparently had to rush home to get ready for a meeting with someone Marina felt was important to her."

"Any idea about who she was meeting?"

"No, but it doesn't seem like she would've needed to get dolled up for someone she was trying to get rid of."

Atticus nodded. "You think there was another mule kicking in the stall?"

"Yeah, I do. I located a summary of the reading I'd done for her and it pointed to a new man in her life. And jealousy projected at the new relationship and her job."

"You don't see FoZ or the roommate figuring into that?"

"Truthfully, I could see both of them figuring into it. But I've been at this for such a short time, I'm open to all comers."

Atticus applauded. "Way to go. Not bad for a newbie. The whole Nancy Drew thing is kinda working for you."

"Gee thanks, boss man. Any suggestions about where to focus next?"

"I wouldn't underestimate the power of the office grapevine. Marina or someone else there might be dying to unload. Tragedies do that to people. Makes them want to share. A nice girl like you; it should be a snap."

"You're full of complements, today. What are you up too?"

"Trying to keep up with the competition."

"What competition?"

"The deli dudes. Maney, Moe, and Jack."

"You mean Nick, Brandon, and Chris."

"Whatever." He shrugged.

"Well, they are pretty irresistible. But I'm old enough to be their grandmother, by your standards."

"You mean dog patch standards?"

I glared at him. "Why is it that those who would never dream of slurring people of color or any other ethnicity feel perfectly comfortable taking pot shots at white Southerners, especially if they happen to be from the mountain South? What's up with that?"

"Now, don't go gettin' all steel magnolia on me, darlin'. Personally, I think hillbilly chicks are hot." He placed his right hand over his heart.

I shook my head. "You're hopeless. But seriously, I do think cultural prejudice made it easier for Burnette to justify closing the case. I'm not sure he was conscious of it, but he spoke of Laura as if it was inevitable she meet a bad end."

Atticus turned his torso and stretched his right leg the length of the bench. "It can get hard to be objective after you've been on the job for a while. You can only take in so much ugly before it starts to get to you." He grunted, coming out of the stretch. "Then there's the budget. When it comes to departmental funding and man hours, there's only so much to go around. In cases like Laura's, with no squeaky wheel around, aggressive investigations are gonna get shelved."

"Guess it's a good thing I have connections." I laughed.

Atticus looked past me, out at the horizon. "To be honest, when you first came to see me I didn't think there was a case. Burnette's a damn good cop and there isn't much that gets by him."

"Then why did you agree to help me?"

"I guess I figured you'd get to the point where you'd see for yourself there was nothing to uncover. And I might have been looking for an excuse to see you on a more regular basis."

I started to protest, but his words rushed past mine. "Now I'm starting to think you're on to something and I want you to promise me that you'll proceed with some street smarts from this point on."

"What does that mean?"

He turned to face me and crossed his arms on the weathered wood. "That means you'll check in with me, if you come up with anything new. No confrontations on your on. And don't discuss going undercover with anyone. Whoever killed your client is probably figuring they've gotten away with it about now. I don't want you to alert them to the fact they've been made. Got it?"

Heat stung my face. Heat not generated by the sun.

I dropped my sandwich back in its wrapper. "So, let me get this straight. You thought my suspicions were unfounded, despite the fact that you used my services to successfully solve a case of your own. And now that you think they might not be, you've decided I can't take care of myself?"

Raspiness gathered in the pit of my throat. I swallowed hard. I'd begun to think of Atticus and myself as partners. The thought that he'd merely been humoring me was hurtful—surprisingly so.

I picked up what was left of my lunch and crammed it into the bag. "You're starting to sound like Burnette," I said.

"What's he got to do with this?" Atticus' pupils had contracted to pinholes, in the glare, his eyes a watering, vivid blue.

I extracted myself from the picnic table. "I ran into him a couple of days ago and he volunteered advice on who he'd be targeting as suspects. If he were me." I tossed the empty tea bottle into the recycling container and glared down at him. "Well, he's not me and neither are you. I can understand Burnette thinking I'm a ditz. But, given our history, I expected more from you."

Funny how the mood of a day could shift so quickly. I turned and stamped off across the sand.

Chapter Nineteen

"Where's Marina?"

I must've been asked that question twenty times, in the last two hours. Patients wanting follow-up appointments, prescription refills, postoperative advice, account balances; all exuding disappointment upon seeing me behind the reception desk or hearing my voice on the other end of the line. All because Marina had taken off for her own doctor's appointment.

I started into my spiel, without looking up. "Marina is out of the office this afternoon, but she'll be back on Thursday. Can I help you?"

"Could you give this to Neil, please?"

A hefty, black-and-white checkered bag, sporting the logo of a local gourmet-to-go eatery—a chef, in a pleated hat, waving from the front seat of a Maserati—edged into view on the counter in front of me. Dr. Landon's sister stood behind it in a sleeveless linen shirt that showed off the distinctive curves of her biceps. She looked a tad flushed, and surprised to see me. I'd been getting a lot of that this afternoon.

"I'm sorry," I said and nudged back the chair to take the package. "I didn't see you there. I don't think we've been introduced. My name's Eileen."

I started to extend my hand and then, on a reflex, scooped up the bag instead. A handshake might seem presumptuous and an unwelcome act of familiarity. Marina liked to keep things formal and, as her stand-in, I should probably follow suit. In fact, I couldn't remember having heard her call Dr. Landon or his sister by their given names.

"Ava," she said and pushed the bag toward me. "Thanks for seeing he gets it." She flashed a luminescent smile.

What did Neil Landon do to inspire such devotion in the women around him? It was a wonder he'd gotten through med school without Marina and his sister there to fawn over him. Granted, he was starting to look more wasted everyday. And I hadn't noticed if he'd eaten lunch. Was monitoring his dietary intake another duty of which I'd been remiss?

"I'll take it back to him as soon as he finishes with his next patient," I said and pulled up my most reassuring smile.

She bent to pick up her handbag. Unless I missed my guess, it was genuine Prada: lipstick red, ruched patent leather, with flawless white stitching on the buckle straps and rolled handles—a little dated for haute couture, but beautifully designed. The brilliant pigment popped the neutral tones of her cropped chinos and shirt and underscored the glow of her finely textured, olive complexion.

"I'm sure you must hear this all the time, but your skin is amazing."

"I believe in walking my talk," she said. She tossed back

a strand of hair and slid the bag over her shoulder. "I'm an esthetician."

"Wow." I paused to let her see I was genuinely impressed. "You and Dr. Landon should go into practice together. He could do the repair work and you could do the maintenance."

Her hazel eyes widened. "That's uncanny, we were talking about that recently." She gave off a girly tinkle of a laugh.

"Seems like a perfect partnership. I've heard him encourage his patients to practice good skin care, and I would think they would want to after the investment they've made. Who better to make referrals to then someone he trusts? You're obviously living proof of the results . . . your own best advertisement."

I was laying it on a bit thick, I know, but a little flattery never hurt. We would probably be crossing paths over the next several weeks and being on friendly terms would give me one more person I could question about Laura. Besides, I was telling her the truth, intuitively speaking. I could see that a partnership between the two of them had the potential to be quite profitable.

I warmed to the topic. "With all the disposable income in the Bay Area, I would think this would be a great market for an esthetician."

She smiled, making the end of her nose crinkle. "You know, since Neil brought it up, I have been giving San Francisco some thought. But I already have a practice in Honolulu. We spent some time there as kids and we like the lifestyle. I've been wondering if the pace there might be better for him."

Given his enthusiasm for the place, I could see that. Life

on the islands did, in theory, move to a saner rhythm. Maybe he and his sister had been discussing a possible relocation the day he'd been reminiscing. I felt a twinge of envy. I wouldn't mind indulging in a little Hawaiian Standard Time myself.

"Of course, the Bay Area is a fantastic place to live, too." She brushed at a microscopic smudge on her blouse, her silky hair obscuring one side of her face. She wore no fingernail polish, but her nails were buffed to a high shine. I had to admit she had the natural beauty thing down to a fine art. It took serious commitment to maintain your face and body to such a degree. In that sense, she was the direct opposite of her brother.

A prickle on my left inner arm reminded me I was still holding the bag and its chilled contents. "Well, good luck with your plans," I said and set it on the back counter with deliberate care. "Dr. Landon's lucky to have you watching out for him."

"Well, he is one of the good guys." She glanced up at the clock behind the desk. "And I'd better get going. Could you tell Neil I'll call him later? And pass this on to him, too?" She pulled an envelope from the handbag and slid it across the counter. It bore the return address of a real estate broker in Novato; the same agency I'd posted to last week.

Was Dr. Landon selling his home in anticipation of a move? Poor Marina. She'd be devastated. Now she had two rivals for his attentions: his sister and Oahu.

"No problem," I said, placing it next to the bag.

I was headed home, eastbound, on the lower section of the Richmond-San Rafael Bridge, my brain churning over the events of the day. "The Roller Coaster," as it was known locally, resembled the creation of a deranged giant with an erector set: two cantilever spans joined by a lowered mid section, giving it a curvy, swaybacked appearance. The proverbial stepchild, it was considered to be esthetically unappealing even by the architect who designed it. Yet its five-and-a-half miles of uncomplaining steel and concrete carried more than seventy thousand cars between Marin and the East Bay every weekday. And the view of the bay it afforded, especially in early evening was, in my opinion, unparalleled.

The sun, a glowing tangerine, hung several hours above the horizon, her fiery rays superimposed over the crawler making its way across the choppy waters. A forest green BMW Z4 convertible with a beige top roared up behind me. The 3.OSI filled my rear-view mirror: a three-liter engine, two-hundred-fifty-five horses under the hood, capable of zero-to-sixty in less than six seconds. Three-thousand-plus pounds of German engineered, sleek, aggressive, driving pleasure. Yours, for a mere fifty grand.

The Z slipped over into the fast lane and kept pace with me for about a quarter of a mile, then popped into sixth and slid in front of the car ahead of me. I watched it purr past the Pt. Richmond exit and disappear in the traffic up ahead. What must it feel like to control a machine like that, to meld with the power of it—to draw the attention of every other driver on the road, if only for a few seconds? Probably not a sensation I'd ever know.

My thoughts recircuited to the profile of Dr. Landon's sister gliding out of the office door: leggy, strong, and perfectly put together. I had to cop to some jealousy there, but it wasn't her physical appearance that was sticking in my craw. There was no way I could deal with the upkeep that a career choice like hers demanded. God knows I barely had the patience for my morning toilette as it was. What I coveted was her air of self-confidence; an accessory far more enviable than her posh, red bag.

My own self-esteem had taken a few hits lately. Truth be told, I had a pervasive sense of not doing anything particularly well these days. I had failed to alert Laura to the danger that was about to overtake her and had made precious little progress toward uncovering what had happened that night at the lake. I wasn't meeting up to Marina's standards at the office, and was still smarting from my exchange with Atticus, yesterday.

On some level, I admired his honesty. It was a mark of his character that he was willing to be that up front with me. And, I suppose, I could get his reluctance to put too much credence into my feelings about Laura. He and Burnette were simply mirroring the cultural paradigm that decrees if a conclusion isn't linearly derived, or based on some randomized double-blind study, it must not be the truth.

It reminded me of the medical establishment's claims that acupuncture is not effective despite two thousand years of recorded history and hundreds of thousands of case studies that show otherwise. Yet the very same body would put themselves foursquare behind pharmaceuticals whose chemical trials, when brought under scrutiny from someone not standing to profit by them, showed evidence of manipulation. All because of a pervasive belief in the value of "hard science" methodologies. In the end, it was simply a question of where you were willing to put your trust.

I wasn't getting Atticus, or even Burnette, as the villain in this scenario; in their own ways, they'd both tried to help. My frustration stemmed from being marginalized because of the way I perceive information. And because I was employing reasoning. I had, for example, a theory: Laura Neff was the victim of a homicide. My hypothesis stemmed from the evidence—that Ecstasy was found in her body following her drowning—and that she'd confided to me, with believable conviction, that she wouldn't do alcohol or drugs. I'd made observations about her accountability, her death, and the events that lead up to it based on intuitive input, suspect interviews, and the police reports Atticus had gotten from the OPD. I, therefore, believed that my findings would confirm she'd been murdered.

Burnette examined Laura's case file and concluded she'd drowned. He looked for patterns to support this observation such as frequency of recreational drug use in Laura's age demographic and her exposure to a family with a history of drug/alcohol abuse. He hypothesized that doing drugs was part of her societal/cultural norm and formed the theory that she'd intended to take the Ecstasy and, as a result of exposure to it, had suffered an accidental death. I could see that his approach had validity. So why were he and Atticus so hesitant to acknowledge that my way of problem solving might be as legitimate as theirs?

Okay, enough with the self-flagellation. No one had forced me to play amateur detective or promised me that making people in authority believe Laura had been murdered would be easy. The decision had been my own, and whining about my insufficiencies and other people's opinions wasn't going to get the job done. I had a reading and some housework to handle tomorrow, but I'd be back in the office on Friday.

And, for once, I had a plan.

Chapter Twenty

Wendell Holsinger was a ruddy-faced fifty-eight with thinning sandy hair, an impressive case of halitosis and a mouth that remained in constant motion. Perched on the edge of the exam table in his patient gown, bloodstained girdle, and black-and-gold-toed crew socks, he'd been jabbering away nonstop since I walked into the room. I'd completed his physical exam ten minutes ago and had, thus far, been unable to get anywhere near my nurse's notes.

"Wen", as he liked to be called, was divorced, childless, a golfer, and recently retired from thirty-four years in the roofing business. He was chomping at the bit to take his new girlfriend, Angela—fifteen years, his junior—to Vegas and spend some of his hard-earned savings. After all, you only go around once, heh, heh, heh, and hadn't he just dropped four grand on this?

He poked a stubby finger at his midsection for emphasis. All he needed was a refill on his Cialis, and he was good to go. Wink, wink, nudge, nudge. When did I say he could get rid of this damn thing? He was, after all, feeling fine. He'd hardly cracked the bottle of pain pills the doc had given him and he wasn't going to get any action as long as he was strapped into this medieval torture device. Heh, heh, heh.

It was my job to review post-operative instructions with patients in order to maximize their recovery, but in Wendell's case, I had little faith that any reinforcement would make much difference. Not with visions of Sin City firing his imagination, blocking out all other input.

He paused to draw breath and I seized the moment. I reminded him that although he'd opted for a wet lipoplasty—one in which solution had been injected into his abdomen, making the fat less difficult to suction out—there could still be postoperative complications. He would probably notice some swelling and bruising when the doctor removed the compression garment and those were typical side effects that might linger for sometime. He needed to keep the girdle in place to support the traumatized tissue. Doing this would speed up his recovery, which could take as long as two months. The doctor would go over the specifics when he saw him.

If he ever got here. Dr. Landon had been late to the office all week, pushing his arrival time back farther with each successive day. Mr. Holsinger had been scheduled for 11:00 a.m. and the clock on the wall read 11:38. The office closed at noon for lunch, and I didn't want to leave late today of all days.

I finished my assessment and was trying, unsuccessfully, to divert Wen from further disclosures about his love life, when the doctor arrived, bleary-eyed and even more disheveled than usual. I passed off the chart and made my escape.

Marina, to her credit, had volunteered to stay and finish up the patient when Dr. Landon completed his exam, for which I was grateful. If their experience with Wen was anything like mine, I doubted either of them would get anywhere near lunch. And I needed to intercept Karin, pronto. Fridays were the only day we were both in the office and one of the days she race-walked in the green space behind our building along with some of the other employees in the complex. Today, I planned to include myself in her workout.

I caught up with her in the kitchen, braced against the sink, lacing her trainers. "Do you mind having some company on your walk today?" I asked.

She glanced up at me. "Not at all," she said, color creeping up her pale, freckled face from bending over.

We headed out the emergency door at the back of the building and the heavy metal door slammed shut behind us. The medical complex consisted of eight two-story buildings built around an enclosed rectangle. The interior of the rectangle contained a grassy area bordered by a sidewalk with a small pond and a fountain, at its center; a source of considerable attraction for the local ducks and birds. Trees encircled the pond, lending the space an air of lushness and tranquility.

"How much distance do you cover?" I asked, noting her long strides.

"Twelve loops average out to a little over two miles," she said. "That's usually what I aim for."

I settled into a cadence beside her. "Have you been race-walking long?"

"A few years." She laughed. "This is about the only chance I get to exercise these days. Once I get home, it's dance class and swim meets and band practice."

"Mom's taxi service?"

"Yeah, my oldest is about a year from getting her learner's permit, so I'm the family chauffeur for now."

"Sounds like they keep you busy."

"It's more like me wanting them not to have much downtime. They both have a lot of interests and I would rather they have full schedules than time on their hands." She brushed one gleaming gold hair from her cheek. "With all the technology kids have at their fingertips today, it's far too easy for them to sit on their butts in front of the TV or the computer. At least this way, I can keep an eye on who they're hanging out with. It's scary how fast kids can form online friendships with someone you don't know and then disappear."

That sounded like as good as segue as I was going to get. "Like the girl you used to work with?" I huffed, already out of breath. "Marina didn't seem to think much of her choice of friends."

A puzzled look crossed Karin's patrician features, no doubt at the abrupt shift in topic.

"Oh. The rapper guy," she said. "Yeah, he was kind of a jerk. You shouldn't judge her by him, though. She was a really nice girl."

"Marina said she was a hard worker."

"She was. Smart and responsible. It's hard to believe what happened."

"I just heard that she'd drowned."

"Yeah, over in Oakland, at Lake Merritt." She quickened her pace. "I've heard bad things about that place."

Spoken like a true Marinite. I'd bet she'd never been closer to the lake, or any other part of Oakland, than 580. It was surprising how people could have such fixed opinions about communities they'd never visited.

"I race-walk there sometimes and I've always felt pretty safe."

"In the daytime, maybe, but I wouldn't be down there alone after dark." She tossed back her hair in defiance of the breeze rippling the face of the pond. "Confidentially, what happened to Laura hit everyone in the office pretty hard. Marina got very upset when we heard the news. And Dr. Landon's been showing the strain."

"He does seem pretty distracted."

"That's a good word for it." She glanced over at me. "He's a sweet guy. Very humanitarian. He does regular trips with medical-relief organizations, you know, like, Doctors Without Borders."

"Really?"

"Yeah, he's got scrapbooks full of the pictures of underprivileged patients he's done cosmetic surgery on. Kids with severe facial deformities."

"That's impressive. I can see why Marina's so devoted to him."

Karin rolled her eyes. "Marina's devoted to having everything clean and neat and wrapped up with a pink bow. And feeling like she's in control. If she actually paid attention to some of the stuff that's gone on in that office, she'd pop a cork."

"Such as?"

"Dr. Landon and Laura, for one."

The sun prickled my scalp. My feet seemed to be moving in tandem with Karin's, but I couldn't feel the ground underneath them. Blood roared in my ears, pulsing to a frantic rhythm that rocked my entire body. I wiped the damp from my forehead and tried to ignore the rushing sensation between my eyes that threatened to disconnect my brain from the rest of me.

Focus, Eileen, focus.

"Really?" I said, my voice shooting up into the stratosphere.

"Yep. I guess he was a real change of pace from that rapper dude. And she was such a pretty little thing—like a breath of fresh air. I don't think he quite knew what hit him."

"So, you saw them together?" I asked, striving for the proper mix of curiosity and titillation.

"Uh huh," she nodded. "I stopped by the office one Saturday, to pick up some papers I'd left there—some consent forms for one of the girl's field trips. When I got to the door I could see them, through the glass, kissing at the back of the hallway. They were too involved in what they were doing to notice me, so I made a big deal about getting in the door, pretending I was having trouble with the lock. By the time I opened the door, Neil had disappeared into his office and Laura was at the front desk looking rosy."

"And Marina never caught wind of this?"

Karin cracked the seal on her water bottle. "Marina is much too dedicated to the image she has of Dr. Landon to see past it. She wouldn't have admitted to what was going on if she caught them on the exam table in *flagrante delicto*."

I burst out laughing. I laughed so hard that I started to hiccup, not only at the picture culled up by Karin's description, but out of sheer exhilaration. I'd been right! The barefoot, tee shirt-stained tarot reader was right! I felt like punching the air.

Karin extended her bottle to me.

"Sorry," I squeaked between the spasms in my diaphragm. "I don't mean to make light of such a tragedy. It's just that your description was so—"

"Dead on?" She grinned.

I took a sip of water. "Well, yeah. Marina does seem pretty stuck in her way of doing things. Do you think she would've objected, if she'd let herself see what was going on?"

"I don't know. I'm sure she genuinely liked Laura, but as you've probably noticed, her commitment to maintaining the status quo is absolute. I doubt that she could've made room in that anal little brain of hers for Dr. Landon and Laura, as a couple. I think she would have thought it a bit tawdry, you know?"

I handed her back her bottle. "What did you think?"

"Honestly, I thought they were cute." She sighed. "He lit up when she was around. It didn't take much to see there was juice between them."

The thick foliage of the oak in front of us rustled.

Karin jumped and giggled nervously. One of the branches bent and, from the tree's depths, a black crow emerged, beady eyes glowing. It glared at us and cawed and fluffed its oily feathers. Then it shot off, into the air, cutting a dark path across the sky.

It was always the unseen that caught you off-guard. Maybe Marina was more than a fussy little office manager. And not as oblivious as Karin thought, particularly to a truth that would seriously screw with her vision of Dr. Landon and of herself, as his most valued employee. Had Laura become a treacherous interloper, in her mind? A threat that needed to be disposed of?

Marina, with her love of precisely aligned mugs and all things floral . . . working her substantial butt off to keep the office just so. The source of jealousy I'd seen in Laura's reading? The Three of Pentacles, upended?

Chapter Twenty-One

"Would you look at those beauties!" Tessa peered at the summer squash, green beans, and ears of white corn nestled in the wicker baskets in front of us. "I don't remember the last time I saw such veg-a-tables."

She picked up a knobby little patty pan and scrutinized it with the care of a jeweler examining a yellow diamond through a loupe. I waited patiently while she assessed the rest of the produce and made her selection. Then she arranged her treasures in the canvas bag I held open for her.

"It's the next best thing to growin' them yourself!" she said.

Personally, I'm more than happy to let other people grow my food for me, as long as they don't coat it in pesticides or try to genetically modify its innards. Which was precisely the reason I loved shopping at the Lake Merritt Farmer's Market. Eating fresh food raised by local farmers as Mother Nature intended: What a concept.

Tessa poked at an heirloom tomato and eyed the purple, red, orange, and yellow offerings. She sniffed a pink one with green stripes and the vendor cut into its ripe flesh and offered up a sample; a meaty, succulent slice with a mellow flavor and the faint aroma of good, rich soil warmed by the sun. A glimpse at Tessa's face told me that she, too, was in a state of nightshade-induced bliss.

"Now, I ask you, why would anyone pay good money for one of those anemic, mealy things they sell at those chain stores when you could be tastin' the likes of this?" A trickle of tomato juice ran down her chin and she patted at it with a flowered handkerchief.

A breeze shook the canvas of the vendor's tent; the kind of chilly air that makes you want to stay in the sun if you're bare-legged and wearing a thin cotton skirt like me. The ubiquitous summer fog had burned off around noon, leaving a sunny, seventy-degree day in its wake. August in Virginia meant wearing as few clothes as possible and, despite having spent the last twenty of them here, the Southern girl in me still refused to accept the lability of Bay Area summers and layer adequately for them.

"So how are Kalie and Mara doing?" I asked.

She slid a plump, golden tomato into the bag and her lips tightened. "That beast is eatin' her out of house and home. But he is good enough natured, I suppose. And a fine watchdog." She chuckled. "One look at that monstrosity would send the devil himself runnin'—not that I mind, you understand. Young women can never have too much protection, these days, with all the messin' goin' on."

She gave me a sidelong glance. "And, speakin' of which, how is your investigating going?"

"Investigating?"

She stopped to admire a pint of black cherry preserves.

"The one about that wee client of yours who got herself drowned."

"How'd you know about that?"

"A little bird told me."

"Would that be a long-legged bird with exotic plumage, like a peacock, by chance?"

"It would, it would," she nodded and returned the jar to the counter. "She also said you'd been keepin' company with a private eye."

Private eye? I hadn't heard that expression in about forty years. "You know, Jessamae imagines romance everywhere she looks. He's an acquaintance that agreed to help me out a little, that's all."

"And do his professional services extend to helpin' you around the dance floor, then?"

I sighed. "The woman's lips should be surgically bound."

"She is a fountain of information, that one. What say we take a sit and enjoy some of my blueberries while we talk."

Tessa maneuvered us through the crowd and behind the food court tents to a spot on the grassy embankment across from the Grand Lake Theater. Clusters of people sprawled on the slope, noshing and sunbathing and watching cars inch their way down Lake Park Avenue. Traffic had slowed to a crawl due to a group of protesters, dressed in black, who'd gathered under the theater marquee with placards protesting the conflict in the Middle East. A passing motorist honked in support of their cause.

Tessa pulled a pint of dusky berries out of her bag. I could hear Atticus' voice in my head warning me about discussing my undercover status. But I wanted to talk to someone about what I'd discovered, if for no other reason than to organize my thoughts. Besides, as a former nurse, it might be worth getting her take on the situation, especially since I'd been all but outed by the Social Director of Glen Avenue, anyway.

"Truthfully, I'm more confused than ever. At first, I assumed my client was killed by her ex-boyfriend, end of story. But the more I dig into her life, the more suspects crop up."

"What did the poor child do to warrant such bloodlust?" Her slate blue eyes glinted, alive with curiosity.

Bloodlust? This was the most worked up I'd seen her in years. She was clearly intrigued. And hyper-focused. What was going on with her?

A black-and-white image flickered before my eyes: Raymond Burr as Perry Mason, broad-shouldered and dimpled with slick, wavy hair and his trademark sly smile. The camera in my brain pulled back to reveal a full screen shot of a thirty-something Tessa walking into his inner sanctum, in a knee-length pencil skirt and twin set with a 1960's bubble cut, stenographer's pad in hand . . . pretty, precise, and poised to tackle her next assignment.

Good lord, she was envisioning herself as Della Street.

I hesitated, glued to the TV screen in my head. "Well, I, uh, I have a couple of theories, but nothing definitive. I've been doing a little undercover work, temping at her old job."

"Aren't you the clever one?" She nodded and passed me the basket of fruit. "Who better than a nurse for this kind of operation?"

I couldn't believe my ears. Despite what I'd just seen, I'd been expecting some level of admonishment. And the mandatory lecture involving terms like *what foolishness* and *this is a matter better left to the police*. Or, at the very least, a *you are in over your head, young lady*. On the other hand, I had Atticus and Burnette for that.

She selected a berry and popped it in her mouth. "So, what have you turned up so far?"

"Four suspects." I ticked them off on the fingers of my right hand. "The ex-boyfriend, a rap producer and maybe drug distributor who wanted to get back with her. A homely, brainiac roommate with a flaming crush on the ex-boyfriend. Laura's work manager, whose devotion to her position and her boss runs to the obsessive. And her boss, a surgeon, who my client was involved with at the time of her death."

Tessa whistled. "What a tangle. Motivation?"

"The first three: jealousy, with varying levels of need to control thrown in. As far as her boss goes, I don't know. He's single, so no angry spouse to contend with. Maybe a lovers' quarrel gone bad?"

Tessa slapped her knee. "My money is on the doctor. If he's anything like some of the ones I've known, he probably likes his hanky-panky, free and easy, on the side—hands roamin' around behind the nurses' station." She wrinkled her nose in distaste. "Disgusting."

My stifled giggle turned to a snort. The thought of any doctor getting amorous with Tessa was too hilarious not to contemplate. Particularly the part where he draws back a bloody stump in place of his hand.

"He probably was done with her and she wasn't goin' quietly," she continued, full steam ahead. "So, he takes her out to dinner, somewhere near the lake, and puts some of that rager drug in her drink. Then suggests they go for a lovers' stroll and pushes her in."

She had clearly given this some thought.

I took a bite of blueberry. "Sounds like you and Jessamae went over this in detail."

"Well, it would be a shame now wouldn't it, if that poor girl wasn't able to rest in peace with all this hangin' over her."

The 'not resting in peace' part, I could identify with. Although the nightmares occurred less often now, in my waking hours I was finding it hard to concentrate on anything but honing in on Laura's killer. Assuming that Karin was telling me the truth—and I had no reason to think otherwise—the new leads about Dr. Landon and Marina were promising. I had to cop to feeling a bit proud, especially since neither Burnette nor Atticus were aware of my discovery.

But that didn't change the fact that I had less than a month to unearth definitive proof from somewhere inside of the office. A nagging sense of urgency told me that the window of opportunity was closing . . . and the only strategy I'd dreamed up entailed getting closer to both of my bosses which, given their respective levels of reserve, was not going to be easy or quickly done. To be honest, I wasn't sure I had that much charm in me.

Tessa's voice cut across my thoughts. "What's the name of this doctor, then?"

"Landon. He's a plastic surgeon in Marin."

"That's an Irish name. I used to know some folks by that

name in Carrickfergus. They were very big in the Ulster in Bloom competitions."

"Ulster in Bloom?"

"Oh, sorry." She patted my arm. "You must excuse an old woman's ramblings. It's like a county competition, you know, for which town can have the prettiest gardens and floral displays. Landon was a bit of a name back there."

"Northern Ireland, huh? His features make me think he's more Nordic, like Scandinavian."

"Well, you know, with all the times that island's been invaded over the centuries, there's all sorts of blood runnin' through our veins." She put the basket back in her bag and winked at me. "With a surname like yours, you must have a drop or two of Ireland in you."

"Yes, from way back though. My people made it to the Virginias shortly after the Revolutionary War and then proceeded to proliferate with the English and German settlers. And I think there's some Native-American in there and some Swiss-French. So, I guess I'm more your classic mixed-breed."

"No matter." Tessa waved her hand. "You should still go see the place. It's a beautiful little island. Even if you're not a child of Eire."

A street performer in a straw hat and patched vest strolled by and blew an air horn in our general direction, eliciting shrieks of joy from the group of children playing tag next to us. Across the street, the only action under the marquee involved moviegoers queuing up for the 2:00 p.m. matinee. The traffic from the market's parking lot was beginning to disgorge itself onto Lake Park Avenue and some of the vendors were breaking down tents. The smell of kettle corn, so pervasive earlier in the day, had thinned to a ghost of its former self. Tessa stood and brushed off her capris.

Somewhere in the back of my brain, a flare went up. "Tessa, what did you just say?"

She shook her head. "You really are too young to be so forgetful. I was talkin' about you payin' a visit to Ireland."

"No, the part about a child, a child of . . . "

"Eire?"

"That's like a folk name for—"

"The old Irish Free State: The Republic of Ireland."

The flare exploded into fireworks: a fiery cascade of spinning color. Eire . . . Ari. A destination, not a name. A place, not a person. Spoken with a Southern accent, they were virtually interchangeable.

"That's a pretty popular travel destination, isn't it?"

She shouldered her bag of produce. "Oh, sure. Now that the trubles have calmed down, it's very popular, especially with you Yanks. Tendin' to the tourists is a big part of how people make their money over there these days."

And who better to be dropping some coin than a rich American physician rediscovering his roots? And what better locale for a romantic getaway? If the office were closed in his absence, no one would notice if Laura slipped away with him.

Or would they? Maybe someone who didn't want Laura getting any closer to Neil Landon did take notice. Or maybe he planned to go on his own and she objected and things got heated. Heated enough to murder her?

Landon didn't seem like he had much of a killer instinct, but then neither did Marina. I hadn't spent enough time with either of them to make any predictions about what they might be capable of. But, of one thing, I was sure; a planned to trip to Ireland shouldn't be that hard to uncover.

And now, thanks to Tessa, I knew where to look.

Chapter Twenty-Two

Morning light stabbed at the back of my eyelids. I rolled over and cool damp rushed up under the covers. I blinked at the red LED display on my bed stand and struggled to open my eyes.

6:58 a.m. What was I doing conscious at this hour on a Sunday morning?

I started to nod off and then something rustled up under the bed; a kind of scrunchy sound that made my skin crawl. With all the holes in the building, the list of possible offenders was endless. *Yuk.* Maybe it was a mouse. On the other hand, I shouldn't have mice. Not with . . .

"Audie!"

She leaped onto the bed with a thud and bound across the bed spread, planting her front paws on my shoulders. I grunted as she dropped her full weight onto my chest. All was quiet in the bedroom, except for the sound of a tabby purring.

"What have you been up to?" I muttered.

Her gold eyes shined as I reached to scratch behind her ears. She'd probably been up for hours. And now her human was awake. It didn't get much better than that. She rubbed her cheek against my bare shoulder and burped: a moist, incredibly fishy burp.

"Whoa, Audie, you stink," I cried and covered my nose. The purring dialed up a notch.

What could she possibly have gotten into, at this hour? Maybe Tessa had left her some scraps on the stoop this morning . . . except that I'd latched the cat door last night. At least, I thought I had.

I peered into her chubby face. "Audie, where did you get treaties?"

"Murp!" she announced, at the mention of her favorite word. She dove off the end of the bed and made a bee-line for the kitchen. There would be no peace now that she'd seen me awake.

I swung my legs over the bed, promising myself a long nap later in the day. Only instead of the nubby texture of my throw rug, my feet pressed down on something squishy: a furry surface, with way too much give for my liking. I shrieked and pulled my feet back up on the bed.

Nothing moved. I couldn't be sure without my contacts, but I didn't see any fur, or scales, or tail scuttling across the floor. I peered over the edge of the bed. My black velveteen change purse lay on the rug next to my sunglasses and a pair of lavender beeswax candles. They'd been pulled from my canvas tote, along with all the other items I'd purchased at the Farmer's Market, and strewn across the floor.

I followed the trail up under the bed. A bag of dried shrimp kitty snacks had been pushed up against the baseboard. There was a jagged tear down the middle and, as best as I could tell, at least a third of the contents were missing. Oh, great. I was about to have a bloated, thirsty cat on my hands. One who would not be especially understanding about not being given her breakfast. Terrific.

I located my bedroom slippers and padded into the kitchen. Audie was waiting by her bowl, evidently not yet feeling the effects of her pre-dawn recon. Maybe if I gave her some water, she'd feel full. I poured some from the water bottle into her dish and she slurped it up. I had a feeling she was going to want a lot more of that before the day was over.

I would need to keep an eye on her. Overeating like that could result in a bowel ileus. I didn't think her little seafood extravaganza would warrant an emergency trip to the vet, but I'd better monitor her. Why was it that pets always managed to get sick or injured on weekends, effectively doubling the cost of repairs? Not that she wasn't worth it.

She jumped up onto the kitchen chair—the one she considered to be hers—and washed her face and paws with focused care. Grooming was a good sign, I told myself, as I refilled her water bowl.

I pulled back the curtain on the small window above the sink. It was overcast and grey and, from the way the ginkgo trees in the yard next door were swaying, windy. I was willing to bet the thermometer wouldn't climb past sixty today even if the sun came out. Good incentive to be housebound.

I put the kettle on to boil. My plan was to devote at least part of the morning strategizing with my list of suspects and my reference manual and I needed some caffeine to get my synapses firing. I retrieved *The Urban Guide* from the bookshelf in the living room and headed back to the stove.

The kettle whistled. I poured hot water over a tea bag, settled in at the kitchen table, and cracked opened the book. Audie was now on her side and sprawled across two chairs; eyes closed, belly only slightly distended. So far, so good.

According to Atticus, the word "evidence" stemmed from the Latin root word, *videre*, meaning to see or, in some interpretations, to apprehend. It was also a term used in some role-playing games to refer to the state in which our belief systems were observed to affect our view of reality; that is, our perception of the world and what was taking place in it. For example, both Marina and Karin witnessed daily exchanges between Landon and Laura in the office, but only Karin saw the romantic relationship there.

Atticus went on to say there were primarily two forms of evidence: physical and verbal. Physical evidence was the stuff of prime time crime dramas—blood stains, tire marks, DNA, clothing, bullet fragments, and even the victim's body—anything tangible that would help the police to reconstruct the crime. Although interpretation of the findings provided by this kind of evidence differed from expert to expert, the judiciary system generally considered it to be the most reliable.

Verbal evidence referred to statements made by those who claimed to have knowledge about some aspect of a crime. Like the *videre* of role-playing, eyewitness accounts varied in any given case and were dependent on the prejudices and beliefs of the individuals interviewed. Therefore, verbal evidence was given less credence by the authorities than physical evidence. The bad news was that all I had, so far, were indirect witnesses: people who could testify to events that preceded Laura's murder. True, I had the dreams and some pretty compelling visuals I'd intuited around some of the suspects, but the only real evidence I had—Karin's account of Laura and Landon kissing—was verbal. And I had my doubts that approaching Burnette or even Atticus with this disclosure would be enough to kick a new police investigation into gear. I needed something more explosive.

Across the table, Audie's right ear twitched; an indication that her postprandial slumber had been disturbed. Then her belly began to rumble and an ominous cloud of kitty flatulence filled the kitchen. Talk about explosive. It was time to make for higher ground. I grabbed the book and my tea and headed for the living room.

Since the physical evidence from the crime scene had already been collected, processed, and analyzed, I was going to have to set my sights elsewhere. From what I'd intuited, all my suspects had means, motive, and opportunity. So, where should I focus my attention? I picked up the deck of tarot cards on the coffee table and pulled out a significator for each of them: the Ascetic with its three-headed dog, for both Ravenwaif and FoZ, the Three of Pentacles for Marina, and the Eight of Pentacles for Dr. Landon.

I held up The Ascetic. I didn't foresee what further disclosures could be gotten out of FoZ. Like the dogs being chased by the cloaked friar, he was the shadiest of my suspects and the hardest to pin down. Always a little ahead and to the left of the law, he embraced the darker aspects of his shadow self as a state of being. I'd never seen anything like the wispy, grimy energy floating around him that day in his apartment.

That he didn't have closure about Laura, I was sure, but the real truth of what had passed between them was going to be tricky to bring out into the light. And if there was any physical evidence connecting him to her murder, I'd be willing to bet it'd been destroyed about five nanoseconds after Laura hit the water. What I really needed was another chance to check him out when his attention was focused on Laura, and I hadn't a clue how to pull that off.

Ravenwaif was the ultimate hermit, sequestered in her dim little hovel like a monk in his cell; hunched in front of her computer, buzzed on junk food, stoking up agro and her infatuation for FoZ. Given her housekeeping skills, there could still be physical evidence of her tie to the murder moldering away in that dump of hers. And if Laura had planned to go to Ireland, there might be a paper trail, such as a ticket or itinerary, in her bedroom. In either case, it was worth another trip to El Cerrito.

I ran my hand over the slick surface of the Three of Pentacles and turned the card upside down. It wasn't hard to visualize Marina as the jealous shopkeep's wife, maintaining a sharp watch over her husband's business and suffering in silence when he promoted an attractive young employee. Perhaps she had caught wind of the romance and Laura's burgeoning influence over her boss. Marina's self-identity seemed bound to her job. Maybe the prospect of having to kowtow to her protégé had driven her to the edge, to an act that would normally be out of character.

If she committed murder, in her mind, Marina would have been setting things to rights. And she would have dispatched her duty with precision, pulling on her latex gloves and tidying up the messy leavings. Had Marina been the one hiding in the cypress, there'd be nothing but a sterile field left in her wake. And I couldn't get a read on her, to see if she had been at the lake that night, while I was in work head; which was the only time we were together. If I could just get her away from the desk and relaxed enough to chat again; to expound on her relationship with Laura.

Which brought me to the reversed Eight of Pentacles. Landon, the warrior/athlete: an individual intent on building a better world or forcing a twisted vision upon it, depending on the position of the card. His own sister had referred to him as " . . . one of the good guys". And, if what Karin said about his medical relief work was true, he more than matched the positive aspects of this card. No doubt, his devotion to helping others had made him attractive to Laura, initially; in that sense, he was the polar opposite to FoZ. But was there a side to him as dark as FoZ's? A secret self even his family wouldn't recognize? A self that reared its ugly head when Laura wanted to move forward with the relationship and maybe make it public?

A planned trip to Ireland, solo or with Laura, should be noted in the appointment book or on the office schedule in the computer. If I could produce physical evidence linking the two of them to a shared vacation then Burnette would have to regard Landon as a person of interest. Wouldn't he?

Now my stomach was rumbling. The cup of tea in front of me was cold and singularly uninspiring. I wondered if it was safe to go back into the kitchen. I tiptoed over to Audie and placed my ear near her belly. A cacophony of gurgles and growls arose, interspersed with snores. The digestive crisis had probably been averted, but I didn't want her eating anything else until I was certain.

All that analyzing had left me running on empty. I could hear the home fries and apple smoked sausage from Mama's Cafe calling. And, for once, I'd be ahead of the rush. I slipped into the bedroom and threw on some jeans and a sweater and ran a brush through my hair. I'd knock on Jessamae's door and see if she was up yet and without company. She would be appalled at my lack of makeup, but what the heck; it would be good to share breakfast with a human for a change.

On my way out, I sneaked a peek at Audie's water bowl. It was still two-thirds full, enough to hold her until I got back. She sighed and rolled over on her back; the tip of her tongue protruding from between her teeth. She was pretty cute, toxic fumes and all.

I reached out to pet her, then changed my mind and tiptoed to the door.

Better to let gaseous cats lie.

Chapter Twenty-Three

I turned the page. Ebony eyes gazed back at me, fringed with a sweep of dark lashes. A little boy with skin the color of burnished copper and an empty gum where his left upper tooth should be smiled for the camera: a preschooler named Armando. A child with Crouzon's Syndrome.

Armando had been born with craniofacial dysostosis, a condition that caused the sutures in his skull to close prematurely, resulting in a profound distortion of his facial features. The photographs that accompanied his medical history revealed a diminutive boy with exophthalmoses (bulging eyes) that slanted downwards, a slightly beaked nose, and a severely underdeveloped jaw. In addition, he had been born with a cleft palate and strabismus (crossed eyes).

His cleft palate had been hastily repaired at the small hospital forty-five miles from his village, and, as a result, Armando was able to nurse and, therefore, survive his infancy. But as he grew, his facial deformities became more apparent and made him the subject of ridicule among his playmates in the community. Like most children with

Crouzons, he was born with normal intelligence and, according to his psychological profile, became increasingly aware of negative reactions to his appearance. His mother's response was to keep him at home with her as much as she could and, as a result of the isolation, his social and behavioral development began to lag.

Through the persistence of extended family members and the village priest, his case was brought up for review before Dr. Landon's medical relief team in South America and, at the age of four, a series of staged procedures were initiated. The sutures of his skull were released, allowing adequate room for brain growth and expansion. Jaw surgery increased the volume of his eye orbits, thereby reducing the bulging effect. The muscles behind his eyes were resected and repaired and the original cleft palate incision brought into better alignment. At the time of Dr. Landon's last visit, eleven months ago, Armando was an active six-year-old, developmentally on target, and preparing to attend public school.

His story was such a testament to what allopathic medicine can offer, I'd almost forgotten where my attention should be. I peeked over the top of the album. Marina was in the process of rearranging Tuesday's schedule and very much occupied. Excellent. The less aware she was of my true intentions the better. Trying to read someone who was on guard was a little like bench pressing a black hole: one big energy suck.

Plus, I was feeling a bit slimy for doing this without her permission, even though I promised myself I'd keep the personal invasion tactics to a minimum. A quick peek through the windows for anything pertaining to Laura and I'd be on my way.

Ava had phoned shortly after my arrival to say that Landon had been sick in bed all weekend with a high fever and wouldn't be coming in today. I'd helped Marina make cancellation calls and reschedule patients and was almost out the door when it occurred to me that this might be my one opportunity to check her out without any patients around. I really didn't envision any future reality in which she and I would be socializing outside of the office, so I'd asked if I could glance over Dr. Landon's scrapbooks off the clock.

I softened my gaze. I wasn't much of an aura reader, but I could see if things were seriously out of whack in a human energy field. In Marina's case, I hadn't glimpsed anything that spelled out total psychopath—at least, not yet. What I was picking up was sluggish energy around her belly which grew denser directly in front of her gallbladder. On closer examination, I could see sludge there and the kind of stagnant current you'd expect in the backwater of a swamp. If I were to guess, I'd say she was about two months shy of a cholecystectomy.

Below her torso, her right knee was emanating what I could only describe as the visual equivalent of static. The joint was struggling to support her upper body and it wouldn't be long before she began to experience pain and weakness there, if she wasn't already. It was clear she was spending way too much time in couch-and-carb mode and was going to be seeing the inside of a surgical suite, for one ailment or another, before the year was out.

What struck me the most was how the energy from her etheric body hugged her, as if she were restrained in a whole body corset. Normally it extends out as far as four to five inches, but hers was contracted, pressed up against her physical body like the kind of energetic aberration I'd seen around patients who'd suffered a recent trauma. Perhaps it was sourced from her intense need to keep control. But I wasn't going to stick around long enough to delve into that.

I silently posed the question, *"How did you feel about Laura?"* Then I closed my eyes and waited ... and waited and waited. No one was picking up on the other end. I could literally feel her psyche resisting me from across the room.

I peeked at her through one eye. She was still on the phone and nothing in her etheric field had changed. Maybe I should rethink the question. Perhaps, "feel" was too threatening a word for her. It could imply vulnerability, something she was probably on guard against.

I closed my eyes, again. *"How did you experience Laura?"* I asked silently. The blank space before me began to fill, first with color, then with form. The seated figure of Laura, charting at the front desk, materialized in front of me.

I was standing behind her, looking over her shoulder. She was writing in a patient file deliberately, carefully choosing the medical terminology to best describe her assessment, pausing now and then to ask for feedback. Only the flourishes and curlicue extensions of some of her letters hinted at the fact that a teenager was doing the charting. Noting this, I felt a surge of affection. And pride. I reminded myself that she was still young as I caught a glimpse of pink scalp peeking through her pale blonde hair, parted in the middle and pulled back into a ponytail; hair so fine the tie around it had been tripled. Hair like a baby's.

My eyes stung.

"Do you need a Kleenex?"

Marina stood planted in front of me, holding out a box of tissues. "Some of those case histories are pretty touching," she said.

"Yes, they are." I nodded, grateful for the excuse for my tears. I pulled out a tissue and dabbed at my eyes. "It, it must make you feel good to work for a doctor who affects those children's lives so profoundly."

"It does." She sighed. "But sometimes I think he will run himself ragged trying to help those who can't help themselves."

"With his medical relief work?"

Marina took the album from me and cradled it against her chest. "Oh that, too. And his work at the free clinic in San Francisco. And Berkeley. And anyplace else that needs him."

"Wow, I had no idea. No wonder he looks so worn out all the time."

She set the album and tissues on the front desk and winced as she eased herself into her chair. I could practically hear her cruciate ligaments whining in protest.

"I was hoping that his sister might put a stop to some of it, but she doesn't seem to have gotten him to slow down any. At least, she sees to it that he gets a decent meal from time to time." She sniffed, apparently indignant at the thought of Dr. Landon having to forage for his own food.

Like he couldn't find decent take-out in Marin. Or San Francisco. Or Berkeley.

"Well, it can be good to have family around," I said, reaching for a topic to keep her engaged. "Are they from the Bay Area?"

"Dr. Landon is from Chicago." Her voice drifted as she scanned the computer screen. In a minute she'd be back in work head. *Think, Eileen, think.*

"Maybe Laura's death is still troubling for him?" I stammered. "I mean . . . Karin mentioned it'd taken its toll on all of you."

Marina peered at me over her reading glasses. "Well, a tragedy like that is hard to up and put behind you. We all cared about Laura and Dr. Landon was very kind to her."

Kind? So that was how she'd labeled it. I watched as she entered data into the computer, her daisy-tipped acrylics clicking over the keys. Could she really be that blind or was she covering for him? Or playing the benevolent coworker to distract everyone from her true feelings?

She paused and reviewed her entries. "It is good to have family close," she said, folding her glasses and placing them in their case with a snap. "I think if Laura had some family around, she wouldn't have gotten into trouble."

"Trouble?" I asked.

"Young girls, today, are too sure of themselves. They think they have everything figured out. But you still need someone to keep an eye on you, to stop you from making mistakes . . . "

Marina's voice trailed off and she stared at the monitor. Only I could see that what occupied her was well past the screen, beyond the confines of the office or the medical complex. In a place long ago boarded up and shut away from the light—a place she returned to often these days.

Pale green walls swam by as she struggled up through twilight sleep. She strained to hear their voices, to understand the words they were saying. Was it over?

Bright lights blurred into glowing balls above her. Thank God they'd finally given her something for the pain. She'd never hurt like that. And now she was so sleepy. But she needed to wake up.

She knew it must be a girl, from the way she'd carried it, like her mother had with her. They'd told her she wouldn't be able to see her. That it would be better for everyone if she didn't. She wished they would let her see her . . . her mother . . . her baby. If only she could raise her head.

A thin wail pierced the air, like a small bird crying for its breakfast. She tried to sit up and fell back onto the pillow, her breasts and belly throbbing. "I want to see her!" she screamed silently.

They were pulling the bedrails up, shutting her in. "Please," she begged, her tongue cleaving to the roof of her mouth. The bed began to move, rolling seamlessly over the waxed linoleum.

The computer ceased humming as she powered it down. Marina stood with some effort and picked up the album, then started down the hall slowly favoring her right leg. It was hard to watch. I hoped my probing hadn't exacerbated her knee. Or a pain far worse.

"Marina, you're limping!" I scolded, in my best big nurse voice. I walked over to her and held out my arms. "Let me take the book back to the doctor's office. You need to rest your knee."

"Well, I . . . " her voice wavered.

I took the album from her and guided her to one of the chairs in the waiting room.

"Where should I put it?" I asked.

She dropped her weight onto the vinyl cushion with a groan; a gutteral sound that proclaimed her utter exhaustion. I know, because I felt it, too.

"In the cabinet, to the left, next to the surgical journals," she said. She leaned forward and massaged her right kneecap.

I wanted to say it will be all right. You did the best you could, given the choices available to you. There are people who can help you find out about your child, help you make contact, if you want. It's not too late. But, of course, I couldn't say any of those things without invading her privacy. And I'd done enough of that for one day.

I switched on the light in Landon's office. An ornate teakwood cabinet sat against the opposite wall at a diagonal from the door; massive and intricately carved. Angry-eyed dragons decorated its burnished surface, spewing fire and clutching pearls of wisdom in their scaly, five-toed claws. Normally, I would have enjoyed taking the time to examine the artistry behind the design and to have an uninterrupted look around. But Marina and I both needed to go home, to leave behind what we'd experienced here today. I pulled open the door and pushed the album into place next to the journals.

The troubled aspects of Laura's reading—distorted vision, jealousy—could all have stemmed from Marina. She'd probably made the decision, on some level, to ignore the relationship between her boss and co-worker because of the conflict acknowledging it brought up for her: jealousy versus her adoration of Landon and her genuine affection for Laura. Couple that with her concern that Laura might be headed for the same kind of situation she'd found herself in so many years ago and you end up with an emotional quagmire that was messy and difficult to access. There was motive to be sure, but, given what I'd just seen, I didn't think it was of the murderous variety. My instincts told me I had bigger fish to fry.

I shut the door. It closed effortlessly, gliding back into perfect alignment with its twin. I brushed my hand across the satin finish, tracing the fine grain of the wood. One of the dragons stared back at me accusing, daring me to delve deeper.

Keeper of your master's secrets, eh? I stuck out my tongue. We'll see about that.

Chapter Twenty-Four

"Can you work wid it?"
"Can you work wid it?"
"Kickin' in da club."
"Can you work wid it?"

"Can you work wid it?"
"Can you work wid it?"
"Shakin' yo dreads."
"Can you work wid it?"

Music pumped out of the opened windows of Blind Dawg Productions—blaring, heavily synthesized, and hypnotic in a brain-numbing kind of way. The pounding baselines and overdubbed vocals made most of the lyrics indecipherable. But I could make out the chorus and it was starting to imprint on my brain.

"Can you work wid it?"
"Can you work wid it?"
"Hollar hyphy at your Bay."

"Can you work wid it?"

FoZ's office was located on Adeline Street, near the border of Emeryville, in an area referred to by commercial real estate agents as "transitional"; meaning a blighted urban landscape of boarded-up buildings where private retail once thrived, now dotted with a shabby and heavily-secured liquor store or two. Not a flower or tree or any other sign of gentrification in sight, just some prickly weeds forcing their way up through the cracks in the sidewalk. It was the kind of place you didn't frequent unless you were bound there by business or misfortune and most definitely the kind of neighborhood you didn't venture into without backup.

As it happens, I had my posse with me: one member who was panting quietly in the seat behind me, the other parked around the corner in an unassuming blue Toyota Rav4. Mara was there for the protection his appearance would lend and Kalie had made herself available in case anything went wrong—like Mara and I disappearing inside the ugly yellow brick building we were parked in front of and not coming out again. Her assistance was something we'd agreed her aunt could never know about and, guilty as I felt for accepting her offer, I was glad they were there.

A large black man, roughly the size of a refrigerator, loomed in the doorway and studied my car. Even in this neighborhood, its sun-bleached carcass was an eyesore. The once red paint had oxidized to a burnt orange and the covering for the rear right taillight was cracked and held in place with electrical tape. The windshield sported a dime-sized hole and the passenger's side door had been keyed, leaving three wavy streaks raked down to the primer. If Atticus' scraper was any example of a proper P.I. car, there should be no question I was a legitimate employee.

Atticus. He wouldn't be too pleased about this either. Especially since I was about to do the very thing he'd warned me against.

Halfway through its fourth repetition the song skidded to a stop and an eerie silence fell over the deserted street. The man in the doorway muttered to himself, then lumbered down the steps. He made his way over to the car laboriously, as if each step required effort; a blue light flashing sporadically from the cell phone inside his right ear. A behemoth of a square-cut diamond stud hung beneath it, pulling down the fleshy lobe.

"You got a appointment?" he asked and bared the metal caps that covered his front teeth.

"Tuesday, one o'clock, with FoZ," I said, and handed him Atticus' card. I could feel myself starting to perspire: a cold, anxious sweat. Mara whined softly and shifted his weight on the back seat.

He took a long time examining the card. Too long. I told myself he had poor eyesight. I told myself he was a slow reader. I told myself he was just doing his job. Then I reminded myself to breathe.

He handed the card back without looking at me and walked away from the car, stopping short of the front steps. His lips moved for a few seconds, then he nodded his slick, bald head, apparently acknowledging communications from inside. A long moment passed before he motioned me out of the car.

I did a sharp inhale, released Mara from the back seat, clipped his collar, and started toward the building.

He glanced down at the canine on the leash beside me. Crossing his beefy arms, he blocked the entrance to the building with his torso. "No dog," he said.

I had anticipated his response. Mara had the appearance of a serious guard dog; the kind that could move into attack mode, unprovoked. He also looked like a canine that could get anxious with disastrous results: an impression I planned to use in my favor.

"The dog comes with," I said, doing my best imitation of a stare down. "He'll rip the car to pieces if I leave him alone."

FoZ's bodyguard looked over at the Lynx, then back at Mara. Then he started to laugh. At least, I think it was a laugh. A noise that reminded me of an incoming tsunami rumbled out of the confines of his thick neck: a sound that put my adrenals on red alert. His eyes screwed up into tight little slits and his double chin shook, bringing to mind a demonic Buddha. I had to give FoZ his props; he'd picked the right man for the job.

The noise stopped as abruptly as it started and he jerked his head toward the opened doorway. "Down the hall," he mumbled and moved a few inches to the left. Mara and I squeezed past him and into the building.

The room was industrial in its proportions, with high ceilings, a catwalk, and a bank of open windows that faced out toward the south side of the building and illuminated the space. Directly opposite us, there was a stage with an elevated platform that contained a jumble of towering speakers and a long table with two turntables, coils of cable, and a wireless mic. A large monitor hung from the catwalk, centered above the stage. In the east corner of the room sat a pool table and a trashcan spilling over with beer bottles and flattened cans of energy drinks. Despite the opened windows, the odor of stale tobacco hung in the air. There appeared to be no one around except for Mara, me, and The Refrigerator—a thought that brought me no comfort.

We walked past the stage and down the narrow hallway that extended past the right side of it. The creepy dog logo spray painted on the door to my left let me know I'd arrived at my destination. I averted my eyes from the empty, staring sockets, and knocked. The smell of clove cigarettes drifted past the crack in the door.

"Mr. Fotakis?" I called out and pushed it open.

FoZ sat behind a sleek metal desk, his face partially obscured in shadow. He was wearing a chocolate brown fedora pulled down over one eye. A silver hoop dangled from his right ear and thick black hair curled up and away from his neck. He looked plenty ripped in a thin, white wife beater. How appropriate.

"That thing your bodyguard?" His sneer revealed a row of even, pearly whites.

I shrugged. "He likes to go where I go."

I bent down to pat Mara's head. He stood at attention, in a state of calm beside me. I was glad one of us was. Not waiting for an invite, I seated myself in the wooden, slatted chair opposite the desk, crossing my ankles and pressing one knee into the other to stop them from shaking. Mara sat, those strange eyes of his fixed on the figure in the black leather chair.

"I'll get right to the point, Mr. Fotakis. Our investigation has turned up some evidence that indicates Laura Neff's drowning was not accidental. Being her ex-boyfriend . . . an ex-boyfriend that didn't want to be her ex . . . well, I'm sure you understand." I paused and smiled, making sure no hint of warmth made its way into my expression.

"One of the people that we questioned is willing to state you were stalking Laura, up to a few weeks before she died. Before I go to the police with that information, I'd like to hear your side of the story."

Only my tone said that I didn't, not really. It conveyed that, as far as I was concerned, anything he might have to say was inconsequential. Like Burnette and Sgt. Johnson were waiting outside. Like he'd be running his next rave from inside city jail. Or from San Quentin.

I checked out his energy field. No disturbances. Not around his solar plexus or anywhere else. But his remarkable eyes had begun to smolder. And the sneer had hardened in place.

FoZ crossed his legs and reclined in the chair. "You've got some cojones, Ms. Ass-sistant. But see, I know Laura's lame-ass excuse for a mother was too piss poor to pay for some three-hundred-dollar-a-day cowboy dick. So, I ain't givin' you shit."

Nice. He hadn't bought the cover after all. Fair enough. I was prepared to tell him the truth—or a version of it.

"Okay, Mr. Fotakis, I'll level with you. I'm not working for Laura's family, but I am working for a friend of hers; a person who cared very much about her who doesn't believe she would have done Ecstasy of her own free will. Or that she died accidentally. A friend who doesn't want her remembered that way."

FoZ stared straight ahead. The heat behind his eyes had begun to dissipate, but he said nothing.

I leaned forward. "Look, I believe you loved Laura. And I think she loved you. We just want to find out what really happened the night she drowned."

And there it was: a cloud of liquid charcoal emanating from his gut, faint but visible. The film floated upwards and intertwined in furls of what resembled cobwebs. They froze in position around his chest, forming a vest. A lump formed in my throat.

FoZ wiped his fingers across his lips. "Aw–ight," he said, his voice hoarse. "It's like I said. I wanted to get back with her. She didn't have a cell, so I called her at work a few times."

He shrugged. "Sometimes she called me back. Things were rollin', ya know."

I didn't, but I wanted him to keep talking. I nodded my head.

"So, one day, she stopped takin' my calls. Said she couldn't talk to me no more. So I had one of my boys check out her place."

He eyed me, daring me to object. Then he shrugged again. "Some nights, she didn't come home."

"How'd you feel about that?"

"What ya think? I was pissed. But she was my girl. I wouldn't have done nothin' to hurt her."

The gauzy fibers around his chest began to pulsate, fluttering like they were being blown about by an invisible wind. They quivered around him for an instant, than settled back into place. My heart—his heart—sunk, leaden in my chest.

"Did you give Laura the Ecstasy?"

He slammed his fist down on the desktop and I jumped. Mara made a sound I'd never heard come out of a dog before and showed FoZ a row of broken teeth. FoZ glared at us both.

"I never brought no X around her, okay?" he snarled. I told you she didn't like that shit." He rubbed the back of his hand over his mouth. "Why don't you go ask that freak she lived with? That bitch is a head, for sure."

"Ravenwaif?"

"Yeah, that ugly bitch in El Cerrito. Laura was always tryin' to be nice, get her out of that hole. So I told her to bring her down to party, here. Freak was thizzin' the whole night."

Of course. Ravenwaif could have slipped the Ecstasy into her food or drink there at the apartment, anytime. She'd made a point of telling me that getting high wasn't Laura's thing. Exposing Laura to something she knew she hated could've been payback for having FoZ; a little taste of humiliation for the way she felt every time she saw the two of them together. Or even a bizarre punishment for having dumped the man she wanted and couldn't have.

FoZ's sullen expression mirrored that of the hip hop artists that papered the walls of his office, posed in their baggy pants, link neck chains, and stunna shades. Only he was prettier and, in his own way, far more dangerous than their glossy personas. It was a seductive combination that meant there'd always be women vying for his attention. But

I knew from the misery inside of him—inside of me—that he was telling me the truth. And all the alpha dog bravado in Oaktown wouldn't soothe the regret gnawing at his insides. He would miss Laura for the rest of his life.

My cell phone rang and I jumped, again. It was Kalie's signal; the one we'd pre-arranged. If I didn't answer in three minutes, she'd call 911. I needed to wrap this up.

"I'm going to have to take that," I said. I stood and picked up Mara's leash. I turned to leave and a hazy scene began to coalesce inside my head and then sharpen: a preview, straight off the six o'clock news. Moving pictures detailing the bloody detritus of urban street justice and the termination of another life.

I turned back to face him. "Mr. Fotakis?" I asked quietly.

The muscle under the hollow of his cheek twitched and he flexed his right hand, opening and closing it until the knuckles pushed white through the skin. This was the consequence I hadn't foreseen; the one Atticus had warned me about. He'd been right about me coming here. The last thing I needed was another death on my conscience.

"Mr. Fotakis, I want you to know what you've told me today will make a difference. And I'll contact you when we find the person responsible. Don't try to handle this on your own. You know that's not what Laura would have wanted."

FoZ watched me for a moment, his dark eyes liquid, unreadable. Then he hung his head, like he had during the interview with Atticus. When he raised it again, all the tension had drained from his face. Only the girdle of grief remained in place, imprisoning his upper body.

He pushed the fedora forward and placed his feet on the desk. "Whateva," he said.

Chapter Twenty-Five

Atticus set the frosted mug down on the wet paper napkin. "Okay, this is the point in the conversation where I remind you, again, what a bad idea it is to let the perp know he's about to be made." In his pleated, collarless shirt and black tux, he looked quite handsome. And thoroughly exasperated.

"FoZ's not the perp." I said.

"And you know this how?" He raised his voice and then lowered it, noticing stares from the silver-haired women sipping wine in the booth behind us. "Okay, okay, I get it."

A smattering of tourists, businessmen, and couples from the OPD dinner/dance benefit had begun to drift into the Oakland Marriott bar for a drink and some private conversation. It was that point in the evening when dress shoes got kicked off under tables and tongues and ties got a little looser. Music from the '80s cover band blared past the ballroom doors and out into the hallway.

I raised my voice. "He says that Ravenwaif is the connection between Laura and the Ecstasy and I think he might be right." I pulled my green silk wrap around my bare shoulders. "I mean, think about it. They lived together; it wouldn't have been hard for her to sneak it into Laura's food or drink."

Atticus sighed. "Alright, I'll bite. Why her?"

"She had a thing for FoZ."

He grimaced. "Did he tell you that?"

"No, I doubt that FoZ even noticed. Let's just say it's something I picked up on."

Atticus shook his head. "Sometimes I wonder why you women keep us around at all, we're so oblivious. Apparently the only things we're good for are lifting heavy objects and satisfying your carnal lusts."

"You wish." I whirled some warmed Remy Martin and took my first sip. The sweet fire of the Grand Cru found my belly, fortifying me against the hotel air conditioning and urging the muscles in my aching legs and feet to let go. It'd been a long time since I'd indulged in such an extravagant pleasure. I should thank Atticus for his generosity; after he'd finished sulking, that is.

"My man," a deep voice boomed behind me.

Atticus stood and clapped Sgt. Johnson on the back. "Sup, brother?" he asked, his smile extending from ear to ear. "You flying solo tonight?"

"Yeah, my wife is home with the rug rat." The detective grinned and offered me his hand. "The psychic, right?" He squeezed my fingers. "Whoa, you're a popsicle!" He jerked his thumb toward Atticus. "Tell this man to lend you his jacket."

"I'll be fine," I said, flourished my brandy snifter. "I just need a little more of this magical elixir."

He towered above the table in cream-colored linen that draped off his broad shoulders and emphasized their muscularity. The suit had quality resort wear written all over it, making him seem simultaneously relaxed and imposing. I had the feeling he was waiting for an invite.

"Please join us," I said and slid across the icy vinyl to make room for him in the booth.

He squeezed in beside me and propped his elbows on the table. "So, Daniel says you've been doing some follow up on the Neff case."

Atticus lifted his mug in my direction. "Well, it started out that way, but my partner here has taken charge of the investigation."

Sgt. Johnson raised his eyebrows.

I was starting to wish I hadn't said anything to Atticus about my visit with FoZ. He was making a bigger deal of it than he needed to and I wasn't ready for any of what I'd surmised to make its way back to Burnette. Not until I had a chance to drop the Laura/Landon bomb.

"Ignore him," I said, trying to sound playful. "I had a chat with a suspect without him and he doesn't approve."

"Not just any suspect, mind you, the prime suspect," Atticus said.

"FoZ?" Sgt. Johnson chuckled. "Well, that's not a bad strategy. Let's face it, man, she's a damn sight prettier than you and Fotakis does like the ladies."

Atticus pointed his trigger finger. "Yeah, well, that kind of talk is not going to get you a Samuel Adams, my friend."

Sgt. Johnson laughed. "I just call 'em as I see 'em."

Burnette and the woman he'd been chatting up at the

station swept into the bar. He had on a charcoal grey suit with a discreet pinstripe and she was dressed in a coral, knee-length cocktail dress that profiled her petite, hourglass figure to its best advantage. A heart-shaped Mexican fire opal hung at her throat and she had one arm tucked under Burnette's. The buzz in the room dropped perceptively as the heads of the other patrons turned to check out the new arrivals.

Burnette scanned the crowd. I lowered my eyes and sent up a silent prayer he wouldn't notice us. I didn't want his disparaging remarks to take the shine off my hard-won progress or the evening. Let him have his fun, just not at our table. My heart sunk as he spotted his partner and Atticus, who waved. Burnette nodded, placed his hand on his date's waist, and guided her past the bar and away from our table. I breathed a sigh of relief.

Atticus took a swig of beer and stood up. "Be right back," he said and headed off toward the happy couple.

"So how long have you known the A-Man?" Sgt. Johnson shouted over the growing din.

It was the same question Burnette had asked me at the barbeque, but this time I felt no need to go on the defensive. From Sgt. Johnson it came across as a congenial inquiry, with maybe even an undercurrent of approval. I took another sip of cognac.

"We met about a year ago," I said and leaned close enough for him to hear me. "I helped him out with another case."

He nodded. "Well, you've got your work cut out for you with FoZ and that's a fact. Wherever he goes, trouble follows, and nothing ever sticks. He's the original Teflon man."

"So I've been told."

But I didn't really want to discuss FoZ. What I'd been hankering for, for days now, was a fresh perspective on the case; one that didn't belong to either Atticus or Burnette. Talk about serendipity.

I cleared my throat. "Sgt. Johnson—"

"Chaz. My name's Chaz," he said.

"Chaz." I smiled, acknowledging the introduction. "Was there anything about the case that didn't sit right with you? A detail that Atticus or I might have overlooked?"

He yawned, deep and wide. Oh jeez, I was boring the man to death. It'd been so long since I'd been out in polite company, I'd forgotten how to act. I couldn't let the preponderance of evidence thing go for even one night. I should apologize.

"Sorry," he said. "The kid is breaking in a new tooth, and no one at my house is getting much sleep lately."

He blinked and rubbed an eyelid. "Yeah . . . there were a couple of things that felt off. For openers, Lake Merritt didn't seem like the kind of place to drop some E and go wandering around alone at night. If I were a kid her age, I would have wanted to be out with my friends or stay home and enjoy the ride."

He made an effort to subdue a second yawn. "And the autopsy report showed she'd eaten right before she died. Doesn't seem like she would've wanted a heavy meal in her stomach if she was planning to party or was feeling suicidal."

"Dinner?"

"Yeah. Steak, pasta, bread and salad. We checked several restaurants in the area and it turns out there was a steakhouse not far from the lake. But no one on staff recognized her picture."

"Anything else?"

He looked out over the crowd and then back at me. "There was one other thing, but it was more a lack of evidence." He lowered his voice a notch. "I'm sure Atticus has told you there weren't many marks on the body."

I nodded. "Wasn't that one of the reasons her death was ruled accidental?"

"Uh huh. There were no signs of struggle, it's true. But think about it; if you were high and fell into the lake, wouldn't you stumble around a little first, bang your knee, or scrape up your legs on your way in? Maybe throw out an arm, get it scratched or bruised trying to protect yourself from falling?"

He was right. I could picture Laura, at the water's edge: disoriented, uncoordinated, frightened. Losing control as the world closed in around her. Like the way I'd felt, that day in the cypress trees. Why hadn't I thought of it before?

Chaz continued. "And even if she did want to kill herself, she wouldn't have been able to dive straight in like with a swimming pool. Where she was found, the lake is only about four feet deep. And the wall around it's rough, like sandpaper. Making a clean entry into the water would be damn near impossible, if you were high."

I was starting to sweat, strapless dress, air conditioning and all. "So, you're saying . . . "

"I'm saying that, except for the contusion at the back of

her head, some small abrasions on her right hand, and a couple of minor scratches on one ankle, the body was clean—a little too clean, in my opinion, for a suicide attempt or a fall into the lake."

An opinion obviously not shared by his partner. I wondered if he'd discussed the discrepancy with Burnette and gotten shot down. Opposing expert witnesses argued these kinds of points at trials all the time. Perhaps he, too, thought the case needed a second look. Maybe that's why he was talking to me now.

Chaz pulled back the sleeve on his suit coat and checked his watch. "Uh oh, I'm gonna be in the doghouse, if I don't get outta here. I promised my wife I'd be home a half-hour ago."

He eased out of the booth. "Are you going to be okay, on your own?"

Was I. He'd given me plenty to think about. In fact, he'd made my evening. I tapped my glass. "I have this to keep me company and my date will wander back, eventually. He'll be sorry he missed you."

I watched him thread his way through the crowd as I savored another taste of Remy.

On the drive home I mulled over Chaz's disclosures. Had he chosen to be forthcoming because he was hoping I would do something with the information? Or was he jerking my chain? The whole thing could be a set-up, some sort of elaborate practical joke designed by Atticus to put me in my place.

I glanced over at my chauffeur, apparently none the

worse for wear despite a full evening of drinking, dancing, and schmoozing. He was humming Van Halen's "Jump," and looking like the ginger cat that ate the canary. What was he up to?

I decided to take the bait. "Chaz Johnson went over some of the autopsy findings with me this evening."

"Yeah?"

"He seemed to think that Laura's death might not have been an accident or a suicide."

"Because of the small number of marks on the body?"

I eyed him. "Yeah, how'd you know?"

He stopped humming. "Cos that's pretty much what he told me when we talked about it."

"So, when were you going to clue me in on your conversation?" I asked.

Atticus didn't respond. We turned off Piedmont and took a right onto Glen. He slid up to the curb, in front of Casa Mariposa, and shut off the engine. The building sat silent and a bit Kafkaesque—jumbled apples, rocks, combs, and hats looming large in the pale moonlight. He turned to face me.

"I'm considering your question, carefully, because the last time I let my thoughts leak out my mouth, it got me into trouble. In case you haven't noticed, I haven't seen a lot of you lately, probably because of an unfortunate tendency on my part for being honest. So I'm choosing my words here. I would have gotten around to telling you once you were done nursing your hurt pride."

"Perhaps it wouldn't have gotten hurt if you'd shown some faith in me." I tightened the wrap across my arms.

"Alright, I'll cop to that. But, if you remember, I told you I believed you were on to something. And now, Chaz thinks there are some holes in the case, too."

"So, the stuff he told me, it's not just the two of you winding me up?"

"So I could piss you off again?" He threw his hands up between us. "No thanks."

"Okay, I accept your apology."

"Whoa, heh, I don't remember making any apologies." He settled back against the seat. "But I have to admit you're good at this fuzzy logic stuff. Scary good."

Maybe it was the compliment or the cognac or the fact that he was kind of cute when he was teed off. Or unexpectedly put together in his formal wear. Suddenly I felt the urge to kiss him. I leaned across the emergency brake and pressed my mouth to his.

He tasted of ale and peppermint. "When did you sneak in a breath mint?" I murmured against his lips, enjoying the sensation.

He pulled his head back slightly. "You obviously haven't read all of my book."

"Your book?"

"Yeah." He grinned down at me. "Chapter 4. The First Rule of The Hunt: Preparation, Preparation, Preparation."

He was right. I should've been better prepared. I was a nurse; I understood medical terminology. I should've asked to see the autopsy report, first thing. I needed to follow up on that. And I would . . . tomorrow.

Chapter Twenty-Six

Laura Neff, Caucasian female, age 19, 5'4" and 118 lbs. with blonde hair and blue eyes, died at approximately 10:00 p.m. on the night of July 5th. Her postmortem was conducted on July 9th and took slightly less than three hours to complete. The coroner's report indicated that the medical examiner, Dr. Frank Ralston, and his assistant were the only people present during the autopsy.

The external exam detailed damage within three areas of her body: a contusion and laceration to the upper outer edge of the left parietal lobe of the skull; three small abrasions on her left ankle varying from five to seven millimeters in length; and a small series of puncture wounds to her right hand consisting of eight pinpoint markings in the middle of her palm, with four deeper grooves in the upper left quadrant of the palm. A photograph showed the groups of markings were separated by one millimeter of unmarred flesh. No birthmarks, scars, or other significant abnormalities were noted and there were no indications of sexual assault.

The internal examination methodically documented the

condition of her body in the following order: cardiovascular, respiratory, gastrointestinal, hepatobiliary (liver, gallbladder, pancreas), genitourinary, endocrine, lymphoreticular (lymph nodes and spleen), musculoskeletal, and the central nervous system. The findings indicated a subdural bleed in the space between the brain and the membrane that covers it, occurring at the left inferior parietal lobule. Hemorrhaging was also found inside the sinuses and passages of her airways. Significant amounts of undigested food, matching Chaz Johnson's description, was present in her stomach and a smaller amount of partially digested food was recovered from her small intestine. An x-ray revealed that a portion of her left parietal skull had been fractured.

Dr. Ralston's summary stated that the presence of blood in her sinuses and lungs indicated that Laura had been alive when she went into the water. He also noted that the significant quantity of undigested food in her stomach indicated she had died within two hours of her last meal. Based on the evidence uncovered by the autopsy, he concluded that Laura's death had occurred as a result of an accidental drowning. An attached toxicology screen noted the presence of 4-methylenedioxymethamphetamine in her bloodstream, and a slight elevation in ketone levels.

I sensed that the ME, the last of a succession of strangers who'd touched Laura's body posthumously, had treated her with as much care as can be given such a brutally intimate process. And for that and his thoroughness, I was grateful. Unfortunately, there was little in the way of the outstanding abnormalities I'd hoped the gross and microscopic evaluations of her tissues would've revealed.

The laceration, contusion, and fracture were all consistent with the kind of blunt force trauma her skull would have sustained when she hit the boom. Struggling for breath after she entered the water would have increased airway pressure which would have, in turn, produced the respiratory hemorrhaging. I'd seen enough victims of drowning in the ER to recognize that pattern. So no inconsistencies or magic bullets there.

But why the elevated ketones? They normally show up in blood and urine testing when the body can't access the carbohydrates it needs for energy and begins to break down fat instead—ketone release being the by-product of this process. Unstable diabetics are prone to ketone elevation, as high levels of glucose will tend to stay in the bloodstream and not make its way into the cells where it can be utilized.

But if she were diabetic, I would have expected to see blood glucose abnormalities in her labs. Plus, the palm of the hand isn't a typical site for glucose testing and the markings seemed too uniform and evenly spaced to have been made for that purpose. More likely they'd occurred when she'd grasped at or scraped against a hard object after she'd gone into the lake, like the ankle abrasions. And since Dr. Ralston hadn't observed any finger sticks on the pads of her fingers where glucose testing is usually done, that pretty much ruled out diabetes. So why was she throwing ketones?

I'd had a patient once who had elevated ketones because of limited dietary intake: a young woman with an eating disorder. But Laura, although slender, was in weight range for her height. So I wasn't getting her as anorexic. Bulimia, however, was fairly easy to hide and, sadly enough, not that uncommon in women her age. Maybe the pressure of being in a secret relationship with Dr. Landon was getting to her and binging and purging had become an outlet for the stress. Her reading had indicated a need to take care of her health during this time of transition. Perhaps, the message was more urgent than I'd realized—another red flag I'd overlooked?

Poor baby. I needed to get back into the office pronto.

Chapter Twenty-Seven

I rubbed the inner corner of my left eye, trying not to smear the mascara I'd hastily applied a few moments ago. A series of wildfires in the Sierras were taking their toll on the air quality, making my eyes and throat itchy and irritated and prompting a "Spare the Air Day" throughout the Bay Area. I'd considered the idea of busing into San Francisco this morning and then transferring to Marin-bound transit, but the thought of a ninety-minute commute in each direction was more than I could bear. I promised myself I'd leave the Lynx in the garage over the weekend to make up for the damage I inflicted on the environment today. I had to get to Corte Madera and the sooner the better.

It was Friday, August 13th. In two more weeks, my time as Landon's medical assistant would come to an end along with any chance I might've had to search through his belongings. A piece of paper was all I needed: a note passed from Laura to Landon, e-tickets to Ireland . . . a snapshot of the two of them taken in a photo booth, away from the prying eyes of anyone who would care. Any kind of physical evidence that announced to the world they'd been lovers.

Which is why I had to make my move now. Karin was in San Diego at dance camp with her girls, and Dr. Landon had a meeting at Marin General and wouldn't be seeing patients until after lunch. My presence wasn't required until afternoon, but I'd come up with an idea of which I thought Marina would approve, maybe even applaud my diligence for; a strategy that would justify my being in the office from eleven o'clock until it reopened at one. With Marina on lunch break, I should have at least thirty minutes alone and more than enough time to check out the contents of the doctor's desk and cabinet.

A rush of moist, air-conditioned air pushed past me and out the door as I stepped inside the office. Normally, the temperature drop would send me running for my lab coat, but this morning it felt welcome, even refreshing. Marina was at the front desk with her reading glasses pulled down to the end of her nose, her neck craned forward as she focused on the computer screen. Next to her, on the counter, lay a napkin, the remains of a glazed, blueberry doughnut, and a torn, dampened packet of artificial sugar in the saucer of her coffee cup.

It was a never-ending source of amazement to me that overweight people would go within a mile of the stuff. Regardless of the color of the packaging, the contents left me shaky and hypoglycemic and grasping for anything sweet to raise my blood sugar; a side effect that didn't seem to lend itself to weight loss. Not that I begrudged Marina a treat. I just didn't think including additives that increased the urge for sugar in a diet already heavy with carbohydrates was going to help her gallbladder or her knee.

She could no longer disguise the limp in her right leg and, by the end of the workday, she could hardly bear weight on the thing. Her orthopedist had recommended a brace that appeared to be doing little to relieve her pain or increase her mobility. The next step would be an arthroscopy and, at least, six weeks away from the office: an absence I'm sure she wished to avoid at all costs.

"Good morning, Marina," I said, shutting the pollution out behind me.

"Oh, hello." She frowned over the nosepiece of her glasses. "Aren't you a little early?"

Her dark eyes appeared huge, behind the lenses, and a bit annoyed at this interruption in the rhythm of her day; like an owl that'd gotten its feathers ruffled. It was so easy to assume the position of her subordinate, I sometimes had to remind myself we shared another relationship, as well—one that needed to remain hidden. Whether she was responsible for Laura's death or not, if she caught me snooping she'd have security throw me out in a hot minute.

"I am early," I said, stowing my tote bag behind the desk. "I got to thinking about how a complete stockroom inventory hadn't been done since I've been here. With your new assistant coming in a few weeks and the training you'll need to do, I thought you might not get to it for a bit. I could handle it this morning while it's quiet, if you like."

Behind the rimless glasses, I could see her weighing the cost of an extra hour of pay against the possible benefits of a well-supplied workplace. Which shouldn't be too painful considering she'd called me off work two days last week, while Dr. Landon was home recovering.

Her face softened an iota. "All right," she said and returned her attention to the monitor. "Page me if you have any questions."

I cleared my throat. "I do have one, before I get started. I noticed that most of the IV solution will expire by the end of September. I was thinking I should mark the bags and pull them to the front."

Marina sat back in the chair, resting her hands on the pink Gerber daises that camouflaged her rounded abdomen. "Stack them on the counter behind the exam table. And make a sign for them—'Use First'—or something like that. Then if we need one, it will be clear where they are."

"Will do." I reached around her for an ink pen from the organizer by the computer. It was a tighter squeeze than usual with her right leg propped up on the trashcan. She had tomorrow's schedule up on ICAL, the contents of which I needed to review during her lunch break. If Landon and Laura had an extensive trip planned prior to her death, it could still be there on one of the monthly calendars.

Marina frowned again and removed her glasses. "And go ahead and prepare an order for next month. And change the size and number of bags. There's no point in paying for IV solution that we don't use. If a patient is in crisis, they should only need enough fluid to get them to Marin General. Five-hundred-cc bags should be enough."

"Discontinue the thousand-cc bags then?"

"Yes. They take up entirely too much shelf space. And make it six bags instead of twelve. I don't think the price break justifies a full dozen, not if at least half of them are going to the incinerator in the end."

And into our lungs, I thought, noting the haze over the eastern peak of Mt. Tamalpais through the window. At around two thousand, five hundred feet, it wasn't much of a mountain—compared to the ones I'd grown up with— more like an overly ambitious hill. But it was a pleasure to take in. Even the eastern slopes, sheltered from the marine layer and the moisture required by the redwood forests to the west, had their own kind of beauty with the needle grass and manzanitas in the foothills giving way to woodlands of oak and pine and, in the higher elevations, an occasional Douglas fir. From this distance, I could make out the patches of tan, grey, mauve, and green delineating the microclimates on the mountain: a vista spoiled, this morning, by a film of brown particulate that hovered above the fog line.

I wondered if the air quality had affected Landon's recovery. Four days was a long time to be unavailable to his patients. Although, as rundown as he was, it wouldn't take much of an opportunistic infection to flatten him. I'd be willing to bet that Ava nursed him all week, pumping him full of chicken soup and antioxidants and campaigning for his return to Hawaii. Not that I blamed her. It was probably costing her plenty being away from her clients and her practice and it would be a lot easier to keep an eye on him from her own backyard.

Somewhere between the saintly humanitarian of Marina's imaginings and Ava's hapless sibling lay the truth of who Neil Landon really was; a man neither of them could see. A man who had chosen to take life, rather than preserve it, as he was sworn to? He certainly acted the part of a soul saddled with a heavy burden, the weight of which was slowly destroying him, as he shuffled around the office like a dead man walking.

It was only a question of time before the practice began to suffer. Who would want cosmetic care from a man who didn't care enough about himself to run a brush through his hair? Something was obviously wrong; a malady that no amount of coddling and gourmet take-out was going to cure. He was exhibiting all the signs of clinical depression: one born out of mourning or a guilty conscience. Or both.

I made my way down the hall and glanced past the opened door of his office. Eyeballing the carved dragons, I savored a sting of anticipation. In less than an hour, I would have the place all to myself.

I pushed open the door to the stockroom and switched on the light. The stacking units appeared full. Due to the patient cancellations, little had been used from last week's supply. The entire inventory would take less than forty-five minutes unless I dialed down my pace.

I made a sign for the IV solution and piled the five soon-to-be-expired bags of D5 ½ NS on the counter opposite the exam table next to the sink. They were surprisingly heavy for a product that was nothing more than plastic, dextrose, sodium chloride, and water. I continued working slowly and methodically, tabulating the stacks of supplies until the phone on the counter beeped. It was almost noon. I took a deep breath and picked up the receiver.

"I'm going to lunch, now," Marina said. "Are you almost done?" She sounded tired and irritable. And not in the best mood for negotiating.

"It's taking a little longer than I thought," I demurred,

trying not to sound rehearsed. "I was thinking I'd go ahead and skip lunch and finish. Since it's kind of a short day for me anyway."

There was a long pause. I was hoping the reminder that, even with the additional time, she wouldn't be paying me for a full day would clinch the deal. I could practically hear the calculator in her head humming, crunching the numbers on the other end of the line.

"All right," she said, in a voice that telegraphed how put-upon she was. "Just remember you'll be locked in. If you try to go out, the alarm will go off." She hung up before I could respond.

Yes! I listened for the alternating beep tones as she input the alarm code, and waited for the sound of her key turning in the lock. Anyone out on the sidewalk could see me through the front window and door, so time was of the essence. I hurried down the hall and around the front desk. I crept low and did a double take to assure myself Marina was nowhere it sight.

The computer screen was dark. She had shut it down before she left and only she knew the password. Great. No chance of any HIPAA violations on her watch. I pulled the scheduling book over in front of me. Most medical offices used a software program or a book designed for that purpose, but not both. For once, Marina's compulsions were working to my advantage.

There were no breaks scheduled for Dr. Landon for the months of September or October, just pages of Marina's impossibly tidy script penciled in with an occasional stripe of perfectly-spaced Wite-Out where a patient had been rescheduled. Two days had been marked for the Thanksgiving break, but even with the weekend that wouldn't allow for a real trip to Europe. I flipped to December.

Christmas fell on a Tuesday and the entire week, including Christmas Eve, was crossed out for the holiday. The early part of the following week was also blocked out with the office reopening on the second day of the new year. January the 3rd bore the notation *'Dr. Landon back in office'* in underscored letters. When taken with the weekend that preceded Christmas, he and Laura would have had twelve days; more than enough time for a lovers' getaway.

I gasped as a delivery truck bounced off a pothole out on Vista Road—a daily occurrence that didn't usually make me want to jump out of my skin. I needed to calm down. I took a deep breath and started down the hall.

Behind Landon's desk, the light filtering through the contaminated air outside of the window cast a dingy pall across the room. The clock on the wall above his framed license and diplomas read 12:15 p.m. If Marina was her usual prompt self, I only had fifteen minutes left to complete the search, twenty at the outside. Thumbing through the handwritten schedule must have taken longer that I thought.

I opened the cabinet doors. The top shelf contained an entire row of bulky medical tomes, most of them too heavy to try and lift. A slew of medical journals and two leather-bound photograph albums filled the second shelf. I did a quick inventory of the spaces between the magazines to make sure nothing was hidden there and then turned my attention to the photograph album I hadn't perused yet.

One damaged face after another stared out at me. My God, how much misery there was in this world. Whether you believed that life's challenges stemmed from choice, circumstance, genes, or karma, it was painful to come face to face with such suffering, regardless of what continent it occurred on. How could someone as seemingly fragile as Landon handle such heart-wrenching circumstances day after day, let alone volunteer to go back for more? Perhaps it was a comfort to know that the sweep of his scalpel cut away some of the unendurable from their lives. I returned the album to its niche and the doors closed with an emphatic click.

The burnished wood of the two cabinet drawers lay silky and cool beneath my touch. I wanted to run my hands over its sleek surface and enjoy the craftsmanship of such a finely made piece of furniture, but I had to stay on task. The top drawer held a hash of investment prospectuses, gift calendars, medical supply catalogues, and several magazines on mountain biking. I surfed through the clutter and found nothing of interest. The contents of the drawer beneath it were equally uninspiring: wrapped samples of prescription strength Ibuprofen and a box half-full of antibiotic ointment packets.

I turned to the desk. It was also a heavy carved teakwood, but its rosy caramel sheen was of a deeper hue. A wireless phone and Landon's black mesh inbox sat on the top of it, stacked high with unfinished charts. I pulled out the top drawer and several uncapped pens rolled across the bottom of it. A handful of loose paper clips, a stapler, a stack of business cards, poorly bound by an overstretched rubber band, and a prescription pad lie scattered about inside. A more careful man would have kept the pad under lock and key, but I guess Dr. Landon figured with Marina around there'd be little chance of a security breach. In the right hand corner, wedged between the drawer and desktop, protruded an engraved invitation from a pharmaceutical firm for a dinner presentation at the Saint Francis.

Two deeper drawers occupied the right side of the desk. The top one slid effortlessly toward me, as if it were empty, then gave off a faint rattle. Inside, a small orange bottle nested against a strip of metal in the back of the drawer.

It was a bottle of Sertraline, an antidepressant . . . prescribed for him on August 5th, one month to the day after Laura's death. The starter dose was fifty milligrams, once a day, and the label allowed for two more refills.

So, he was bathing his grey matter in serotonin in an attempt to make himself feel better. Which could explain his increased malaise, decreased appetite, and Ava's prolonged visit. She was probably sticking around to help him monitor his symptoms and response to the drug.

I eyed the bottom of the drawer and the item against which the bottle had been resting: a rectangle only slightly smaller than the drawer's inner dimensions. I pried the metal edge free of its confines and flipped it over. It was a matted, framed photograph of a teenage Dr. Landon standing behind what I took to be his parents; one hand on each of their shoulders. He had inherited his mother's coloring and the athletic build of his father as well as the other privileged genetics of being born into this handsome, obviously well-heeled family.

But the camera lens had captured another impression, as well. On closer inspection, dark circles were visible under his mother's eyes. And everyone's smiles seemed tight; their mouths stretched and wan. The tendons on the back of Landon's hands sat raised and taunt as if he were gripping his parents' shoulders instead of resting his hands on them, and there was visible tension along his father's jaw line. Artifice was such a dominant feature of the picture, it was no wonder he kept it turned over. I placed it face down and repositioned the bottle on top of it.

The lower drawer was crammed full with biking accessories: gloves, pant clips, a metal water bottle, and several pairs of thick white tube socks. I closed it, walked around the desk, and took in the whole of the cabinet. Was there anything I'd overlooked?

"Eileen?"

I shrieked and whirled in the direction of the voice. Neil Landon stood in the doorway with a briefcase.

"Oh, Dr. Landon, you scared me!" I gulped and pressed my right hand against my flailing heart. What possible reason could I have for being here in his part of the office, with the doors locked and Marina at lunch?

He coughed into his fist, his nose red and raw. He was clearly waiting for an explanation. And, unfortunately, so was I.

"'Tis . . . sues," I stammered. "I stayed in to finish the inventory during lunch and it occurred to me that you might need some tissues, with your cold and everything. I didn't see any on your desk. Would you like me to bring you a box?"

He stared at me, his eyes pink and watery. "Yes," he said, blinking. "That's probably a good idea." He brushed past me and set his briefcase next to the desk.

I walked across the hall to the stockroom on legs of rubber. I couldn't let him see that my fear was about more than having been startled. I leaned against the exam table for support. *Just get the man some tissues.*

Then inspiration struck. If I was going to play the role of nurturing assistant, I may as well go whole-hog. It would lend my story credibility. After all, he was used to having women take care of him, probably expected it. I reached for the petroleum jelly.

He was standing by the window, staring out at a day that had turned even more overcast. I set the tissues and foil packet down on the desk. "You might want to put some of this on your nose," I said and pointed at the ointment. "It will help to keep it from getting more chafed."

He glanced over his shoulder at the items on the desk. His swollen, puffy eyelids made my eyes hurt just to look at them. "Thanks," he wheezed and turned back to the window.

I pulled the perforated top off the tissues and bent down to drop it in his trash can.

The top drawer was ajar. I'd failed to notice in my rush to get through his desk and now it was too late. There was just enough space to arouse suspicion: a half-inch gap that revealed his desk was not the way he had left it. A half-inch gap that would disappear with one simple brush of my hand—and become a confirmation of guilt if he'd already noticed the space left by my probing.

The dragons glared, forked tongues extended, claws

poised to strike. The skin on the back of my neck prickled. It was a warning; I'd seen something I shouldn't have.

If I only knew what it was.

Chapter Twenty-Eight

Except for the musty smell, Laura's bedroom remained unchanged from my last visit. Sadly, the funk that permeated the rest of the apartment had begun to attach itself to her belongings as well. There was mildew flourishing nearby and, if my sinuses were any judge, plenty of it. I pushed open the window and watched the thin yellow curtains lift themselves to the incoming breeze.

The moans coming through the wall told me Ravenwaif had scored a critical hit against the orc she'd been fighting when I'd arrived—vanquished now, at the hands of her blue skinned warrior. Unwashed and clad in pirate-themed pajamas at 5 p.m. on a Saturday afternoon, she'd stepped "ATK" long enough to open the door, utter a monosyllabic grunt, and then return to game play; leaving me to make my way down the hall. Which was okay by me. She'd agreed to let me take a second pass at Laura's things, and that was all I cared about.

I took a gulp of untainted air. This room was my last hope for unearthing tangible proof of an intimate relationship between Laura and Landon. If I didn't turn up something

here, today, I was SOL. The good news was that there was
precious little to go over, especially in the way of items that
I hadn't already searched. Laura was too young and
financially challenged to have acquired much in the way of
material possessions and it showed.

I walked over to the chest of drawers and opened the
top one. The flimsy particleboard contained three bras, a
week's worth of cotton bikinis and two sets of folded
drawstring pajamas. There was a pair of black and brown
tights and a half-dozen pastel crew socks in the second
drawer, and a set of pale yellow sheets in the one below it. A
peek under the bed revealed an empty expanse of beige
carpeting. On a whim, I pulled back the coverlet and her
pillow. A hint of citrus rose up to greet me.

I ran my palm over the quilt, enjoying the feel of the
worn feed sacking. It was as though comfort had been sewn
into the padded, nubby texture of the fabric and the
subdued colors of the eight-pointed stars. The delicate
stitching along their edges had been evenly applied; the
thread gently securing the cloth and binding it, placed there
by a steady and patient hand. Folk legend allowed that
modern day quilting patterns arose from the practice of
women sewing magic symbols into their quilts: powerful
enchantments that protected their menfolk when they
traveled and their children while they slept. Someone had
loved Laura enough to leave her this gift of protection.
Unfortunately, it hadn't been enough to keep her safe.

I felt suddenly, impossibly, weary. I plopped down on the
edge of the bed and scanned the room. The IPOD and the
alarm clock were positioned as I remembered them. So was

the tiny mother of pearl jewelry box and the other items in the bookcase. I leaned forward and plucked the romance novel from the shelf.

It was a bodice ripper, the cover depicting a couple in Regency attire, entwined in a heated embrace. It wasn't difficult to envision Laura tucked up under the quilt, reading it, imagining herself in the arms of Landon, the shaggy anti-hero. The back cover proclaimed an epic saga of forbidden romance and familial intrigue set against the backdrop of early nineteenth-century Britain. Heady stuff for a nineteen-year-old in love.

I placed the novel back on the shelf and pulled down the art text. It was heavy and cumbersome, by comparison, the front cover depicting a solemn figure in voluminous, burgundy robes clasping a tome. At his feet lay a carpet of intricate color and design with ribbons of carnelian, mauve circlets, and sea blue rectangles outlined in black, interspersed with twirling gold knots. Celtic knots. It was an image from the Book of Kells.

A thin booklet slid from the inside cover onto the carpet. I leaned over and picked it up. It was a pocket-sized travel guide to Western Ireland.

The outer right corner was curled as if it'd seen some use. A passage on the first page had been highlighted in yellow marker and the picture of a rugged coastline circled. I raced through the glossy pages, my fingers sticking to them in my haste. There were more outlined passages: castles in County Clare, shops espousing the virtues of Tipperary crystal, the pubs of Lower Shannon. On the bottom of the back inside cover, under an advertisement for dry stout, I spied a familiar scrawl, written in black felt tip pen: *Can't wait. Love, Neil.*

Four words. Four little words that corroborated Karin's story. A piece of physical evidence that established the secret relationship between victim and lover and provided a motive for Laura's murder—a damn good motive. One even Burnette couldn't ignore. I flipped the magazine closed and slipped it into my bag.

I wanted to sit and enjoy the moment, but the smell was getting to me and I needed to blow my nose. I closed the bedroom door behind me and stepped into the bathroom. The roars of an enraged griffin filled the hall.

There were no tissues on the vanity or the top of the toilet. But there was plenty of mildew; dark, furry splotches of it on the shower curtain, the wall tile, and the ceiling. I grabbed a couple of toilet paper squares and dabbed at my nose. It was time to thank my hostess and leave.

I tossed the paper into the trash. The wastebasket looked ready to explode; the contents pushed down repeatedly and with such force that the thin plastic bulged in every direction. A discarded ink cartridge and corn chip bag lay wedged between the wastebasket and the wall and, against my better judgment, I picked them up and dropped them into the trash. A small orange cylinder rolled out of the chip bag.

I extracted it from the damp plastic. It was an empty bottle, uncapped, and stinking of mold. I examined the label. It was a prescription for Clonazepam, one mg. My head started to thud. The prescription was for Laura.

Why hadn't she told me? And what was it doing in the

trash now, all these weeks after her death? I knew the medication only too well. When I was working the floors, it was heavily prescribed: thin blue pills with the perforated K, for the pharmaceutical name, Klonopin.

Thin blue pills. What was it Jessamae had said? *". . . you never know what you're getting when you buy that stuff . . . each new batch . . . looks different. Maybe that poor baby didn't know what she was taking."*

The bathroom door hit the wall as I jerked Ravenwaif up and out of her chair.

"Hey!" she cried, struggling to wrench her arm free. "You crazy bitch!"

"What have you done?" I shouted. I pulled her to me and shoved the bottle in her face. "Tell me what you've done!"

I let her go then or I would have hit her. The motion sent her spiraling backward; her short, flabby arms flailing as she fell onto the couch. I lunged forward. Her snarky indifference had morphed into wild-eyed, unadulterated fear. None of the virtual battles she'd logged had prepared her for the sight of a flesh-and-blood madwoman, in her face.

Her mouth crumpled and she started to blubber like a three-year-old. Tears tracked down her cheeks and mucous streamed from her nose. She looked like a Cabbage Patch doll that had been left out in the rain; her sallow, bloated face disintegrating before me. What a mess.

I stomped into the bathroom, peeled off some toilet paper, returned to the couch, and thrust it at her. Blow your nose," I said.

She complied with a noise that was both wet and repugnant.

I thrust my face within inches of hers. Her body funk was righteous, but I held my ground and carefully enunciated every word. "I know you hated Laura because FoZ was in love with her. But she didn't deserve to die for that."

Her red-rimmed eyes widened. "How did you—"

"It doesn't matter now. Your only hope of undoing even a little of this is to tell me the truth." I held the bottle up in front of her. "Did Laura have a seizure disorder?"

Ravenwaif sniffed and nodded slowly.

"Was there anything else in the house, that afternoon, she could have confused with her medication?"

Her lower lip started to tremble. She bobbed her head.

"Tell me what happened."

She raised the glob of wet tissue to her nose. "I . . . I was gonna take a hit that day, but she came home early. I heard her keys in the door and I panicked. She was such a freak about anyone getting high, so I stuck the E back in the bottle, in the cabinet, where I keep my stash. Only I must have put it in with her medicine instead."

She glared back at me. "She never took it anyway."

"She wasn't taking her prescription?"

"No. She hated the stuff." Her voice rose to a high-pitched whine. "I tried to tell her."

"Was she having seizures?"

"I don't know. I don't think so." She shrugged, her rounded shoulders drooping in their sockets. "Like I said, I didn't see her much."

She squeezed the paper into a sodden mass between her thick fingers. "She was on some kind of high protein diet, something she'd found online. She said it would stop, you know . . . the fits."

So Laura had been self-treating. And doing her own research. There was some evidence that high protein diets could help control seizures in some cases, but only under the direction of a physician; the kind of help she'd probably resisted getting. Which means her condition was unstable. God only knows how long she'd been noncompliant with the Klonopin. She could have seized anywhere—in the car, at work, or by the lake.

"When did you realize the Ecstasy was gone?" I asked, making an effort to soften my tone.

"Around 7:30, a few minutes after she'd left." She swallowed. "The X made her have a fit, didn't it? And then she drowned." Torrents of tears raced down her face. She pushed her fists into her eyes and wailed.

I grabbed her wrists and pulled her hands down. "Ravenwaif, I need you to hear me. I'm going to have to go to the police with this. But I don't think the Ecstasy or a seizure killed Laura. I think someone who wanted her dead may have seen she was ill and took advantage of the condition she was in that night."

I squeezed her hands so hard she winced. "I need you to think. Did she tell you who she planned to meet?"

She shook her head violently from side to side. Tears flew off her chin and trailed south, leaving damp spots on the front of her grey tank top. I let go of her hands and the wet ball of toilet paper she was clutching. She pressed her swollen, blotchy face into the ugly beige chenille and sobbed. God, there was so much misery in this world.

*　*　*

I decided to take surface roads home. Evening traffic would be equally heavy on the freeway or San Pablo Avenue and I wanted time to think. Ravenwaif had finally admitted to hiding the pills from the police and, later, flushing them down the toilet and tossing the empty bottle in the trash. Lucky for me she was such a wretched housekeeper. It would be my word against hers about the Ecstasy even when I presented them with the orange bottle now nestled inside my bag. If she denied what I told the police, there would be little I could do about it and, short of a murder confession, no action would likely be taken against her. I hadn't volunteered that information, but she was a smart girl and once she got past her initial panic, she'd figure it out.

Still, that didn't diminish the moment.

The mantra "I did it, I did it, I did it" drummed in my ears. I wanted to go out and celebrate. And maybe brag on myself a little. It might be fun to give Atticus a call when I got home and see if he wanted to grab a beer. I still hadn't had a chance to tell him about Landon and Laura's relationship, let alone the magazine and Ravenwaif's confession. I couldn't wait to see the expression on his face.

The prolonged squeal of brakes pierced my deliberations. I cringed and waited for the crunch of metal on metal. A white Escalade, two cars back, came to an abrupt halt, narrowly missing the bumper of the Honda CRX behind me. I couldn't see the driver of the SUV through the tinted glass windows, but the Honda owner seemed paralyzed; recovering, no doubt, from the sight of a vehicle three times the size of his bearing down on him. I'll bet he'd spend the next couple of days with his eyes glued to his rear view mirror.

I knew the feeling. Ever since Landon had walked in on me in his office, I'd gotten pretty antsy, myself. A raised voice in the hallway, an unexpected tap on the door, a shadow scurrying across the floor—anything could make me skittish. Although he'd done nothing to indicate he was suspicious of my actions. As far as I could tell, he hadn't even mentioned the incident to Marina.

I turned left on Ashby Avenue and headed east. Up ahead, a steady stream of cars wheeled past the lone palm tree in the Whole Foods parking lot and out into the street, groceries swaying in their backseats as they bounced off the curb. Telegraph Avenue was congested with pedestrians making their way home to their families and their weekend plans.

How many years had it been since I had rushed home to someone? So long ago that I'd lost count. But my date with Atticus had stirred up feelings. Emotions so long buried they were barely identifiable. Emotions that demanded recognition even in daylight. Emotions that left me asking myself if I could create space in my life for someone other than a fat, ridiculously cute feline.

I took a left on Broadway and stopped at the light. A green Z4 convertible with a beige top blew past me on its way down Pleasant Valley Road. First on the Richmond Bridge and now in my neck of the woods.

Earth tones must be more popular than I thought. If I had that kind of money, I'd go for a bit more flash: candy apple red or teal blue. Not that I was complaining. I patted the cracked dash of the Lynx. You'd never get fifteen years of reliability out of one of those high-strung thoroughbreds.

Twilight had begun to arrange itself over the East Bay Hills as I cruised down Piedmont Avenue. Maybe I'd reconsider that phone call to Atticus. It would be lovely to settle in with Audie and some pasta and a Brit flick. He probably had plans, anyway.

I parked in the garage and made my way up the back steps, a tad winded. A quiet night in was sounding better and better. I stopped in the foyer to check my mail. A teenage girl with spiky, violet-tipped hair rattled by the front entrance, crouched low over the front end of her skateboard. A few yards behind her, a Z4 was parked along the curb: a green-and-beige Z4.

It had to be the same one that'd passed me on the way home. How many cars like that could there be in this neighborhood?

I squinted to make out the dark blue letters on the vanity plates. G-O-G-N-T-S. GO GIANTS.

I pulled back against the wall, into the shadows. The front seat was occupied by a lone figure with a dark baseball cap pulled low, the face hidden under its brim. A person making no attempt to get out of the car. A person watching Casa Mariposa.

A person watching me.

Chapter Twenty-Nine

A macaw watched from the banyan as I trudged up the hill. It blinked once, twice, then twisted a horny beak to gnaw at an insect crawling between its neck rings. An anemic breeze stirred the roots of the tree and gnarled tendrils creaked along the ground, scooping up clods of damp earth. A cloud of red dirt drifted across the broken pavement.

I inhaled the pungent scent of mold. A monstera hung low over the road, its fronds edged in fungus. Moist air clung like a wet towel and enveloped me in the reek of decaying flowers and mango fermenting in the sun. Fecundity and rot: the eternal cycle of the rainforest.

I peeled the soaked cotton from between my shoulder blades. Tar bubbled underfoot, the heat palpable through my cheap flip-flops. The soles of my feet stung, but I was nearly within sight of my destination now. The falls sang a few yards down the road and I smiled at the thought of dangling my legs over the pool and watching the currents race past. Maybe I'd climb down the rocks and take a swim. By the time I was done, the afternoon trades should be blowing.

Two centipedes darted out from the underbrush and scuttled across the path. The banyan's branch dipped, relieved of its burden. A shadow passed overhead and bird cry drowned out the sound of water rushing down the rock face. Heavy footfall shook the forest floor.

I started to run . . . down the hill, past the turnout and the rippling water . . . over the cracked asphalt, and into the woods. I tripped over a log, tore my knee open, and kept running. Limbs snatched at my eyes as I dodged left and right, plunging deeper into the jungle. I blew out a flip-flop, threw it aside, and raced gimp-legged through the undergrowth.

My lungs were bursting. I dropped behind a cajuput and waited. Gnats flew at my face, buzzing, and I sank lower trying to hide behind a bank of fern. The road was barely visible now for all the foliage, but I could see the shade cast by their enormous bodies; shade so encompassing that it shut out the sun.

There were two of them, monstrous and scaly, their coated tongues lolling between jagged teeth the size of stalagmites. They were the guardians of this place: yellow eyes rolling in their sockets, bloodshot, searching the forest for signs of movement. An outsider had awakened them; an intruder, who'd gone prowling where she didn't belong.

It was the dragons and they had come for me.

Chapter Thirty

"Gah!" Atticus retched. "Whut is dat stuff?" He shivered and collapsed back on the sofa, his knobby knees jutting out from under a purple terrycloth robe.

"It's herbal tea," I said. I retrieved the velour throw from the floor behind the couch and covered his legs with it. "It will soothe your throat and help you to relax."

"And dat?" He pointed at the small bottle of caplets I'd set on the coffee table, within his reach.

"That's the master virus blaster. You should take six of those four times day."

He extracted a crumpled handkerchief from the depths of the overstuffed cushions and blew his nose. "Isn't dat a lot?" he murmured through the hanky.

"Not for someone of your weight." I held up the bottle of Vitamin C and rattled it. "And you should try to get down at least five more grams of this today. From the look of you, you need all the help you can get."

He collapsed onto the two pillows I'd taken from his bedroom. Even with his knees bent, his bare feet stuck off of the end of the couch, covered only by the fringe from the throw. His hair was matted to his forehead and the skin between his nose and upper lip had been rubbed raw. Dusky half-moons hung beneath eyes that struggled to focus. Like many of his gender, when confronted with the prospect of getting sick, he'd chosen to ignore his symptoms, and was now properly KO'd by the mother of all flus with no vitamins, supplements, or cold remedies to be found anywhere in the house.

He nestled more deeply into the pillows. Maybe we should both take a nap. The hourly visitations—down a flight of stairs to the window on the first floor landing—had left me jumpy and unable to sleep. The Z didn't depart until well after midnight, and I lay awake until nearly three a.m. listening to Audie snore and wondering if I'd slipped into complete paranoia or was, in fact, being stalked.

"So, yur not going back to Marin, right?" Atticus' voice drifted up from the folds of his pillowcase.

"I don't know." I muffled a yawn, picturing Marina's face if I failed to show up tomorrow. She was still trying to accommodate the last of the patients she'd cancelled last week, so Monday was going to be a busy one. I hated to leave her with the extra patient load to deal with on her own. "Maybe I'm overreacting. It is possible someone with a really nice car, who is a Giants fan, has a friend in the neighborhood. It could be a coincidence."

He coughed into the dingy handkerchief. "Coincidences are highly overrated, in my opinion, and I don't think dis is one of dem. Not after whut you found out about him and the vic. Dollars to donuts, dat car belongs to Neil Landon."

"But doesn't that seem kind of obvious, parking directly

across the street from my place? Wouldn't he think I'd notice?"

"He doesn't know 'bout yur freaky abilities." He flopped over on his back. "And, if he's as messed up as you say, he prob'ly doesn't care if you do spot him."

I didn't want to admit it, but, even in his fevered state, what he said had the ring of truth. Landon did seem to be unraveling. The respiratory infection had left him downright skeletal and he'd barely spoken a word to Marina and I on Friday. He'd spent the rest of the afternoon coughing and brooding, and the food that Ava brought in had gone untouched. One of his patients had even pulled me aside to ask what was wrong with him. At the time, I'd put it down to his not being recovered from the flu, but now I was starting to wonder.

I flashed back to his face as he turned from the window, the lines of it etched in what could only be called despair. It was the visual equivalent of Laura's voice in my dream, as if he'd glimpsed a future that held nothing but sorrow. Had the realization I'd searched his office pushed him over the edge? Laura could have told him about the reading, possibly even mentioned my name. What if he'd made the connection?

Atticus turned back to face me, hunching the cover up around his shoulders. He groaned and fell into a doze, his respirations deepening. His lips parted and he started to drool on the pillowcase. I waited until I could see his eyes moving under his upper eyelids and then eased out of the armchair.

"Whut are you doin'?" he wheezed.

"You'll feel better if you get some sleep," I said, softly. "I'll call and check in on you, later."

"Noooo," he whined, making a show of raising his head. "You haven't finished telling me about Ravenwart."

"Ravenwaif." I sat back down in the chair. I'd seen this reaction in pediatrics enough times to recognize the scenario. The little boy inside of him didn't want to be left alone, or succumb to the rest he really needed. No problem. The antivirals and the shot of whiskey I'd slipped into his tea should be kicking in any minute.

"So, yur-not-goin'-back-to-da-office, right?" he repeated, one word colliding with the next.

"I'm considering taking your advice."

"I'll call the DMV and Burnette Mo ... Mon ... day." He drifted off, dead to the world before his head hit the pillow.

Maybe I would stick around for a few more hours. He really should get another dose of vitamins and herbs before I left for the day, and I could catch some shuteye while he napped. I pulled the throw from the back of my chair, tiptoed to the couch, and patted it into place around his feet.

He muttered and smacked his lips.

What if Atticus was right? Criminal behavior was his area of expertise. His ability to anticipate the responses of the people he'd investigated not only made him good at his job, but had also kept him alive. Maybe I should take his warning to heart. In his book he'd stated that once a person had committed murder, repeating the act became progressively easier with each kill. And in my case, there would be no attachment to override, like with Laura—only an obstacle that required elimination.

But what if the travel guide and Karin's statement weren't enough to get a confession? What if he slipped off with his sister and any evidence hidden in his office disappeared forever? After the dream last night, I knew I'd overlooked something.

Atticus stirred and kicked the blanket off his feet. There were beads of sweat on his forehead and his hair was soaked. His breathing was slower and less audible. The fever had broken. He'd feel better when he woke up. A hot shower, a cup of miso soup, another round of supplements and he'd be a new man. The worst was almost over.

The trail, in my dream, and the forest and the water . . . they weren't Laura's memories; they were pieces of my own, from my trip to Oahu and Waimea Falls. When I'd mentioned it, all the joy had drained out of Landon. Hawaii was the key to everything: that was the nightmare's message. The answer was in the office, within sight of the dragons.

Which meant one last trip to Corte Madera. One more day of Marina and Landon and risking exposure and I'd be done. To be safe, I'd let Atticus know when he woke up.

The worst was almost over.

Chapter Thirty-One

A lazy sun stretched across a sky that had the appearance of a windswept autumn day; perfectly cloudless and blue. The first hint of crimson and yellow had already begun to peep through the ginkgos and maples that bounded the neighborhood. In another week, trails of kids in blue and white uniforms, super-hero-themed backpacks, and trainers too clean to have made their way past the first day of school would be racing up Lake and down Piedmont Avenue toward St. Leos.

The waning of summer and the tourist season always reminded me of how much of the Bay Area I had yet to see. There were an embarrassingly large number of places I hadn't been; a guidebook full. Maybe I'd take a break before I went back to the salon. They weren't expecting me until after Labor Day anyway. My budget dictated a staycation, but that was okay. A ride on the Napa Valley wine train, a day trip to Carmel, a drive through the mountains to Santa Cruz: any kind of getaway to mark the end of my undercover career and the return to my lovely, boring life.

Maybe I'd ask Atticus to come along.

On the drive to Marin, I tried not to obsess over the fact that he hadn't yet called about the title to the Z. The thought of Landon sitting outside of Casa Mariposa in the dark, plotting God-knows-what, had seriously screwed with my ability to play the diligent employee. I was uneasily situated in that nervy place between creeped-out and ready to come up swinging if he so much as looked at me sideways, which wasn't a useful head to be in considering what I needed to do to get this day behind me. Plus I'd reached my saturation point with all the pretense—Landon pretending that Laura's murder wasn't eating him alive, Marina pretending that they hadn't been lovers, and me pretending to be a detective.

Thanks to the dream last night, I'd narrowed my search area down to Landon's desk and the spot directly in front of the dragons. With any luck, I should be able to take another pass at it this morning without being noticed. Monday mornings were Marina's day to reorder supplies and she was nothing if not a creature of habit. The good doctor hadn't made it in before ten o'clock in weeks so, unless his sister had managed to pull him out of his funk over the weekend, he should be safely out of the way my first hour in the office. Now if I could only get there.

Traffic, which had been fairly cooperative until Larkspur, had jammed into a bottleneck, and for no obvious reason. There was no rear-ender, unusual glut of cars, or police or rescue activity visible; only 101 crawling the last two miles to the office. Not the start to the day I'd had in mind.

I glanced at my wristwatch as I wrangled the Lynx into a spot in front of the office. 9:03 a.m. Marina wouldn't like me parking so close to the front door, but I needed to get inside pronto. Besides, what was she going to do? Fire me?

Through the plate glass I could see her at the helm, her head bent to the side, the phone cradled between her chin and shoulder. She must have called the vendor the split second they opened. Damn.

I hurried through the door and around the front desk and hung up my tote bag. As the door swished closed behind me, she glanced up and then returned to the supply list. I peeked over her shoulder. The ruler she used for maintaining her placement underscored *ace bandages*. I had less than ten minutes.

I scurried around the desk and slipped into my lab coat. As usual, there was a pile of incomplete charts in the outbox waiting to be signed-off by Dr. Landon. Perfect. I could always profess ignorance later if Marina objected to me taking them. And none of that really mattered since this was my last day. A little bubble of happiness welled up inside of me at the thought. I picked up the stack and headed up the hall.

I'd conjured up my cover story on the drive in. Depositing the charts in Landon's inbox, I went to the cabinet and pulled out a photo album. I opened it to the picture of Armando and laid it across the top of the desk. If I got caught in his office, I could always pretend to be admiring Landon's handiwork. And I knew enough about the case file to comment on it. But I needed to hurry. Marina had already made it to the Dakin's solution.

I pulled the top drawer open carefully and braced it against my body to avoid shifting its contents. I need not have bothered. The stack of business cards had escaped the confines of the rubber band and spread themselves throughout the interior over the paper clips, pens, and loose pen caps. The pharmaceutical invite, minus one of its corners, lay crumpled in the corner. In its place, the prescription pad was now wedged between the desktop and the top of the drawer. What a pig's breakfast. I resisted the urge to dislodge the pad and slid the drawer closed.

Marina's voice trailed down the hallway. "A dozen boxes of latex gloves, size medium . . . "

I leaned over the contents of the bottom right drawer. The biking gear appeared undisturbed since the last time I'd gone through it, which was no surprise since I hadn't seen the Bianchi in weeks. The only thing not visible were the riding gloves. I pushed the socks aside and groped for the feel of padded nylon, my knuckles scrapping wood. The scent of tobacco rose up from the drawer.

A scream filled my ears: the sound of pure, undiluted panic. What the—? I shot upright and banged my knee on the drawer, slamming it closed in the process. The impact nearly knocked me to the ground.

The dragons leered as I grasped the edge of the desk for support and a wave of nausea enveloped me. I took a deep breath and tried to steady myself. The nausea receded an iota, and I loped around the desk and to the doorway, my right leg threatening to give way with every step. I peered around the door, out into the hall.

Between the front desk and the waiting area lay the figure of a man, spread-eagled, his feet facing the front door. A man with a full head of disheveled light brown hair.

I limped down the hall and bent down beside him. Landon's chest rose and fell in shallow waves, his mint green scrubs accentuating a complexion the color of putty. He could have been a resuscitator dummy for all the animation in him, stretched out on the carpet. I picked up his left wrist and palpated it. His radial pulse was weak and thready.

"Dr. Landon, can you hear me?" I shouted.

He moaned, and tried to sit up. I pushed him back with surprisingly little effort.

"Marina, can you get my stethoscope?"

She didn't respond. I turned to find her, stock still, behind the reception desk; her fluffy, brown hair poofed out around her face like a frightened cat's tail. Her hands were pressed to her mouth, the orange poppy nail appliqués a stark contrast to the white of her nail beds. At least she'd stopped screaming.

I raised my voice. "I need you to get my stethoscope out of my tote bag. And wheel over the portable blood pressure monitor, please?"

A few seconds passed—time in which she seemed to orient herself to her surroundings and what had been asked of her. Slowly, she turned toward the cabinet where the sphygmomanometer was kept. She retrieved it and wheeled it up beside me, then limped back to the desk and returned with my stethoscope. Cold, clammy hands passed it off to me.

I pressed the bell against the apex of his heart. His apical pulse was weak and rapid, but not irregular. I moved it upwards and listened again to confirm the pattern of the beat.

His breath smelled downright fetid. His forehead felt warm to the touch and his lower lip was chapped and peeling with the imprint of teeth sunk deep into the tissue. When pinched, the skin on his hand took a full three seconds to rebound. The man was obviously dehydrated. And his electrolytes were probably out of whack. Maybe Ava had given up mothering him and gone home.

I wrapped the cuff around his arm and waited for the readout. 88/58. I moved the cuff to his other arm and took it again: 90/62, way too low for a man of his size.

Terrific. I was going to have to start an IV on him. It'd been over three years since I'd been near a needle and I didn't think he was going to be an easy stick. An athlete like him should have veins like ropes, but his looked brittle and hard, like shriveled-up pasta. And my knee was starting to throb. Within a few hours I was going to have a bruise the size of Wyoming.

This day just kept getting better and better.

I glanced up at Marina. Her face had settled into a semblance of her normal reserve. Her pupils were dilated and she was a bit pale, but it wouldn't be long before she was back. Giving her directions was going to take some finessing, now that she was regaining her composure.

"I think we'd better get him over to Marin General, to be on the safe side, so I would go ahead and call 911. And maybe you'd better contact his sister."

Her chin jutted out a skosh and then she began to move in the general direction of the phone.

I leaned in toward Landon's ear. "Dr. Landon, I need to start an IV on you. Do you have diabetes or kidney issues?

He shook his head.

"Any allergies that we should know about?"

He opened his eyes and blinked against the light. "No," he whispered.

"I don't want you to try and get up. Do you understand?"

He nodded his head and closed his eyes. I stood with some difficulty. Behind the desk, Marina barked out orders to dispatch, her eyes trained on the patient.

I made my way back up the hall, my knee begrudging any attempts at weight bearing. In the supply room, I slipped on some gloves and picked out a thousand-cc bag of D5 ½ NS from the soon-to-be-expired pile on the sink. I opened a pack of IV tubing, spiked the bottom of the bag, turned it upright, and hung it on the hook above the sink. Squeezing the drip chamber, I watched for air in the tubing as fluid flowed toward the distal end. I twisted the cap off, let the air and a small amount of solution escape into the sink, and recapped it. So far, so good.

I grabbed a starter kit off the second shelf and then hung the bag on the lone IV pole that Marina kept by the door, raising it high enough to prevent the tubing from dragging on the floor. Now all I needed was an angiocath. I'd normally use an eighteen or twenty gauge on a man Landon's age, but, given the condition of his veins, something smaller would be easier. For both of us. I dug through the angio container. Not a twenty-two in sight. Great.

I rolled the pole down the hallway and retrieved some paper towels on my way past the kitchen. Kneeling on Landon's right side, I positioned the pole to my left and layered the towels under his arm. Then I peeled back the top of the kit and fished out the tape. Tearing off a four-inch strip, I split it in half and stuck the ends to the sleeve of my lab coat.

I tightened the tourniquet above his elbow and scanned his forearm. The skin pinked up, but his veins remained flat from elbow to fingertips. He groaned as I released the tourniquet and reapplied it more tightly. Marina scowled at me from behind the desk.

"Dr. Landon, I'm sorry if I'm hurting you, but you don't seem to have much in the way of veins today. You are right-handed, correct?"

He nodded, his perpetual cowlick flattened in the carpet pile.

His dominant arm should have a better blood supply than this. The only vein that protruded was the antecubital, in the crease of the elbow. I could probably get in there, but the paramedics wouldn't like it—too easy to dislodge when transporting him, too easy for him to bend and clot off the line. I snapped at the top of his right hand with my index finger. Nothing.

I turned it over. A crooked strip of green swelled below the wrist, at the ulna. I pressed on it gently and it sprung back. I opened the alcohol wipes and cleaned off the area, hoping the tiny bulge wouldn't disappear before my eyes.

Marina cleared her throat. I could feel her anxiety expanding to fill the room . . . as if I didn't have enough of my own.

I removed the twenty gauge from the pack and pulled back on his parched skin, well aware of Marina's eyes on the both of us. Piercing it, I inserted the needle and threaded it into the vein as gently as I could. Landon grimaced, but, to his credit, stayed still.

And there it was, like a hello from an old friend: flashback, in the chamber.

I advanced the catheter and released the tourniquet, pressing on the top of the angiocath. The stylus slid out easily and I stuck it through the paper towels into the carpet below. Removing the cap from the IV tubing, I connected it to the hub and dialed up fifty-cc an hour: enough to initiate hydration and as fast as I was willing to go without a doctor's order. I checked the insertion site for signs of swelling, taped a chevron around the hub of the angiocath, and secured it with another strip.

In the distance, I could hear the sound of an ambulance alarming its way into the medical complex. The paramedics would bolus him en route to the hospital and this bag would probably get swapped out for one with additional potassium. He'd be well hydrated by this time tomorrow and much more alert. And, hopefully, in good enough shape to have a chat with the police.

A red and white van sped into the parking lot. The cavalry had arrived.

Chapter Thirty-Two

A massive lump squirmed under the throw rug. I tapped it with my big toe and it froze in position. I tapped the lump again and a muffled squawk arose from the rug. A third tap brought the edge of a grey paw into view, batting wildly at the multicolored fringe. The phone rang and Audie shot across the room and disappeared into the kitchen, leaving a misshapen ball of knotted rags in her wake.

She'd been wound up all day; cutting wheelies in the living room, racing in and out of her cat door, and leaping up on the couch every time I started to nod off. I, on the other hand, was using the purple-blue mass that had bloomed on my right knee as an excuse to do as little as possible. Including answering the phone.

"Hey, psychic fiend, are you in?" Atticus' voice boomed out of the phone's speaker. "If you're there, pick up . . . okay, I guess you're not there. Probably out pimping more work for the OPD. So, I checked with the DMV and the Z4 is registered to a Neil Landon of Greenbrae. Which means that you should, under no circumstances, go back there. I filled Burnette in and he and Chaz will be headed over to

Corte Madera ASAP. So, call me."

He hung up before I could disengage myself from the futon, which was no surprise given the speed at which I was moving today. Still, I didn't want Chaz and Burnette to make an unnecessary trip to Marin. Or give Marina the opportunity to inadvertently alert Landon to their intentions and have him slip out of California before they could question him.

I dialed Atticus' cell and got his voicemail.

"Hey you, thanks for the update. I'm not going back to the office and I don't think that Landon is there today, either. He fainted at work yesterday and is probably still at Marin General, so you might want to let Burnette know. And I'm thinking about taking a few days off before I go back to work, so if you're going to be around, maybe we could do something non-investigative for a change."

Non-investigative? I repositioned my knee on the pillow and replayed the invite in my head. I was seriously out of practice with the whole asking boys out thing. And maybe getting ahead of myself, since I didn't know how mobile I was going to be the next several days.

The cat door clacked as Audie raced back into the living room. She skidded to a halt in front of me and began to groom herself furiously.

"What is up with you today, Cat?" I asked.

She stopped licking and stared up at the window, rapt, as if a school of herring had just beached themselves on the window sill. Then she resumed her toilette. She was making a point of ignoring me; something she'd gotten down to an art over the years. That, and selective hearing. If I so much as uttered the first syllable of a word like *dinner*, I'd have her immediate attention.

"Audie, I thought you'd be happy I was home today. Why are you acting like such a spaz?"

She turned her back to me and flopped down on the rug. Maybe she was punishing me for spending the last three weeks away from her. Not that I was going to miss the eight-hour plus workdays or the commute. Or watching Landon come unhinged.

Coward that I was, I'd left my notice on the office voicemail early this morning before Marina arrived, citing my knee injury as the reason. Even if Landon made it back to the office later in the week, she could make do with a temp. Besides, if anyone could sympathize with knee pain it should be her, although I doubted, given my premature departure, that she would.

Poor Marina. I wondered how she was going to deal if Landon got charged with Laura's murder. However upsetting that might be for his sister, she could pick up her life back on Oahu. But I was pretty sure Marina didn't have one outside of the office.

Audie rolled over on her back and growled. She was sound asleep; the muscles in her face twitching, paws batting the air. I often wondered what she dreamed about, stretched out on the floor with the sun on her belly. Taking down an oversized mouse? Chasing squirrels? Swimming upstream with the salmon?

I glanced at the clock in the kitchen. 4:17 p.m. and I hadn't eaten yet.

No wonder I was so wasted. I'd better see what I could

scare up. My knee wasn't going to heal on ice tea alone.

I lifted my knee off the pillow and grabbed my glass en route to the kitchen, trying to remember the last time I'd shopped for groceries. I pawed through the meager contents inside the refrigerator and came up empty. There were stacks of cat food, three cans high, filling up half of the kitchen shelves, but nothing fit for human consumption. Not even a bar of chocolate. Tessa was right; my eating habits, or lack thereof, had become abysmal. However . . .

I hobbled back to the fridge. Inside the freezer, next to a lone bag of frozen green beans, sat one of those rectangular glass containers with a lid that locked on all four sides. On the top, the date, 7/31, had been penned in precise script. *Yes!* It was a hefty serving of Tessa's turkey/bean soup: red lentils, yellow split peas, summer squash and organic sausage, all lovingly assembled and slow cooked in her crock-pot.

I pulled out a saucepan and put it on the stove to warm and the savory smell of Tessa's homemade chicken stock began to permeate the kitchen. From the size of it, there should be more than enough to get me through today, maybe even a little left over for Audie. And I could put off shopping until tomorrow.

I should, however, attempt a walk after I ate. It seemed downright sinful to stay indoors on such a sunny afternoon and it would do me good to get out of the apartment if only to make my way down to Piedmont Avenue. Especially now that I didn't have to worry about Landon, lying in wait outside my doorstep, with all the attention that would be trained on him today.

I leaned against the stove and listened to my stomach

complain while the soup defrosted. I really did need to get out of the habit of putting off eating until I was hypoglycemic. Lifting the glass lid, I inhaled the scent of chives.

It was almost ready, except for the rectangle of ice in the middle. I poked at it with a serving spoon and gave the contents a quick stir. The creamy mixture began to bubble and I sent up a silent thank you to the Martha Stewart of Glen Avenue.

I grabbed a bowl, filled it to the brim, blew on it, and sampled a too-hot spoonful from the stovetop. Despite the singed tongue, it tasted incredible and so thick, tangy and full of ingredients that no crackers or bread were needed. I couldn't believe Audie hadn't already roused herself and bounded into the kitchen, demanding her fair share. It wasn't like her to be so nonchalant about Tessa's cooking.

I took a peek into the living room. She was no longer on the rug. It wouldn't be long now.

I hiked my leg up on her chair, retested the temperature of the soup, and dug in. Wonder how Landon was faring on Marin General grub? I hadn't had a chance to finish going through his desk. Or get his album back in the cabinet. Not that it really mattered now.

There were only two items in the drawer I hadn't reexamined, anyway: the Sertraline and the picture. A bottle of pills and an overturned frame. Anti-depressants and a strained family photograph—both physical reminders of Landon's secret and abiding unhappiness.

Clatter, closely followed by a loud thud, signaled impending disaster in the bedroom. I put down my spoon and caught a glimpse of Audie tearing around the corner like the devil, himself, was on her tail. Now what?

I lifted my right leg down off the chair and limped into the bedroom to investigate. The curtains were still on their rods and hanging in place and there were no overturned lamps or toppled furniture. Nothing had been knocked off the nightstand or the bookshelf. Apparently, the damage was minimal.

I took a step forward and sharp metal poked at my instep. A tangle of necklaces and pendants sprawled across the hardwoods in front of the dresser. Audie had apparently gotten into my jewelry; an impressive undertaking, given her girth and the distance she would've had to jump from the floor to the necklace stand.

I bent over and scooped them up off the floor. Maybe it was time to consider investing in some new cat toys. I shifted my weight to my left leg and rested against the vanity, teasing the chains apart and hanging the necklaces back on the tiered jewelry stand. The pain in my knee had lessened; I should finish the soup and get that walk in while I was in the zone.

I made way back into the kitchen and plopped down into the chair. Inside the bowl, a few bite-size pieces of zucchini and squash rested in a shallow covering of broth, with not a scrap of turkey in sight. The cat door swung back and forth, indicating a recent and hasty departure. It looked like I'd be making that trip to Piedmont Grocery after all.

Freaky cat. I sloshed what little remained of Tessa's soup down the disposal and rinsed the bowl with hot water. My right hand started to tingle.

I stopped rinsing and examined my hand. In the center of my palm there were tiny indentations, sensitized by the warm water from the faucet. I recognized the pink markings instantly; they were from the pineapple pendant, the one I'd nearly stepped on. I loved the intricate detail of the design, but it was so sharp I never wore it against bare skin.

I ran my fingertips across the pinpoints. There was no mistaking the pattern: the four upper ones gouged by the pointed edges of the leaves with smaller impressions, underneath, from the body of the pineapple. And I'd barely held the thing.

Oh, my God.

Chapter Thirty-Three

Eight pinpoint markings in the middle of her palm . . . four deeper grooves in the upper left quadrant . . .

The coroner's report fluttered to the living room floor.

She would have been no match for Landon's sister that night, peaking on Ecstasy, struggling with her by the water. Not with a woman practically the size of her lover. A woman she would have been eager to please, to win the approval of.

It would have been easy to draw Laura into a secret meeting, on the pretext of getting to know her better. A little girl-talk over dinner, woman-to-woman . . . just us girls. Laura probably admired the pendant, sitting across from Ava at the restaurant, as I had at the office— fascinated by its sparkle and the simple elegance with which Landon's sister had put herself together.

The Eight of Pentacles: Ava, not Landon. I had misunderstood the person and the message. It wasn't about a lovers' quarrel, or Landon trying to rid himself of Laura. Or Laura not seeing him or his motives clearly. It was a warning to be on guard against a jealous sister's obsession; a sister very much aware of their budding relationship and the threat that relationship posed to her future plans for her brother and their business.

A tall, athletic woman, with specialized skills: the embodiment of power and success. A striking, confident female with a vision she was determined to see made manifest, and an ability to keep her true motives hidden. Why hadn't I made the connections?

All right, I had to focus. I'd call Atticus, then figure out what to do next. I grabbed at the handset and knocked it out of the cradle. Retrieving it from the floor, my fingers fumbled for the redial button. The shrill, triple-ascending tones of a non-working number rang in my ears.

Fine. I had his number on my cell.

I rummaged through my handbag and found it, beeping piteously under a pack of tissues. The battery was low, but I had enough juice for a short message. The call went straight to his voicemail.

"Atticus. I need you to call me as soon as you get this. I found something that . . . that's too detailed to explain over the phone, but Landon isn't Laura's killer. His sister is. Call me as soon as you can, on my landline. Thanks."

I plugged the cell into recharge. Maybe I should call Chaz Johnson, in case Atticus had gone out of town. No, I'd better wait. Wherever Atticus was, he would get back with me. And he'd be far more likely to generate Burnette's cooperation than I would even if he had to do it long distance.

What I needed to do was calm down. This would be a good time for that walk, except for missing his call. Maybe a few laps around the backyard would do the trick. If I left the back door open, I could still hear the phone.

The back steps burned the bottom of my feet as I descended into the grass. There was no sign of Audie on the stoop or in the yard. The little rat was probably sleeping off our lunch in the shade somewhere.

The afternoon had turned stifling and windless and even the flowers bowed in submission to the glare of the westbound sun. The bird of paradise and the asters and the calla lilies looked particularly peaked. Was the drip system on the blink?

I crossed the yard and checked the beds along the northeast fence. Brown-edged fuchsia and the curled jasmine petals littering the ground confirmed my suspicions. I might as well water them now while I was down here, and let Tessa know later. Provided I could find the hose.

A search along the perimeters of the fence yielded nothing but perspiration. Ditto for the pegs behind the stairs. Which means it was probably in the garage. I pushed past the gate and waited for my eyes to adjust to the darkness. There on the back wall next to the storage room, it coiled on the spindle, waiting to be pressed into service.

I was halfway across the garage when I caught it: a smoky essence that prickled the inside of my nose. And footfall whispered up behind me. I whirled in the direction of the sound.

A sinuous arm shot across my chest, compressing both of my arms, and I rocked back on my heels. I hung there for a second, immobilized, and breathed in the stench of tobacco. My right heel connected with a kneecap and I lunged forward and twisted inside of the hold, driving an elbow into my attacker's diaphragm. A sharp intake of air let me know I'd found my target.

Then fire shot up the side of my neck and the cool concrete floor rushed up to meet me.

Chapter Thirty-Four

The bay flew by the window. I pushed my bangs out of my eyes and reached up to rub a small knot throbbing at the back of my neck. A circlet of cold metal gouged my left temple.

"You need to keep your movements small and slow. Do you understand?"

I flinched and nodded my head slowly. The ash-grained cockpit of the Z wavered. I blinked and the photophobia receded slightly as my pupils attempted to adjust to the light piercing the windshield and the sight of a semiautomatic pointed directly at my head.

It was a vicious little thing with a snub nose that tipped upward: the insignia 3032 TOMCAT visible, in my peripheral vision, on the steel barrel. The gun was less than five inches long and the grip fit Ava's gloved hand like it had been custom made for her. In fact, she looked at ease in her black tee shirt and yoga pants and SF Giants cap. With her hair tucked up under it, she could have been Landon's doppelganger.

The resemblance was so eerie that, for a second, I hoped

I might be dreaming. But the seatbelt stretched across my bare arms and the silky purr of the engine that propelled us down the highway told me that this was not my mind conjuring up one of its alternative realities. I was caught in a trap of my own making, with a woman who embodied evil in a way no omen could.

The smell of freshly-smoked cigarette clung to the car's interior. "Where are we going?" I rasped.

"Back to the office." She downshifted into third and redirecting the snout of the Beretta at my head.

The clock on the dash read 5:15. I must've been out for close to thirty minutes—time Ava had made excellent use of. She'd gotten me out of the garage before the majority of Casa Mariposa's other tenants got home from work. And across the Richmond Bridge just ahead of the commute.

An ugly thought blasted through the last of my brain fog; she was no newbie at this. It was she who'd tailgated me on the Richmond Bridge . . . she who'd waited in the Z outside Casa Mariposa. And, judging from her dexterity, this wasn't the first time she'd handled a gun or used her Vulcan neck pinch on someone's carotid. Or waited in the dark to kill. God, I hope Atticus had gotten my message.

I was being driven to a secondary crime scene, where, statistically, my odds of surviving dropped exponentially. I'd always told myself that if anything like this ever happened I would unlock the door and jump out of the car, no matter what. But the sight of those two-ton metal boxes speeding past left me paralyzed. That, and calculating how many seconds it would take for me to undo the seat belt and unlock the door before she blew my brains out.

I'd watched enough true crime TV to know that I had to come up with a plan if I was going to survive. Every minute that passed increased the odds of this ending badly—for me. I needed to shift the balance of power and soon.

I cleared my throat. "You know that cigarettes cause premature aging, right? Doesn't seem like a very good example to be setting for your clients, what with walking your talk and all."

"I wouldn't concern myself with my clients, if I were you. Or with trying to be clever." Her eyelids flickered. She raked over my body with the kind of detachment a scientist might show a lab rat; a look that brought with it a surge of panic so intense the breath went out of me. Bile rose up in my throat and, for a second, I thought I was going to throw up on the leather upholstery.

Breathe, Eileen, breathe. I forced breath down into my belly, exhaling from a spot just below my umbilicus. I dropped my shoulders and let the tension travel wherever it needed to go. A slow and steady pulsing rose up in the center of my gut. The anxiety began to dissipate, along with the nausea and the fear. I'd been wrong; I was strong. And cunning. This woman was no match for my skills.

The Lucky Drive signpost rolled by overhead. We were less than a mile from Corte Madera. By the time we got to the medical complex it would be vacant; a daily occurrence I'm sure Ava had taken note of.

But there was always a chance that someone in the adjacent offices was working late. It was also possible that Atticus already knew I had gone missing and had alerted the Marin police to the vanity plates. Otherwise, it would be me pitted against Ava and, given my back and her muscle mass, I didn't have a prayer of winning a fight that depended on brawn alone.

A few pieces of gravel blew out from under the tires as we turned down Vista Road. There were no cars in the parking lot, just a lone white SUV speeding past the complex toward Mount Tam. Ava slid quietly into the space directly in front of the office, shut off the engine, released her seatbelt, and got out of the car; every movement fluid, with no wasted motion. She switched the gun to her left hand and leaned down into the Z.

"I want you to get out of the car slowly," she said, holding the gun gangsta-style and down low enough that it couldn't be seen from the road. "We're going to walk up the steps and into the office. As you can see, there's no one around, so any attempts at running will merely get you killed now instead of later. It makes no difference to me." Her lips parted in a smile. "Comprende?"

Once again, nausea threatened to spoil the Z's interior. Not only did she have more than a passing familiarity with martial arts, but she was ambidextrous. My insides went rigid with fear. Then a flash of self-confidence pushed the sensation into the background, like a painter stroking one layer of color over another. It was the same experience as before; a rush of self-assurance that was totally alien. Alien, like I'd been mainlining testosterone.

Alien, because I wasn't the one sourcing it.

I'd kicked into full empathic mode; maybe due to my heightened emotional state or because Ava viewed me as so easily expendable that she'd let down her guard. Whatever the cause, a link had opened up between us, like two computers interfacing. And right now I was downloading a picture of a woman so determined to keep her distorted view of the world intact that she'd eliminate any perceived threat to it: Laura, myself, or anyone else that stood between her and Neil Landon.

"Did you hear what I said?" she raised her voice and inched the gun forward. She'd misread my lack of movement as a lack of deference. Good. Now I knew how to screw with her head.

"Yeah, I heard you." I smiled like we were good friends involved in a minor tiff.

I lingered over unlocking my seat belt. Then I fumbled with the door latch. She slipped around the Z, threw the door open, and yanked me to my feet. My shoulder tendons screamed as she twisted my right arm behind me back, using more speed and force than necessary, given her fitness level. My eyes watered as she jammed the gun into my kidney and shoved me forward.

Maybe I could turn her agitation to my advantage. I knew the green area pretty well. There weren't enough trees back there to provide any real cover, but if people were inside any of the buildings in the quadrangle, they'd hear me shouting. If I could distract her long enough, I could get back there. It would be tricky with no shoes, but I might be able to outdistance the bullets.

Maybe.

The Beretta prodded me toward the first step. I lurched forward and pretended to stub my toe. The momentum pulled Ava off-balance and she stumbled and lost her grip. I twisted away from the gun and stepped sideways, inadvertently scratching her arm. She cursed and let go.

I started to run.

In an instant she was behind me: centered, pulling me into her, scraping my bare feet across the hot sidewalk. I gasped as she jerked my arm back into position. That smoky scent of hers had grown muskier. At least, I'd made her break a sweat.

"I said, move!" she hissed, encircling my wrist with her thumb and middle finger and pressing the tender inner flesh.

I went limp and forced her to drag my full body weight up the last two steps. She cursed and slammed me against the door, jamming her left foot between mine, pinning me in place. I scanned the reflection in the glass and searched for some kind of activity on the street, praying a passing motorist would notice me flattened against the front of the building, held at gunpoint by a person twice my size in a baseball cap. I could hear the murmur of cars on the freeway less than an eighth of a mile away, on 101.

But there was no traffic moving in front of Landon's building.

Ava unlocked the door, pushed me through it, and paused long enough to punch in the entrance code. With the door unlocked and the alarm disabled there would be no chance of me setting it off and bringing down the complex's security. And they wouldn't be making their rounds for several more hours. Marina was long gone and the mailman had made his final pickup. She'd choreographed this well; we were completely alone.

I choked back more bile. "You might want to put

something on that," I said, and nodded at the raked flesh on her inner arm. Three rivulets of bright red blood trickled from the torn skin, down her wrist and into the gloves. My right arm tingled at the sight of them.

She wiped at the wound with the other sleeve. "Move," she snarled and pushed the gun into my back. She marched me past the darkened kitchen and down the hallway. "In there," she said and shoved me into Landon's office.

I stumbled, not on purpose this time, and regained my footing a few inches shy of the desk. The photograph album was still there lying open. I turned to face her, my hands in the air. "I feel really honored being let into the inner sanctum and all, but what are we doing here?" I drawled.

She advanced toward me. "There's no need for you to keep up the pretense, Ms. McGrath. I know you're working for a private investigator and that you've been snooping around in here. Neil told me he thought you'd been going through his things. So now you're going to save me the trouble of hunting for his medication."

She motioned me around the desk. "He says it's in the drawer with his family's picture."

I froze in position. "His family? I thought you were—"

"His sister?" She smiled again, her lips stretched tight across opalescent teeth. "We are family, in a way. I was a friend of Neil's sister, Alice. I spent so much time at their house when we were in high school, he nicknamed me his little sister."

"So Marina just assumed you were related?"

"Yes," she sighed, impatient, as if the mention of Marina's name had interrupted a pleasant reverie. "That fat cow would believe anything I told her. Alice died when she was a teenager." Her voice deepened into a melodious, honeyed tone. "She drowned in an unfortunate accident."

So that's why everyone in the photograph looked so unhappy; they were in mourning. Like the absence of markings on Laura's body, it was what was missing from the picture that mattered. No Ava. No Alice. And no sadness coming off her at the mention of Landon's real sister. But she looked so much like him. What were the odds of two unrelated people sharing that kind of resemblance?

A hodgepodge of images danced before me; like cutouts from old photographs spliced and glued erratically, torn edges curling back on themselves. Half-formed memories crawled over one another and darted out at me like angry insects from a rusting can . . . a madwoman's collage of twisted remembrances.

A teenager with purple blotches of acne, stringy hair, and thick-framed glasses painstakingly transformed into the sleek female in front of me. A bright girl with a gift for mimicry and a hunger for a place in the world light years away from her single mother's one-bedroom apartment in the shadow of the L. A hunger that bordered on obsession.

A hunger that had driven her to kill—more than once.

"You . . . you had yourself cut to look like Neil Landon?" I stammered.

She shrugged. "Successful people share certain physical characteristics. Neil and I see that in our practices all the time."

"So, you killed Laura Neff because she wasn't attractive enough?"

She transferred the gun back to her right hand and patted at her wounds absently. "I killed Laura Neff because she was weak. And stupid. When I tried to explain to her why continuing her relationship with Neil would be impossible, she became irrational. She ran away, across the street to that park. By the time I found her she was twitching, slobbering, having some sort of convulsion. She grabbed at me. It was disgusting." Her mouth puckered in a show of distaste.

She examined the streaks of dried blood on her arm. "Bad breeding always shows itself. Neil would have seen it, in time."

"That's funny, he had everyone here thinking he was in love with her."

Her eyes came up to meet mine. Her jaw clenched and the veins in her neck bulged through creamy, bronzed skin. I could feel the jealousy rear up in her like an angry stallion, kicking a hole in that wall of self-possession she presented to the world. Landon and I weren't the only ones still haunted by Laura.

The green-gold flecks around her irises glittered, as she warmed to the task at hand; the message behind them unmistakable. She was going to shoot me as soon as I laid my hands on the bottle. Of that, I was certain.

"But, why Landon's sister?" I blurted, stalling for time. "Surely she didn't suffer from bad breeding?"

"She took me in out of pity. Me!" She smirked. "Thought she'd rehabilitate me, then show me off like a pet bird. But when she saw Landon and I were in love, she got jealous. Started scheming to keep us apart."

A funnel of rage twisted in my gut—her gut. "Get on with it," she snarled.

My time had run out. I stole a glance at the window. I'd been right. The trees and shrubs in the green area were too closely trimmed to provide any real camouflage. Even if I could distract her long enough to get past the back door, a bullet would nail me before I could scream.

I kneeled down and pulled the drawer open. The Sertraline rolled to the back and landed against the corner of the frame. Ava passed the tip of her tongue over her lower lip, flicking at it with sharp little movements.

I grasped the bottle and came up out of the crouch, standing slowly. I held it up so she could see it and extended my hand. She reached for it and I let the pills roll off my fingers and onto the table. The bottle came to rest at the fold in the book, next to a picture of a little boy with a mop of black hair and a missing front tooth: Armando.

For a split second, she hesitated, and then grabbed at the Sertraline. In an instant, the picture was in my hand. Fragments of glass and scarlet droplets flew across the desk as it connected with her head.

I was in the hallway by the time she screamed. I darted inside the supply room, locked the door, and flicked on the light. On the sink, by the pile of outdated IV bags, sat the phone. I lunged for it and tripped over the exam table pedestal, sprawling across it as I grabbed for the handset.

There above the cradle, in Marina's impeccable hand, was security's emergency number: #666. I punched it in. The phone rang twice and an operator came on the line. In the hallway, Ava raged, and threw her weight against the door.

"Gunfire, in Neil Landon's suite. Call security now!"

I hung up, raced back to the door, and flicked off the light. The room was doused in darkness, but, in my mind, I could see the layout: metal shelves on the right wall, exam table in the middle, and the cabinets and sink on the left. A sink with just enough space for a person my size to crawl under.

Ava kicked the door, cursing it. I took a few steps forward and groped for the table. The zing of casing on metal reverberated out in the hallway. I stretched out my hand and found the table's edge as she pumped a second bullet into the lock.

The door flew open, knocking the IV stand on its side. I scuttled under the sink as the room flooded with light. The baseball cap was gone and her tangled hair trailed down her back, the ends uncoiled from their confinement. Blood oozed down the right side of her face and congealed over her eye and chin.

She backed up against the metal stacking units and swept the room with the gun, steadying it with both hands. I could see her chest heaving, feel her heart beating. It was engorged, pulsing—the blood singing in her arteries and veins, thick with anticipation for the hunt. And the kill. She had me pinned down and she knew it. And she was counting on her left eye to tell her where to aim the business end of the Beretta.

I slid my hand up to the counter top and hooked my fingers around a bag of IV fluid. It was pliant in my hand and icy to the touch. Shockingly so.

I pulled the bag into my chest and counted to three,

visualizing the full weight of it smashing into the left side of her head. I darted out from under the sink and lobed the bag toward the metal shelving. The gun went off as I flicked off the light and cleared the door.

I was in the hall when the bullet found me, biting into my leg with a fierce fire. Shouting and heavy footfall rushed up behind me. The carpet fibers tore at the soles of my feet and a warm gush of fluid dripped down my leg, pooling between my toes.

Then the emergency door slammed closed and I was twisting, freefalling; my head exploding with light.

Chapter Thirty-Five

The Pacific crashed against the shore and pulled back again. I could hear raised voices in the distance, oscillating in volume . . . voices so loud they were starting to make my head hurt. I wiggled my toes in the sand and watched the tide rush out to sea.

Up ahead, on the beach, two teenagers danced in the surf, her blonde hair and his darker curls wet with ocean spray. He was shorter than her and his limbs were underdeveloped and pale, as if it'd been some time since he'd been outdoors. One hand rested gently on his shoulder as she guided him across the sand, delight coloring her heart-shaped face. It was peaceful here, listening to their laughter and the rhythm of the sea. I could drift off to sleep, if it weren't for the shouting.

I could also use a drink. Something girly with an exorbitant amount of tropical fruit hanging off the side, in a chilled, hurricane glass; a blended drink, the color of a tropical sunset with a bright green straw. If those people would quiet down, maybe I could get the waiter's attention.

"Hey," I yelled and my head nearly split from the effort. The shouting stopped, but the thudding behind my temples didn't. Geez, it was bright here. Too bright. I squinted and groped at the edge of my towel for my sunglasses.

"Eileen?"

A fuzzy, orange blob materialized overhead. A blob that sounded a lot like Atticus.

"Welcome back," he said. His big mitt enveloped my hand. Then his face went blurry and red. In fact, he looked downright sunburned. Maybe he'd been on vacation, too.

"Why is your face so pink?" I rasped.

"It's nothing." He patted my hand. "How do you feel?"

My field of vision expanded, edged in a cottony haze, and the red glow from my index finger morphed into a pulse oximeter. Nearby, a cart rattled down the hall.

I reached for the mauve, plastic cup on the bedside table and my vision blurred. "Where's Ava?" I asked.

"In custody."

"And Landon?"

"They're on their way to question him now." He pointed at the ceiling.

How ironic. Landon and I in Marin General and Ava behind bars. Boy, was I thirsty.

"Can I have some water, please?"

Atticus jumped to his feet and banged the tray table against the bed. "Sorry," he said and handed the cup to me.

I took a gulp of ice water. It was no Tahitian Breeze, but it would do. A surge of panic shot through me. "Audie. She's in the backyard—"

"Hey, you're not supposed to get excited." Atticus retrieved the cup from my hand. "She's fine. Your landlord is keepin' an eye on her."

I dropped back on the pillow. The green checks on the lavender-and-yellow bed curtain overlapped, superimposing themselves over one another in uneven layers. Head pain, memory loss, and squirrelly vision: the concussion trifecta.

"What time is it?" I asked.

"It's about nine-thirty. You've been out for almost four hours." His face glided back into focus—still flushed—and, I could now see, decidedly forlorn.

"Okay, who died?"

Atticus dropped his weight onto the small wooden chair by the bed and it tipped backward. He caught himself before he hit the wall and righted the chair, banging his shoulder against the tray table. The water pitcher fell over and he grabbed it and set it back on the table, with a thud, as a thin stream of ice water dripped from the spout and over his fingers. He muttered under his breath.

"Atticus, if you want me to hear you in my incapacitated state, you're going to have to speak up."

He wiped his hand on the side of his jeans and eased back into the chair. "I said this whole thing was a bad idea."

"Sounds like you've been talking to Burnette."

Atticus peered at me through the bedrails. "You don't miss much, do you, Little Bit?"

"Well, there are a few details I'm still foggy on. When did you get my messages?"

"Yeah, about that." Atticus took a swipe at his mouth. "I had a court case in Lake County this afternoon. Signal reception is pretty spotty up there so I called you on my way down out of the mountains. I didn't check my messages until I made a pit stop in Vallejo and since you didn't give me much to go on with the sister thing, I figured I'd swing by your place and we'd discuss it."

He leaned forward in the chair. "By the time I got there, your landlord and neighbor were on a tear. They'd found your backdoor open and Audie squalling her head off. When we saw your car was still in the garage, I called the Marin police. Turns out they were on their way."

"So, security must have called them."

"They did. But there was already a pair of patrolmen en route when the dispatcher got that call."

"What?"

"According to the arresting officer, the original call to dispatch was made by someone who said he was on Vista Road and claimed to have witnessed a tall person in a baseball cap struggling with a shorter individual outside of Landon's office. A short time later a second call came through from complex security with a report of shots fired. When they arrived on the scene, the police found a man holding Ava in a half-Nelson in the hallway who'd apparently disarmed her as well. By the time they'd located you on the back steps and taken her into custody, both he and the white Escalade in the parking lot had vanished."

I hit the button on the inside of the rails and raised the head of the bed a few inches.

"Did they give a description?"

"Yep. A large, bald African-American male in his thirties, with metal caps on his front teeth."

"The Refrigerator?"

Atticus cocked his head to the side. "Well, heh, I didn't know you were on a first name basis, but it fits FoZ's BG. I'm guessing he had him tailing you. Probably wanted to find out what you knew."

"So, he saved my bacon?"

Atticus nodded. "More than likely. I mean, the police weren't far behind, but his timing was pretty good."

The Refrigerator and FoZ: my knights in not-so-shining armor. I was going to need a little time to digest that one.

Atticus cleared his throat. "Hey, I really should go get your nurse. She told me to let her know when you woke up."

"There's a call button right here." I pointed to the nurse's hat on the squawk box looped over the bedrails. "And you don't have to go. I won't be getting any sleep tonight anyway. They'll be doing neuro-checks and vitals all night—head injury stuff."

Atticus rubbed the back of his neck. "I'd better go. I've got to make a stop on the way home, and I promised I'd call your landlord and let her know how you were doing."

He stood and the chair squealed in protest as he pushed it back against the wall. His big face loomed over me, tired and a little drawn. "Is there anything else you need?"

I reached for the ice water. "Yeah, a drink. And tell Tessa and Jessamae that I'm doing fine. And thank Burnette for his help . . . tell him we couldn't have done it without him."

A slow, broad grin spread across his ruddy face: the full Spencer treatment. Not quite a tropical sunset, but it would do.

Chapter Thirty-Six

"You are my Audie, my silly Audie."
"I love you more than I can say."
"Cos you're my kitty, a furry mystery."
"And you brighten up my rainy day."

Audie kneaded the blue feed sacking under her paws and sighed, watching the rain swirl around the trees next door. She'd spent the majority of the week on Laura's quilt, curled up among the stars, next to me on the futon. Even her excursions to the backyard had been few and far between, as if she were afraid that if she was gone too long, her human might disappear again. Tessa and Jessamae had been only slightly less vigilant, working in shifts to assure themselves I wouldn't lapse into a coma.

Ava's capture and the back story hit the Chronicle, the Oakland Tribune, and the Marin Independent Journal before I was released from the hospital. The Trib and the Independent ran it on the front page with Laura's headshot next to a picture of Ava, half of her face crusted in blood, being thrust into a squad car outside of Landon's office.

Atticus, as the principal investigator, got his three minutes of fame: resplendent, on the local news, in his red and yellow macaw shirt.

When the whole story came to light and Karin realized that Laura's belongings had not been returned to her family, she took it upon herself to rectify the situation. She tracked down Ravenwaif—a culture clash I would've paid money to see—boxed up Laura's possessions and located one of Laura's aunts, who insisted on leaving me the quilt as a gift. Since it was too small for my double bed, it'd found a home on the futon where Audie had taken immediate possession of it.

Since my return home, the phone had been ringing off the hook. I'd finally been forced to turn off the ringer and leave an outgoing message stating that once I'd recuperated from my injuries, I'd be glad to do interviews and follow-up on anyone interested in receiving a reading. It was going to take a while to pick through the messages, but, with any luck, they would provide me with gainful employment for some months to come.

The media coverage had done nothing to hurt the reputation of A. Spencer Investigations, either. According to Atticus, regional sales of his book had shot through the roof and his caseload had tripled. And he'd been bombarded with requests for speaking engagements throughout Northern California. The A-man was, in short, in his glory. And he'd been hinting at the possibility of bringing me on board as a consultant.

As appealing as the prospect of steady money sounded, I couldn't wrap my mind around any decisions right now.

Other than a tendency to tire out and an occasional bout of fuzziness when I stood up too fast, I wasn't feeling half-bad; but my doctor had suggested I take it easy for a few more weeks. For the moment, being tucked up in my garden gnome pjs with a belly full of Tessa's stew and listening to Audie snore felt like the right place to be.

A thunderclap rattled the roof and brought her awake with a grunt. It was unusual to have any kind of rainstorm in summer, let alone one that involved such dramatic presentation. She eyed me through heavy lids, then tucked her nose under her tail and fell back to sleep. The churning sky had darkened into premature twilight with swollen clouds scuttling across the face of it, their contours etched in black. The wind howled and hurled nickel-sized raindrops against the windowpane.

I should call FoZ. I owed him and the Refrigerator a debt of thanks, regardless of their intentions. Because of them I'd gotten off with a mild concussion and a bullet graze instead of ending up on a metal tray at Marin General. Guess you never know what form your salvation might take. At the very least, I hoped FoZ would find peace in knowing he'd been instrumental in taking down Laura's killer.

The doorknocker clanked, barely audible above the rolling thunder. It was probably Tessa coming by to collect her dishes and make sure I was still conscious. I stood slowly, letting my brain adjust to the change in altitude, and padded across the room and opened the door.

In place of my silver haired landlord stood Burnette; a very wet Burnette, dripping in the hallway. With Tessa and

Jessamae coming and going so much lately I'd gotten lax about checking the peephole. Now, I'd have to invite him in. *Damn.*

"Your phone didn't seem to be working, so I followed one of you neighbors in," he said, and stamped his feet on the rug. "I hope I'm not disturbing you."

"Oh, well, uh . . . I was just resting." Suddenly very conscious of the one-inch gap between my tee shirt and drawstring pajamas, I stepped back to let him past and closed the door. Laura's blanket lay rumpled and empty, its former occupant having slipped soundlessly from view.

Burnette cleared his throat. His eyes looked bloodshot like he'd been putting in some long hours and, without the benefit of a raincoat or umbrella, he was pretty well drenched. I guess the summer storm had caught him off guard, too.

"I won't take up much of your time," he said and reached into his dark blue suit coat. "The Marin police found an earring at the crime scene and I thought it might be yours." He extended his hand. Inside of a small zip lock baggy, nestled a dandruff diamond in a tiny white gold post.

I reached up to check the second hole in my earlobes. Sure enough, one of my earrings was missing.

"Yeah, I guess it is mine." I took the damp plastic from him. "In all the excitement, I hadn't noticed it was gone."

"I also wanted to let you know that Ava Ravel will be charged with Laura's murder as well as Alice Landon's."

"She confessed to both?"

"Yes." Brunette wiped at his forehead with the back of his hand. "While on vacation in Hawaii with Dr. Landon's family, it seems she sensed a cooling in her relationship with his sister. Knowing that Alice wasn't much of a swimmer, she insisted they take a bike ride through one of the parks there. She'd tampered with her bike in advance and, when it came apart, Alice fell into the pools below. With a little help from Ava."

"At Waimea Falls?"

"I believe so, yes."

"And Landon never suspected anything?"

"Apparently not. He said the family put it down to a tragic accident. He went off to college and lost contact with Ava. When she resurfaced, eighteen years later, with a story about opening a practice in the Bay Area, he bought it—hook, line, and sinker. He said she'd only recently brought up his moving back to Oahu, so he didn't get suspicious. Just took her attention for an act of friendship."

"But she said he'd brought up the two of them sharing a practice . . . and that she and Landon were in love when they were kids; that Alice didn't approve. She said that's why she killed her."

"That's evidently not the way he saw it."

"So there was never a romance? Not even a teenage infatuation?"

"Not according to him."

So Ava really was delusional: the Eight of Pentacles turned on her head. All for want of a man who would never love or need her the way he had loved and needed Laura. After all those years, after all she'd accomplished, she was still obsessed with Landon. Talk about distorted vision—two lives lost and a third one wasted.

Regret would dog us all. What if Laura had taken better care of her seizure disorder? Or been raised to have enough self-confidence to not be duped by Ava, less flattered by a secret meeting? What if she'd told Marina, or Landon, or even Ravenwaif about Ava's invitation? What if I'd been more adamant about driving home the cautious aspects of her reading?

Burnette's irises had taken on the color of the storm outside; a steel grey that I'm sure some women found attractive. Even wet and rumpled, he had an intensity that never let up, one I found exhausting. It was time for him to go.

I summoned a polite smile. "Well, thanks for the earring and the update. I'm sorry you came all this way in the rain."

I have to give the man credit; he knew a dismissal when he heard one. He hesitated for only a second and then turned on his heel, his wet shoes squeaking on the hardwood. He opened the door and glanced back, his eyes pinning me in place.

"It took a lot of guts to do what you did. I have respect for that."

Whoa. First the summer storm and now an actual acknowledgement from Burnette. The earth must be spinning off its axis . . . or I was.

A streak of lightning split the sky. The room tilted as I groped for the phone stand and, in a flash, Burnette's hands were around my waist steadying me. They were damp and cold against my bare skin, but they got the job done.

This wasn't fatigue or post-concussion vertigo. It was the third-eye head-rush that hits when the universe is talking to me in its Big Voice. And it was happening in front of Burnette, for the second time. How ridiculous.

I could smell his cologne. And tell he'd been drinking. Not much and definitely not beer; probably no more than two fingers of liquid warmth. Just enough to take the sting off a bruised ego and whatever memories Laura Neff had stirred up for him.

She had left her mark on all of us. But this time there was no prickling maul or scalded chest or imprint of pain not my own. Only the brush of wet fabric across my cheek. And the faint taste of a fine Irish whiskey.

Acknowledgements

This book would never have made it to print without a constellation of knowledgeable and kindly souls who were willing to undertake this adventure with me.

I would like to thank my readers: Betsy Showalter, Cyd Krilitech, Judith Messick, Sarah O'Sullivan, Frances Hill, and the late Fern Fix. Your insights and encouragement made me a better writer.

I would also like to thank Myla Lara for her artistic vision, my editor, Lyn Worthen, for her expertise, and my partner-in-crime, Scott Pearson, for his journalist's eye.

Many thanks to the faculty and staff of the Book Passage Mystery Writer's Conference for opening the door and pointing the way.

My special appreciation goes out to Richard Thomas Banegas whose kindness to a stranger will not be forgotten.

Hugs to my buddy, Lee Nyberg, for her wisdom and heart.

And finally, to Robert MacDowell—I couldn't have done it without you, babe.

About The Author

Eloise Hill is a nurse, psychic, and writer who has been in love with the Tarot since she picked up her first Rider Waite deck at the age of eighteen.

She worked for thirteen years in a variety of acute care settings before deciding to pursue a career in writing and all things intuitive. In addition to giving psychic/tarot/rune readings, she teaches classes on various subjects of interest including using the Tarot for personal transformation, practical applications of the Elder Futhark Runes, and the basics of tea leaf reading.

A native of the Shenandoah Valley of Virginia, she currently resides in Northern California, in a cottage by the sea, where she is hard at work on the next installment of the Eileen McGrath Tarot Series.

She can be contacted at www.eloisehill.net.